ROXIE DIDN'T WANT TO COME DOWN THE STAIRS OF THE BROTHEL.

The room was full of armed men dressed in gray. Most of them big. Most of them drinking. A few had brothel whores pressed against the wall. Dead men were all over the floor. Some piled on top of each other, some impossibly crumpled. The women were in shock and the men didn't seem to notice.

William Quantrill was drinking from his flask because he didn't like the brothel whiskey. The parlor stank of blood, powder and death.

OTHER BOOKS BY JAKE LOGAN

RIDE, SLOCUM, RIDE
HANGING JUSTICE
SLOCUM AND THE WIDOW KATE
ACROSS THE RIO GRANDE
THE COMANCHE'S WOMAN
SLOCUM'S GOLD
BLOODY TRAIL TO TEXAS
NORTH TO DAKOTA
SLOCUM'S WOMAN
WHITE HELL
RIDE FOR REVENGE
OUTLAW BLOOD
MONTANA SHOWDOWN
SEE TEXAS AND DIE
IRON MUSTANG
SHOTGUNS FROM HELL
SLOCUM'S BLOOD
SLOCUM'S FIRE
SLOCUM'S REVENGE
SLOCUM'S HELL
SLOCUM'S GRAVE
DEAD MAN'S HAND
FIGHTING VENGEANCE
SLOCUM'S SLAUGHTER
ROUGHRIDER
SLOCUM'S RAGE
HELLFIRE
SLOCUM'S CODE

JAKE LOGAN
SLOCUM'S FLAG

PLAYBOY
PAPERBACKS

SLOCUM'S FLAG

Copyright © 1981 by Jake Logan

Cover illustration copyright © 1981 by PEI Books, Inc

All rights reserved. No part of this book may be reproduced, stored in a retrieval system or transmitted in any form by an electronic, mechanical, photocopying, recording means or otherwise without prior written permission of the publisher.

Published simultaneously in the United States and Canada by Playboy Paperbacks, New York, New York. Printed in the United States of America. Library of Congress Catalog Card Number: 81-80091. First edition.

Books are available at quantity discounts for promotional and industrial use. For further information, write to Premium Sales, Playboy Paperbacks, 1633 Broadway, New York, New York 10019.

ISBN: 0-872-16856-5

First printing July 1981.

PROLOGUE

With a thrum, the bats hurtled underneath the low branches of the pin oaks, taking mosquitoes by the hundreds. They found avenues in the trees where seemingly none existed, and lifted and dove with the uncanniness and the faintly audible chirp of their kind. They charged and lifted and withdrew, veering sharply upward. There was a final shrill call in the dusk and they were gone.

In the deepest shadow of those trees, a man's arm raised and then dropped. Silhouetted against the lighter color of the horizon, the arm looked like a dark semaphore.

The sleeve of the coat was the same deep brown as the woods themselves: the brown of butternut.

Once the arm dropped, the sound of the feet rushing was very like the noise the bats made, and with imagination, the squeaks of their leather harnesses were not unlike the chirps of the bats.

It was November 4, 1864, Kansas Territory, not too far from Tuttle Creek, just north of the town called Fairing.

The maples had flared red, the walnuts had already lost all their leaves, and the oak trees were shedding their yellow plumage with each successive frost.

Under these trees, the ground was six inches deep in leaves, but it had rained that afternoon, and the leaves were no longer crisp and brittle.

Though the pin oaks were bound with Virginia creeper and knotted honeysuckle ropes, somehow the hurrying feet missed the anklebusters—almost as if the feet had eyes.

There can be heard through the forest a sustained rush, without a command or a human voice, and as silent as men can be. There were nearly fifty men under the broad crowns of the stocky pin oaks, and taken together, they sounded like a tree when it falls—the sustained whoosh as its branches gasp and clutch at the air.

One man dives forward, tripped by a root hidden under the thick blanket of leaves. His body executes the fall, and when the man's chest hits the ground, the air leaves him with a thick grunt and rattles past his throat like a death complaint. Teeth gleam around him, his companions flashing their grins in the dusk, but neither he nor they exchange a word.

A quarter mile upslope, fifty horses are tethered, and around them sitting quietly, five men wait as pickets. These pickets don't smoke or talk, and the only noise in the clearing is the noise of the horses, grass pulling, foot shifting, farting, and belly rumbling.

Near the high crumbly banks of Tuttle Creek, the trees stood farther apart. Nearness to the water made snobs out of them. Here, close to the big house, the trees had been cleared away for firewood.

The odor of the evening fire rises from chimneys at both ends of the long ramshackle building before the smoke falls to hug the ground in the forest, interbreeding with the ground fog and the brief spurts of men's breathing. They draw up. They group together. Again the arm raises against the sky. Again it drops and another short rush takes them a hundred yards nearer.

Those beyond shelter simply drop to one knee for concealment when they stop. Tuttle Creek is on the downside of the house; the porch, yard, hitchrail, and road on the uphill. Above the road is a long ten-acre meadow shaped like a brick with its narrow edge fronting the road. In the summer months they make hay in this field, and after the last of the hay is up, horses graze there. Tonight that bare field is covered with boulders, though a moment ago it was bare as a baby's butt.

One of the boulders raises an arm, this time in a

more complicated motion, a circling gesture. Three other boulders detach themselves and join the signaler. Though they speak, their lips barely move and their voices, like the hiss of a grass snake, vanish just a few feet away.

The other stones are patient as stones and don't move and don't talk either.

Noise from the big house: a man's deep laughter, a woman's shriek of pleasure, the sound of glass tinkling, the crash of men's boots on wide board floors.

There are fifteen horses drawn up at the hitchrail of the house that calls itself the Light of Love. Ten of the horses bear McClellan saddles and dark blue saddle blankets. A couple of boulders relocate at either end of the hitchrail. They settle.

The remaining horses are not uniform in type or harness. Two are young and fast, two middle-aged, and one animal is hipshot and positively senescent.

Below each blue saddle blanket is a rifle scabbard. Every one of these is empty. The two strong horses carry a rifle scabbard and a pair of pistol holsters each. Also empty.

The big front windows of the house are closed against the autumn chill and covered with heavy swag drapes, but through crevices in the drapes, a man can see movement, a flash of blue, a gesture of crinoline. The windows upstairs are lighted too—more dimly than downstairs—and the drapes are pulled together more carefully.

As though a stream dividing, two files of men rush around the hitchrack and freeze in an instant when the front door opens. The sound of a fat man laughing is very loud. The tinkling of a player piano. Someone inside is working a concertina with more enthusiasm than skill. The light inside spills across the porch, across the empty walk that is only plain dirt but lined neatly with clay flowerpots and flowerpots made from old tin cans. The light reaches the hitchrail and washes across the horses' heads.

8 JAKE LOGAN

The light just touches the cheeks of a watcher hunkered down next to the horses, motionless, his eyes locked on the big man framed in the doorway. Big man—shirtless—in pants and union suit, with his braces hanging loose at his side. A revolver at his side in a covered military holster. The man fumbles wth his buttons for a moment and steps to the edge of the porch, and then the sound and the odor of a man taking a piss. He groans. The watcher grins slowly. The light illumines only one plane of his face, and in this light his cheek looks very severe, almost Indian. He doesn't move any more than any Indian would either.

Before he returns indoors, the big man whoops to the night and the stars and to Bacchus and Venus too. "Watch out, girls," he hollers. "The Red Rooster's back."

When he slammed the door behind him, he shook the unpainted gray clapboards.

Behind one of the closely drawn curtains on the second floor, Sallie Webster took four fingers of good bourbon for herself and pondered the foolishness of women.

"You been ruined, girl," she explained patiently. "And once a girl's been ruined, she's got two choices she can make and both of them come down to the same thing in the end. Either she can find some man who ain't particularly choosy for bed and bride, or she can work here at the Light of Love." She eyed the ruined girl skeptically, wondering if she should offer her a glass. Girl was so damn young—couldn't be a day over seventeen—an adolescent's fleshless figure. Well, she'd been plenty fleshy a couple months ago when she was carrying her brat and she was still smarting from some of the jokes she'd had to carry with it. She was lucky: the brat died. "Here," Sallie said, handing the girl her own glass. "Medicine. Drink it down. It'll ease you over the tough parts."

The girl had long very dark hair drawn on either

side of her face in severe braids. She had a pair of big dark eyes that caught your attention next; but her nose was too small and her mouth was a mite too generous for her to be really beautiful. And her breasts were still child's breasts. Swollen now. Not too long ago she'd had her baby hanging on them. Sallie thought she'd lose considerable of her charms when they shrank. The girl was more a wood's colt than a woman grown and that was the truth. She tasted the whiskey as though it were going to kill her, and made a face like it had.

Outside, the Light of Love was unpainted. Inside, the rooms were fairly plush. Sallie's bedroom was perhaps the grandest of them all, with a carpet on the floor that covered the whole floor—not just one of those scatter rugs—a real carpet, made on a loom. Her bed was shiny brass covered with a pink silk coverlet. The brass lamps on either side of the bed cast neat circles of brightness above matching tables. The room featured a green velvet love seat, where the girl sat, slumped in dejection; a tall cherrywood chifforobe where Sallie hung her carefully chosen gowns and shifts; and in the corner, a small triangular secretary where she did her accounts every morning—a fairly satisfying part of her day because business couldn't be better. She set her bottle on the writing surface and sighed as she poured herself another generous portion. "Look, honey," she said gently, "I won't be the one to force a girl . . ."

Sallie Webster was a big woman, blond and tall. Her golden hair was drawn up in a great bun, secured with a dark red mother-of-pearl comb. Her gown was low-cut to show the fullness of her breasts, and it drew in sharply at the waist to delineate the graceful swell of her hips. Her eyes were yellow, wide, and kind. "Look, honey," she began again.

The girl drained her glass of whiskey with a perceptible shudder and a thin cough.

Sallie didn't care for the sound of the cough. She had five girls working the Light of Love and not a lunger among them, thank God. She came closer to the girl, but didn't see any of the signs: neither the pallor nor the brightly colored spots on her cheeks. She had the look of the consumptive, but she was demonstrably underfed. "You sick, child?" Sallie demanded, and the harshness in her voice surprised her.

The girl spoke, her voice soft and musical. "No," she said simply. Then, misunderstanding the thrust of Sallie's question, she added, "The man who had me, he was . . . clean."

As the girl blushed, Sallie sighed. "I wasn't askin' that," she said.

Apparently the girl didn't hear, or hearing, chose not to, because she went on. "He was a . . . 'a prominent citizen.' "

"Yeah," Sallie said in a slow drawl. "They're all prominent, every damn one of 'em."

The girl lifted her innocent eyes begging for belief. "If I was to tell you his name, you'd know it. Half the folks in this part of Kansas would know who I meant. He's a 'prominent citizen.' "

"Honey, I don't care if he was Jeff Davis himself," Sallie said. "I ain't interested in your sex habits except one of 'em. Remorse isn't in short supply in any sportin' house and you won't find it absent here. Just sit around the kitchen on a Sunday mornin' with your head still full of the whiskey you drank last night, not even washed yet from the hands of all the men who handled you, and I tell you you'll know remorse. If you want to regret the man who ruined you, that's your business. Save it for Sunday mornin's. Or take it out the door with you right now. Nobody'll put out a hand to stop you."

While she spoke, an image came into Sallie's mind, a mental picture of this afternoon when two different girls had knocked timidly on her door. Sallie had promised to give this girl a try because she liked the looks of her and felt sorry for her. The other girl (who'd come along a couple hours later) was hard faced, stood a little peculiarly, and had smaller breasts than this child had. Sallie had shown her around the house (as per request) but informed her that another girl had just been hired and she should come back in a week or two.

"God knows there ain't any shortage of job hunters," Sallie had noted.

A raucous shout from downstairs. A voice at the foot of the stairs. "Sallie! You and the wench gonna come down here or are we gonna have to come up and drag you down?" The demand was stern enough, but the voice was full of good humor, so Sallie cracked the door to the hall and shouted that they'd be down in a few minutes and he should keep his damn pants on, by God.

This gibe brought a laugh from downstairs and a cheer too. "They're waitin' on us," Sallie explained. She went to her dressing table, ignoring the girl as she checked her hair, dabbed some perfume on a hankie and then to her breast, and then darkened her right eyebrow slightly. She was thinking of this child's looking for work in the war-ravaged countryside. Wasn't much work for an unattached woman in the best of times, and these days, women were useful in the kitchen or the bedroom and that was all. A lone woman walking in the streets was likely to get plenty of propositions but most would suggest a recline. The farms had been burned all along the Kansas-Missouri border, and General Order Number 10 had emptied every damn town for twenty miles from the line. Factories made munitions, foundries made guns. Wherever miners could scrape saltpeter off cavern walls, they set up charcoal works to make gunpowder, and down by Joplin, the lead mines were heavily busy, but none of that was work for a woman.

"I don't suppose you have a family," Sallie said without turning around.

"No, ma'am. Father and Mother were killed by jayhawkers, and Brother Joe is off with the army. I haven't heard from him in fourteen months and have come to fear the worst."

Sallie Webster finished her own makeup and faced the girl. "Honey, I should probably turn you out tonight. This here is a sportin' house and you don't look to be cut out for the life. There's plenty others that are." Sallie was remembering the second girl—the hard-faced one—Jess, she'd called herself—who'd prowled through the house that afternoon. If she was to lose this child, Sallie'd go with Jess. The roads were crawling with women just like her. "I wouldn't be doin' you any favor," Sallie said. "You'd end followin' the soldiers around and carryin' another brat, or you'd get raped and killed on the pike or just starve to death. I'll put it to you plain. I'll take you in, but I got an old darky for a cook and I got another darky that cleans up the leaves and scrubs the floors and the two of them together do the wash and all the linen. Kitchen help I got. What I need for you to do, honey, is to lie with the men who come here for that attraction. I won't say it's always the pleasantest work in the world, but it ain't as bad as you've heard it to be in church and like places. I'm fair with my girls. You'll eat and even put a few dollars away for the time when you want to go elsewhere." Briskly she stepped beside the girl and turned up the wick in the kerosene lamp to illuminate her face.

"I thought I could . . ." the girl began.

"Honey," Sallie said, "probably a couple million women came to the place where you are sometime in their life and most of them just made the best of it. I ain't sayin' you must, but you'd be fifteen kinds of fool not to." Deciding, suddenly, Sallie went to her cupboard secretary, and with a key she kept inside her bodice, she unlocked the strongbox. Handed the girl a coin, a three-dollar gold piece. "Here," she said. "This'll buy you a place to sleep and something to eat for the night. Fairing's only an hour walk from here and the moon's full. Get off the road if you hear riders and stay crouched until they're by. The hotel in Fairing's the best place to stay, though you should check for bedbugs. Go on, now. Git."

Slowly the girl lifted her face and her eyes were wet, but her jaw was set strong. "I will do it, Mrs. Webster."

"Sallie."

"But I don't know how."

"Knew enough to get yourself a brat," Sallie remarked, not unkindly. "What you got to do is learn to like some part of the men, not all of them. That's the trick to it."

As she spoke, she led the girl to her own mirror and patted her face with her own powderpuff. "First, we'll put some color in those cheeks," she said. As she worked, she told the girl to focus on something in a man that seemed likable. Every man had something likable. "If you don't like his eyes or his smile, admire the way he walks or jokes or carries his damn hat," she advised.

The girl sat demurely as Sallie Webster created a whore's mask for her face, and when her face was finished, she rose steadily and stepped to the mirror where she examined herself. Her hand went to her throat. Swiftly, her fingers unbuttoned three pearl snaps that topped her plain cotton dress. The pulse fluttered in her throat.

Sallie Webster said, "Tomorrow morning, first thing, we'll go into Fort Riley and buy you some clothes that are a little more suitable."

The new whore pulled her dress down over her shoulders, but the dress was a high-throated schoolmarm model and she looked ridiculous.

"What did you say your name was?" Sallie asked quietly.

"Julie."

In a false cheery voice accompanied by a little clap of her hands, "Well, we'll just have to change that now. How about Lavonne? Or Roxie?"

The girl admired her schoolgirl's shoulders in the mirror. She was indifferent to the names.

"Roxie it'll be, then," Sallie Webster said.

Roxie swallowed a couple deep swallows of bourbon. "Those men downstairs, they're all soldiers?" she asked.

"Most of them, yes."

"Soldiers and jayhawkers?"

"The jayhawkers stop by in the evenings when they're in the neighborhood. We get top dollar here, Roxie. And anyone well behaved, with money to spend, is welcome here."

"It'll be hard for me to lie with a jayhawker," the girl said simply, without dropping her eyes from the mirror. "It was them that killed my family."

More assured now, Sallie Webster said, "Well, dearie, in a couple days you and me'll have another little talk. And maybe we'll see if there isn't some way to sow confusion among the jayhawkers. I ain't particular fond of 'em myself."

Another bellow echoed in the flimsy house. "Damn it, Miss Sallie! Can't you hurry on down?"

And once more she went to the door and called out sweetly that she wouldn't be much longer and the new girl would come right along too. They were just making themselves pretty, that's all. She shut the door with satisfaction. Her eyes surveyed the girl. "Honey," she said, "you look like one of those half-dog and half-cat creatures you see in the travelin' shows. No sense lettin' you go downstairs like that. No sense at all."

And she threw open the drawer to her chifforobe and sorted quickly through her scarves and underthings until she found what she wanted, a large feather boa, dyed green. It was fluffier and lighter in color than the girl's dress, but it added whatever Sallie was looking for. "It's just what the men want, honey. Make-believe. And it's up to you and me to give it to them. You about ready?"

And the older woman proffered her arm and the younger one took it. "Welcome to the world's oldest sisterhood," she said.

The upstairs hall was uncarpeted and very narrow. The builders hadn't believed in wasting space that could be put to better use in the rooms that lined the hall.

The girl kept her eyes down on the rough pine plank floors. She wasn't particularly afraid. She didn't even wish she was elsewhere. She was here, that's all there was to it, and here she would stay because here she would eat.

Sallie talked a torrent of well-meaning advice. "Get the money first, honey, before he's out of his clothes. Once he's fired his salute, you won't be worth much to most men." And, "Tonight, you pick the one you want. You won't ever have to go with any man you don't want to. You have my word on that."

The watchers outside the house of the Light of Love couldn't hear what the two women said, but their footsteps were quite audible, and the four men beside the window at the bottom of the stairs drew back into the surrounding darkness; shades within shades.

The figure in charge of the party stood dead center in the front yard, his hands on his hips. Sidelights illuminated the front door. Beveled glass—it looked like. Must have come all the way from St. Louis. Or Kansas City. But Kansas City, which was nearer, certainly didn't have glassworks able to make glass this fancy. The figure stared at those flowing sidelights with the avidity of a gypsy woman with her crystal ball.

The sounds of dancing inside. More a crashing sound than a dancing sound, as if bears were going through their paces. The music of a concertina pumping out one old favorite after another, "Barbara Allen" and "Foggy Mountain" and the old hornpipe tunes, which were special favorites. The squeezebox was playing a hornpipe and the men's feet crashed on the planks and men whooped and cheered. The motionless figure took a flask from his coat pocket and drank long and deep. When he replaced the flask, it clinked on one of his pistols, but nobody was near enough to be alarmed.

The whiskey was the finest Kentucky bourbon. Once, not such a long time ago, it had belonged to a judge. It slipped down the man's throat spreading the warmth through his body and making his fingers tingle.

The concertina stopped wheezing. A chorus of whistles and cheers. "Hey! What's this? Where have you been keepin' her, Sallie?" "What's your name, pretty girl?"

The girl raised her chin defiantly. She didn't look at the red-faced Yankee sergeant grinning so broadly at her. "I'm Roxie," she said, and in some instinctive seizing of an ancient craft, her voice came out in a slow seductive drawl instead of the breathless fear she felt.

The parlor of the Light of Love was its largest room and, by all accounts, the grandest. The clock over the mantelpiece chimed on the half and the hour, and the fireplace was always stuffed with burning cedar logs, which perfumed the room and deadened the stink of the soldiers' cigars.

The parlor took up the width of the building and extended for fifteen feet on either side of the entry door. When the building had been built—as an inn—the parlor had been the common room where wayfarers ate and the poorest slept. Windows on one side of the room overlooked Tuttle Creek, not that there was much to see at this time of night, and windows on the upslope side faced the road. The fireplace was broad and shallow, casting welcome heat across the unpainted wide plank floors in waves. Right now, a couple soldiers had their backsides as close to it as they could get.

Big as the room was, it was overfull of furniture. Settees and elaborately carved daybeds lined three walls. Love seats and ottomans thronged the center of the floor. Now, everything had been slid together to make space for dancing. A black man worked the concertina. He was a hand taller than six feet and wore a neat red vest and gray trousers. He was barefoot and perspiring.

Sallie made the introductions. "Jocko, this here's Roxie. She'll be stayin' with us a spell."

The black man's smile was soft and wide. "Yes'm. Good to have you here, Miss Roxie."

"Anytime any man gives you trouble, you just yell for Jocko here," Sallie said, loud enough for every man in the room to hear. "Once Jocko gets done playin' with 'em, they won't be troublin' no poor helpless females again."

And Jocko's smile got even wider.

The men in the room were soldiers and Kansas Jayhawkers of the poorer sort. The jayhawking business was the same as most small enterprises. For those who didn't get in on the ground floor, opportunities and rewards were few. These three men hadn't decided on their endeavor until last year—1863—and by that time, most of the pickings were thin. For their trouble and a year's hard riding, each of them had his horse, his clothes, and his guns as rewards, plus the twenty dollars each carried from that old secess' they'd gunned down outside of Fairing. He should have had more money than sixty dollars, him being a minister and all.

These three men wore homespun clothes and two pistols each. One had buck teeth, the other two looked to be brothers and dressed alike. Their black slouch hats were identical and they hadn't removed them. Two of Sallie's girls sat on their laps and the men's hands stayed under the girls' skirts throughout Sallie's introductions. Their hands were busy.

The soldiers were part of C Company, Second Battalion, Fourth Engineers. New Hampshire men, they'd been assigned to Fort Riley in a group. They were a clannish lot—sons of farmers and small merchants who eked out a living on New Hampshire's inhospitable bony ridges. Shunned by the western soldiers and treated with suspicion by the sutlers and merchants at the fort, these soldiers had withdrawn into their own clannishness. They worked hard all day and at night traveled the roads around the fort, trying out one brothel after another. The Federal soldiers were paid with gold; the Confederates with scrip discounted ten to one and local bank scrip was no better. These Yankee soldiers were suddenly very wealthy men—wealthy as bankers. They had most of what they wanted and understood none of it. Girls and whiskey were theirs for the taking. The work they did—deepening the trench fortifications at Fort Riley—was simple and undemanding. The feelings of the people who lived on the Kansas-Missouri border were as strange to them as the religious customs of the Hindus. Evidences of hatred were everywhere. On the road tonight they'd passed six bodies between Tuttle Creek and the fort—just two hours distant. Human bodies in the ditch identifiable only by the clouds of heavy-bellied vultures that raised up at the New Hampshire men's approach. Some human bodies dangled from pin oaks on either side of the road. Impossible to tell who they were after four or five days in the weather. Jayhawkers or guerrillas, they were just as dead and looked alike too.

None of the bodies wore boots. Boots were scarce on the Kansas-Missouri border.

Most of the New Hampshire men came from average homes. Not the homes that dominated the brow of the hill—the homes that lay just below it. Their richer neighbors bought substitutes to do their fighting. Their poorer neighbors were assigned to the East where Grant waged his fierce campaign against the Army of Northern Virginia. These New Hampshire men went to war but managed to secure duty far from the worst fighting. Most of the men were in their middle twenties, which was pretty old for soldiers. Most of them were drunk, and one had already managed to get sick and had passed out on Sallie Webster's best settee; his feet dangled over the end of it.

A sergeant led the detachment of New Hampshire men, and he was a year or two older and had a better capacity for liquor. He was the one who'd asked the girl for her name.

"Roxie," she replied sturdily. "And I'm here for a good time." The coquette's eyes sped around the room seeking the man she hoped for. She didn't find him until her second traverse, but then she laughed and stamped her foot and—just avoiding the sergeant's outstretched hands—she made toward him. " 'Lo there," she said brightly to a young soldier slouched beside the fireplace. The soldier's name was Sam. Sam was the youngest of the New Hampshire men and his constant good humor had made him a favorite with his brother soldiers who treated him with the affection men have for pets or unblooded boys. Sam had made no secret of his shyness with women and on their previous forays had never found courage to go with the brightly painted girls. He'd taken his ribbings with good humor and some exasperation.

He was lanky, towheaded, bony wristed with big hands and a slow off-center smile. Right now his eyes were big as half-dollar pieces, and if there were a retreat right through the solid wall pressing against his back, by God the boy would have found it.

Roxie held out her hand as she approached, and the boa flowing from her shoulders added a certain grandeur to her walk. "You're a good-looking man," she said, in the tone of voice she might have used to describe a horse. She liked the look of him, that was all. But it was more than enough for Sam, who blushed scarlet and examined his boottops with extraordinary interest. She stamped her foot. "I'm Roxie!" she said, as though she were laying down a gauntlet.

"Sam," he mumbled.

And Sallie Webster laughed and clapped her hands and said, "Ain't she something? I knew she had that special something. Jocko, how about a song? How about 'Buffalo Gals'?"

And as the concertina began its wheeze, Sallie Webster flopped herself down in the Yankee sergeant's lap. He'd meant to follow after Roxie, but the bundle of woman in his lap was too much to move and too much fun to dump on the floor. So the sergeant grumbled and his hand strayed, right off, to Sallie Webster's bodice.

A couple soldiers danced with each other, whooping and battering the floor with their boots. Outdoing each other. A smear of motion at the window—as if a bird had headed for the glass but veered at the last minute.

The sergeant had Sallie's right nipple between his finger and thumb. Sallie was silently counting heads and calculating how many double eagles she'd put in her strongbox tonight. "Oh honey," she said, "how come you do me like you do?"

"Buffalo Gals, won't you come out tonight, come out tonight. . . ."

Roxie got close to Sam and took both his hands in hers. You can find the greatest romantics inside a whorehouse, and the whores and their soldiers smiled and felt good about the two youngsters. The boy was a virgin, of course, though he denied it, and his fellow soldiers were anxious to erase that stain on the boy's manhood.

The girl didn't hear their chuckles or their laughter because suddenly she was quite taken with this young man. The man who'd ruined her had been the executor of her family estate. He'd taken her money and her maidenhead too, and the loss had been a whirl of leather couches and the smell of cigars and fine whiskey. His hands had been hard on her and insistent, that day in his office above the bank, and he'd torn her underclothes as casually as he'd torn away her maidenhead.

Sam swallowed and his Adam's apple seemed to stick for a second before it found its proper place.

"I want to have a good time," Roxie said, surprising herself, because it was quite true. After the months of fear and pain and privation and worry, she was warm and with a young man she liked, and her baby—dead less than a month—was forgotten for now as she put her troubles behind her.

"Sure," Sam said. He licked his dry lips and croaked, "Sure. I can dance a little. Can you dance?"

And Roxie nodded and smiled eagerly and felt like laughing because her heart was so light in her chest. As they stepped to the makeshift dance floor, Sam put one hand around her shoulders and gave her a squeeze she could feel all the way through the boa, and she wondered how she'd look tomorrow with gowns aplenty.

The soldiers dancing made way with ill grace because all of Sallie's girls were occupied and two of them already on their way upstairs and there wasn't anything else to do but dance or drink the rotgut whiskey the Light of Love provided. Sallie never had good whiskey, and when she was called on it—as she sometimes was— she replied that if she'd wanted to run a saloon, she would have, by God, and that was the end of the matter.

The displaced soldiers took their drinks to the fireplace and turned to let the heat wash over their backs and buttocks. Plenty of time. They'd each have a woman before the night was out.

Sam and Roxie danced clumsily at first, with unexpected turns and jostlings, and it was a good three minutes before they found each other's rhythm. The boy was simply metrical, stepping his deep steps and swoops exactly on the beat, as if this rectitude was important to him, and the girl was more frivolous, dependent on improvisation. She was lighter than he was, and better coordinated, flitting into his arms and out again seeming reluctant to be captured.

The boy saw through her cosmetic whore's mask. He saw a girl like the girls he'd danced with in New Hampshire, except this girl was a woman who'd soon go to bed with him, though it didn't do to dwell on that part of it because when he did, he panicked. Her hands were feather light but strong. Her smile was shy.

The sergeant was busy with his other hand now, inside Sallie Webster's gown, and she was turned half to him so he could have the access he required.

Jocko's squeezebox was very loud and he was sweating, his face covered with a fine sheen of sweat.

The three jayhawkers were sitting on a couch passing the bottle between them, and if one of them wasn't drinking, another one was. A few of the soldiers wore that look on their face that meant they weren't able to see what stood directly in front of them, and Sallie had already written them off. Tonight they'd be whiskey customers only.

The boy was perfectly satisfied dancing with the girl, but Roxie suddenly grew nervous, skittish as a colt imagining obstacles in the play of shadows under the trees. She pressed her lips to the boy's ear and whispered, "I think we should go upstairs. Where we could be kind of private."

The boy went beet red, all except the tips of his ears, which were white as frost. "Well . . ."

"Let's go upstairs, honey," she whispered.

"Uh . . ."

She tugged at his hand and with a curious half-stumble he followed her, like a dog that's never been on a leash before.

Though the sergeant didn't notice, Sallie gave the girl a broad wink as she led her swain toward the stairs. One of Sam's friends opened his mouth to cheer the boy but figured he'd reserve his comments until the boy came back downstairs.

As he followed close on her heels, Sam was aware of her body—the way it moved—inside the old faded dress. Half a step above him the boa rustled and tossed.

A tingling in his hands. A dryness in his mouth. His groin was electric.

Roxie led the boy down the long hall past the thin cubicles to the door of the room she'd been in before—Sallie Webster's own bedroom. As they passed one room they heard a man groaning and the steady loud song of the bedsprings. The sound made the boy hungry and took the edge off Roxie's appetite. The man sounded just like a pig—that's what she was thinking.

When she hesitated before the door, the boy reached past to swing it open.

The bed looked very large.

The boy was surprised because he'd never thought a whore's quarters could be so fancy. Awkwardly he turned the girl and tried to kiss her, but managed to put his nose into her eye. She said ouch and took two steps back until the bed interrupted her progress. She sat. She rubbed her eye.

"I'm sorry," he said. "I'm not used to this."

She said, "Neither am I," and rubbed her eye. Her smile was shy but impish somehow. "Well, Sam. How we gonna get our experience since we ain't got any?"

He pushed the door shut behind him with his heel. He returned her grin. "They say practice makes perfect," he said.

She nodded. She said, "Miss Sallie says I should collect from you before we go any further because when we're done, you won't care for me no more."

And he went into his pocket for his money and didn't want to ask her how much so he took it all out—must have been twelve dollars—and laid it on the secretary and said, "Will that be enough?"

"Sure," she said without taking her eyes off him.

He laughed kind of awkward. "Guess I won't be needing this," he said, and his hands went to the heavy brass buckle that held his pistol belt. The belt was plain and highly polished. It held his bayonet as well as the heavy revolver. The pistol was very heavy as he draped the whole rig over the chair. Then he stopped because he didn't know what came next.

The girl removed her boa and unbuttoned those same three buttons at her throat, and this time, when she lowered the dress to bare her shoulders, she was lovely and not awkward.

Sam sat down to remove his boots and socks. The girl kicked off her shoes. She patted the bed beside her. "Here," she said. "Come, keep me company."

He lay down beside her, and this time his kiss was

right on the mark and her lips were sweeter than any honey he'd ever tasted—even the basswood honey that comes first in the spring.

Her breath kissed his cheek and the feel of her pressed against him was wonderful. His hands were shaking pretty badly when he tried to open her dress and the damn buttons were tiny, but his fingers—big around as horse sausages—finally stumbled through the job.

Her breast was silk to his touch, soft as down, and he stroked it delicately as a man might judging baby chicks.

"Oh," she said.

A drop of milk at her breast, but he didn't know that and didn't know about her baby. She opened her legs as much as she could and threw one leg over him.

Her skirt, thus, was rucked up well above her thighs, and his other hand found her womanhood.

"Oh," she said again. And her kiss was furnace-hot. Hot as a tin cup left in the sun in July.

The two intertwined and their hands flew over each other and he opened each button of her dress as if each were protecting some ultimate secret. Then he rolled away from her and looked deep into her dark eyes. He thought he could drown there. He thought he'd seen eyes like that on wild creatures, the deer and doe rabbits he'd hunted as a boy. He tangled his hands in her hair, her braids twining like ropes.

He lowered his eyes when he unbuttoned his shirt and dropped it on the floor. Though it was chilly enough to see one's breath, he wasn't cold, not at all. He looked at the girl. Her eyes searched his, and as his hands fell to his pants, he blushed again. He turned half away from her because he was embarrassed at his erection and he got unbuttoned quick as he could and held her body to his own. Her lips opened to him again and she lay back and let her knees fall wide apart.

He climbed over her hip and stretched out on her, on her breasts and on her belly.

He thrust. He skidded. Thrust again.

And the world exploded.

YIP-YIP-YIP-YIP-YIP-YIP. It sounded like a banshee's shriek or the screams of a thousand coyotes. It was the Rebel yell, and it made the hair stand up on the boy's neck and his erection got cold, already it was shriveling. His ass felt very naked.

A tremendous crash of gunfire downstairs, one shot running over another as they raced pell-mell for their targets. Among the pistol shots, the harsher cough of shotguns. Screams, men and women.

Another roar of gunfire, as if a second wave were chasing the first. The boy was on his feet now, shivering; white goose bumps were all over his naked flesh. His cock was small and glistening as though it were a kangaroo baby surprised outside its pouch.

Footsteps pounding up the stairs, more than one man, that's for sure, but hard to tell how many and again that YIP-YIP-YIP. A door crashed open and once more the shots echoed through the frame house. Another woman's scream joined the chorus from below.

The boy's hand was shaking as he reached for his gunbelt and his fingers quivered so badly he couldn't work the holster flap. "Quantrill," he whispered. "My God, it's Quantrill!"

The girl rolled off the bed and took Sam's arm. In a very great hurry, she flung open the door of Sallie's chifforobe and pushed the boy toward it.

Down the hall another door was kicked off its hinges. Once more the walls vibrated from the crash of pistol fire.

"Down here, Cole. This room's empty!"

The boy stood among Sallie Webster's fancy gowns like a corpse standing up. He didn't protest when the girl hurled all his clothing in after him. He didn't say a word when his heavy riding boots slapped into his ankles.

"This one's locked up," sounded the voice just outside her door. The girl had only an instant to grip her dress together before the door came inward, knocked askew by a man's heavy boot.

Two Colt revolvers eyed her below a pair of eyes just as terrible as the pistols'. The man was a giant in a tremendous slouch hat with a feather stuck in the crown, and a wide silk scarf for a hatband.

The man's shirt was red, marred by darker red splotches of blood. He stepped through the broken door his boot had opened, his cold eyes searching the room. "Evenin', ma'am," he said, and the soft voicing of ordinary courtesies frightened her more than death threats would have. She felt faint. "Your man around, ma'am?" the intruder asked with great politeness.

That cleared her head faster than salts. Her eyes hurt and immediately began watering.

"No. No. I can't. I'm sick. . . ."

Swiftly the man dropped to one knee to check the space under the bed. Then without any further search, he backed swiftly to the broken door touching his hat with one of his pistols. "Go on downstairs with the others," he said. "Sorry to bother you."

And then he was gone. Roxie's fingers flew over the buttons of her dress. Her dress looked awful, but that couldn't be helped. She looked at the boa on the floor, but it looked strange to her and not particularly attractive.

She stepped out into the hall very swiftly, as if her instant compliance could draw the teeth of any suspicion. Or maybe she just wanted to put distance between herself and the boy.

She walked down that narrow hall in a daze, her hand to her face. She was biting her knuckle.

All the doors were thrown open to reveal each room's whore's bed, dresser, and water pitcher.

The doors were shattered. In the first, the broken-out window was the only witness to what had gone on. That and the pocks in the walls and the blood smear beside the window and the smell of black powder.

The room at the top of the stairs had a man's nude

body draped over the end of the bed with his ass in the air like a carelessly misplaced bag of laundry. His back was a red ruin, and the blood had run down across his head and down the sides of his face, ruining it too. His clothes were draped carefully over the wooden chair beside the bed and a whore's kimono was hung on the far wall.

Roxie didn't want to come down those narrow stairs, but she knew she had to follow the bearded man's orders so she took one step at a time.

The room was full of armed men dressed in butternut brown. Most of them were big. Most of them were drinking and a few had women pressed against the wall. One had his pants down around his ankles and his bare bony rump pumped against the woman who held him upright. Her face was very distant, as if she were on some other planet.

Dead men all over the floor. Some piled on top of each other, some impossibly crumpled. One, the sergeant, nearly torn in half from shotgun blasts. The women were in shock and the men didn't seem to notice them.

One good-looking man with vague distant features stood in the center of the room. William Quantrill was drinking from his flask because he didn't like the Light of Love's whiskey. Several of the butternut-clad guerrillas still had pistols in their hands, not pointing them, but simply present as though they were part of their musculature.

The parlor stank of blood and powder and death. Roxie felt the gorge rise in her throat, and she closed her eyes and breathed through her mouth until the reaction was under control.

The guerrilla finished with his whore, stepped back, and lifted his pants. With his other hand, he touched his hat in thanks. He said, "Much obliged."

Though the whore was fixed to the wall, skirt high, womanhood visible, no other guerrilla moved to take his place.

Some of the guerrillas were laughing heartily. "That boy over there, now he came closest to gettin' to his iron. Hell, he had his hand on his holster."

"And how about that Yankee upstairs? Hell, he was workin' hard when we killed him."

Laughter. "If we hadn't killed him, his face was so red, his heart was gonna burst."

A single shot upstairs. Everybody stopped. Ears cocked.

Quantrill stepped to the foot of the stairs and said, quite loudly, "Frank James?"

"Found me another one." The voice was low and gruff. "Hiding amongst the lady's gowns. I gave him a little tap."

Quantrill thought that was very funny. He laughed. His laugh was high and shrill, like a horse's laugh. "Right beside the right eye," he said.

1

John Slocum's boots were stuffed with newspaper and soled with cardboard. Slocum was one of the lucky ones. Most of the men wrapped their feet with rags.

The November rain sluiced into the woods and drove a few scraps of leaves into the mud. Slocum pulled the horse blanket around his shoulders and tipped his gray slouch hat over his eyes.

A teamster sloshed by, thock, thock, thock, the mud sucking at his feet. A ruined bucket dangled from his hand. In it, the teamster had half a dozen whiskey bottles, a couple of pounds of fence staples, and four old iron gate hasps. The battery had enough shot for three rounds per gun and enough powder for six. The battery commander, Captain Varner, meant to make up the difference with grapeshot.

Slocum was on foot, of course. On poor rations, a man can fight longer than a horse, and by sparing his big gray, he'd get fifteen or twenty minutes hard riding from her when the time came. The horse was drawn up with the battery horses behind the caissons, which was no big obstacle, but wasn't much of a target either.

The battery commander was a taciturn squarehead from the Valley. Captain Varner had seen service (as he was wont to remark) under the dukes of Coblenz, and a better gun captain didn't pull a lanyard on either side of the line.

Not that there was a line, really, not in this damned wilderness. The second growth slash pine, alder, sycamore, and low cedar grew so dense, a man couldn't see a hundred yards to his front and no more than that to the side. Units lost contact with units on their flanks —men and supplies hurried from the rear often went astray. Galloping cavalry patrols found themselves willy-nilly behind enemy lines and had learned to fire before asking questions.

Slocum's battery was a cork. Whenever the Yankees mounted an attack, this battery wheeled into the breach. Four twelve pounders—twelve-pound Napoleons to be exact—rifled with a half twist. General Lee ordered all the six-pound guns melted down in favor of these heavier models because—as he put it—"A six pounder isn't worth the lives of the men who serve it."

The guns had seen hard use and their gunners worse. One of the Napoleons started life with a Michigan regiment that had been overrun at Second Manassas. It shot like the three guns made for the Confederacy by Danford and Smith in Chattanooga. No truer, no worse.

Two of the guns bore deep cuts in the metal from shrapnel. The shrapnel had cut the guns and their crews alike. The guns lived to fight again another day.

This morning, in the rain, nobody manned the guns. Beside each gun, an oil-soaked torch sputtered and spat and sent its wavering plume of greasy smoke into the sky. The lanyard holes were plugged and leather stoppers exactly capped the muzzles. The battery was about as relaxed as it ever got. Only Captain Varner had served with the battery for more than a year. All its original gunners were long since moldering under the earth and the present contingent had been drawn from everywhere. Two gunners had been seamen with the Confederate navy until the *Monitor* sank. When the waves closed over the iron decks of "the cheesebox on a raft" for the last time, that spelled finis to any maritime dreams Richmond had, so two of Varner's gunners had had considerable practice on a heaving deck but none hauling four tons of obstinate iron along crooked paths in a vast inland jungle.

Some of the other gunners had been farm boys just short weeks ago. They knew the pitchfork and were learning the ramrod because it was the easiest position to learn, though you always had the chance of having the wooden pole blown clean through you if the gun trainer didn't cap the vent at just the right time.

Any European manual of war will tell you no battery artillery can exist in a vacuum. Artillery must be protected by a screen. The French insist artillery should be provided with a detachment of infantry. The Prussians claim artillery can function behind stable lines with a small cavalry screen.

That was John Slocum's job. He was the cavalry screen. Him and one oldster on a big jenny. The oldster carried one brand-new .52 Spencer carbine and a double-bit ax, tied behind his saddle. He never said two words to John Slocum. Every time the Yankees attacked, he killed officers with his carbine and laid about with the ax when the Yankees got close enough.

John Slocum had a suicide job. That didn't bother him too much. For the past four years, he'd seen most forms of death and hadn't thought himself immune to it. Beauregard, Buell, Jackson, and now Lee. He'd fought in northern Virginia and as a sharpshooter in Missouri. He'd been one of the last men through Vicksburg before Grant seized the fort, and closed the river to the Confederates.

John Slocum had just twenty-one years behind him, and he figured somewhere about two or three days in front.

So long as General Lee had room to maneuver, he took on one Union army after another and destroyed them all with feints, superior tactics, and finer intelligence.

Until Grant.

Grant's policy of warfare was as simple as it was terrible. Press the enemy; never lose contact; fight every day until they surrender or die.

From the day Grant took the field against the Army of Northern Virginia, it was doomed. Day after day, week after week, month after month, he pressed, he attacked.

The weary Confederates killed two to one, but it

didn't matter. The Confederates fought on shorter and shorter rations and that didn't matter either. The ammunition grew short and much of it was captured directly from the Yanks; it didn't matter. Grant wore them down and killed them.

John Slocum was assigned to the battery just three weeks ago and already half the faces behind the guns were new faces. Hell, he hadn't made a single new acquaintance. Why make a new friend just to bury him?

John Slocum's hair was black and thick. Black enough and shiny enough to suggest Indian blood. He'd heard rumors there was a little Cherokee back in the family, but didn't care one way or another.

He wore the cavalryman's slouch hat, with gold braid, because young as he was, he was a full lieutenant in the CSA. The hat funneled the rain down the back of his neck and the duster he wore was no account.

The water sloshed inside his boots as he squished through the mud. Strapped across his back was a Henry carbine he'd taken off a Yankee cavalryman. Somebody called the Henry "the gun you can load on Sunday and fire all week." It held thirteen .44 caliber cartridges in the tube under the barrel and Slocum had four spare tubes tucked behind his belt against his back. The Henry cartridges were almost waterproof, but he kept the rifle muzzle down out of habit. Over his right shoulder saddlebags dangled. Inside the saddlebags he had four revolvers. Three of them were Colts—two Colt Navy .31s and a Colt Dragoon, which was a .44. His fourth pistol was a J. W. Dance—the Confederate armory's imitation of the Colt. Its metal was too soft and ill fitted, and Slocum meant to get him another Colt as soon as he got close enough to a Yankee cavalry officer. Only the cavalry fought with revolvers and you didn't see much cavalry in these damn woods.

The whistling roar of cannon fire over their heads. The Confederates didn't look up. It wasn't more than the noontime salute. One of the gun crews had a good-sized fire and most of the men stood around trying to dry their clothes. Only good thing about a battle in a forest: you don't lack firewood.

The battery stood athwart the crossroads at Burr Hill—just a country crossroads between Culpepper and Chancellorsville. Three of the guns were set in the road itself, their muzzles offering a sour welcome to any travelers. The left and right guns were in the forest on either side, muzzles elevated full, like mortars. A thin line of skirmishers—Louisiana Tigers—were three hundred yards on down the road, and Slocum supposed they'd give the battery plenty of notice before they were overrun, but he wished he could see better.

He shaded his green eyes. Raindrops and mist.

The Confederate right had been engaged for two days now—Sheridan's men against A. P. Hill. For two days and nights the distant tumble of cannon had come from that one direction and from the sounds, the battle had gone first to the Yankees, then to the Confederates, same as usual. The battery had no feelings about it except, perhaps, "Better you than me, brother."

Army rations that had never been enough to stretch a man's belly had dwindled each year of the war and now John Slocum's belly stuck to his backbone as if it were the same organ.

He marched back and forth behind the battery—it helped keep him warm. Their right flank was anchored by Hood's Texas Rifles and their left was nailed down by more Louisiana Tigers. The Tigers were Cajuns and a man couldn't understand half of their funny high-pitched jabber, but they could fight all right.

The air smelled of cookfires, artillery fires smoldering deep in the woods, and the stink of unburied men and animals. Slocum thought it'd take years to sort out the tangled bodies lying out there in the rain, and even then they'd never get everybody right.

Lee lost eight thousand men in six miles of forest and Grant lost half again that number.

The gun crews stood around the fire or made their

sassafras tea (coffee had been nonexistent since the start of the Union blockade and tea had vanished a full year ago), smoking their pipes or roll-your-owns. Nobody talked. Didn't seem like much to say. They would die here along a forgotten road in this forgotten forest for a cause nobody remembered too well. They fought because they were too stubborn to break.

The cannon on the right increased tempo, the concussions following one on another as if they were pursuing something. Nobody looked up. One man had built a low shelter with his duster. He was reading something. Testament, most likely.

Slocum came up beside the battery commander. The two of them calmly searching the mist.

"Reckon they're out there?" Slocum asked conversationally.

"They will come. They will come, Mister Slocum. You can bet your boots on that."

"I wouldn't bet these boots on a sure thing," Slocum smiled.

The earnest commander didn't get the joke. "Yes," he said. "The Yankee troops will drive against this flank if our left flank holds, and they will drive against this flank if it doesn't hold. We will kill a few here on this road and wheel our caisson and run, because it's no sense losing guns that are out of ammunition. Perhaps there will be more powder and shot some other time."

It sounded unlikely, Slocum thought, but Confederate supply had worked similar miracles before.

A single shot, barely audible through the rain. Both men's ears perked up. Neither spoke until it was clear the one shot wasn't a prelude.

"When it's wet, sound travels not so far, I think," Varner said.

"Uh-huh."

For the first time the commander turned to examine the young man standing beside him. Though Captain Varner was not an imaginative man, Slocum made him nervous. Cold as he was, hungry, there was something terrible about the young man. Varner couldn't figure it. "You have fought only in this war?" he asked.

"It's all the war any man could want," Slocum said.

"I ask if you are a professional soldier," Varner insisted stiffly.

Slocum wasn't less confused. Any man had to be professional in this war if he was to survive. He said so. He said also that he was a farmer's son and hoped to farm himself once the war was over.

Varner had been a grain merchant before. "In Parnassus, Virginia." Because he had a better than average education, he added, "Parnassus was the Greek mountain thought to be the home of gods."

"Do tell," Slocum said politely. He pulled a piece of old hardtack from his haversack. He'd meant to make supper of it, but the rain was getting to it. Roughly he pulled off a piece and handed it to Varner. The stubby commander nodded his thanks. His heavy teeth chomped down.

Another shot somewhere up there. Varner wiped his mouth on his sleeve. A few gunners stood up and strolled back to their guns. The raindrops were smaller now, more like a fine mist, but the visibility wasn't any greater than it had been.

One gunner bent over his muzzle cap, examining the lashing. Another peered down the length of the barrel and moved the tail piece very slightly with the aiming bar.

One ammo bearer stretched up to the sky, hands high over his head, and flexed his fingers. He ambled back with his buddy toward the barrels of gunpowder.

Most of the men were facing front. Only a few still around the warming fire.

A brief rattle of shots that settled down to a steady brisk exchange of gunfire. The snaps and whistles over their heads told the battery the Tigers weren't doing all the shooting.

A whistle, a roar, as the Yankee artillery opened up.

In this mist, the Yankees couldn't see to correct, and the balls crashed way off to the right. A shrill scream from a wounded man (horse?).

Varner didn't give any orders. His gunners moved back to their guns, speaking softly, like men returning to the job after lunch. Nothing new in it and the snap and pop over their heads wasn't new either. When one Yankee bullet dropped short and whanged against the bell of a Napoleon, ringing it for everybody to hear, its crew laughed and one man bent to pick through the mud, hoping to find the bullet for a souvenir.

Slocum climbed out of the roadbed. The banks were four feet higher than the road itself and downed timber would offer him some protection. He wouldn't have much work to do until the last—when the Tigers passed back through the battery, but then he'd have his hands full. The other sharpshooter—the old man—climbed onto the back of his big jenny behind the guns and waited, same as he always did. He'd empty his Spencer, unlash his ax, and jump into the melee around the guns.

Men had ramrods in their hands, though they wouldn't have any use for them until the guns had fired. The gunners stood beside the leather muzzle caps.

Faint yells through the mist down the road but impossible to tell whose. The shots were a steady roar. Slocum eased himself down in a stump hole where most of him would be out of sight, and laid his saddlebags on the bare earth before him.

A horse charged up the road from the rear. Its rider wore the braid and epaulets of a member of General Lee's headquarters staff. Still on the run, he dismounted where Varner stood, with his arms behind his back, placidly puffing his pipe, waiting for the battle to catch up to him.

The two men put their heads together, briefly. Varner pointed and the staff major hurried toward the spot where John Slocum was laying his spare ammo tubes out where they'd be easy to get to.

"Lieutenant Slocum?"

Though the major's uniform was as tattered as Slocum's own, at least the damn thing was clean. The major had one sleeve pinned up and the left side of his face wore the long puckered scar a triangular bayonet makes.

"I'm Slocum."

The major didn't waste words. Slocum didn't catch his name but the message was clear enough. Lieutenant Slocum's presence was required urgently at General Lee's headquarters.

Slocum had no idea why. "Not just now," he said quietly. He threw his Henry to his shoulder. The Henry wasn't awfully accurate over two hundred yards, but in this mist he wouldn't get any shots that long. Slocum explained, "There ain't but twenty Louisianans up front there and they'll fall back when it gets hot and we're gonna be seein' some puke blue uniforms comin' at us. So I just reckon I'll just stay where I'll do some good." He jacked a round into the Henry's chamber.

"I'm from General Lee himself. . . ."

"You already said that. When the battery moves, I'll come with you." Slocum shot a glance at the man's empty sleeve. "If you're meaning to wait, you better be ready to fight."

Out of the mist a retreating figure stepped, then another. The Louisiana Tigers retreating unhurriedly. Every few steps they'd kneel and fire into the mist. Slocum couldn't see what they were shooting at. The staff major unflapped his pistol holster and Slocum opened his saddlebags. It doesn't do to let cap and ball pistols get wet.

A couple more Tigers popped out of the mist, walking backward calmly, keeping to either side of the road. One of them held his arm funny and Slocum could see the streak of blood washing his sleeve.

Slocum knew that the Louisianans had left some men behind this time. Weren't so many as the day before.

Varner was hollering to the two guns up on the bank.

They were to depress their muzzles and their fire for point-blank work. "Load with grapeshot."

One of the Tigers went down. Now the barrage over the battery's head was louder and more determined. The Yankees were getting near. The man who'd fallen got up again. He limped behind the guns.

The one-armed major settled down in Slocum's stump hole. "How many?" he asked in a listless voice.

Slocum shrugged. "Enough to move the Tigers," he said.

The last Louisiana Tigers were even with the guns now.

"Infantry," they said.

"Regulars," they said.

"A battalion—at least."

"Now you know," Slocum said.

Once the Tigers slipped past the guns, their part of it was over. Like Slocum, they'd supply covering fire when the attack came. Unlike him, they'd heave on the gun carriages and lash down the muzzles when it was time to skedaddle.

The major had his pistol out. He removed his hat and tilted it over his revolver, a small roof to keep it dry. He was one of those men who grind their teeth unknowingly and he was doing it now.

The flat blap of muzzle blasts and winks deep inside the fog. Varner was pacing behind his guns, like a man with nothing more on his mind than a Sunday promenade. His gunners in place, the gun captains had their hands on the lanyard, ready to pull.

"My knees are getting cold," the major said. "I always stiffen up when my knees get cold or wet."

Both men were kneeling in the mud. "Yeah," Slocum said.

And the next moment they were there, a thick clot of Yankees hurrying through the rain. They had those long bayonets on their Springfields and they broke into a hard run as soon as they spotted the cannon.

"Fire."

And the cannons bucked back against their stakes, and the gun captains covered the vents as the men with the ramrods sponged out the red-hot barrels. A second later, the powder bags and shot were inserted and again the ramrods dipped into the muzzles. The three road guns fired again, on Varner's command.

The only Union soldiers in the road were dead. Most of the survivors had crawled up the banks into the forest. Their officers were shouting commands.

The guns fired again.

As usual, the first ranks were kids. Men who knew better held back and let the recruits and green troops take the point. The forest was a foot-tangling, ankle-twisting, stoop and twist mess of short trees, vines, and saplings. The Yankee charge wasn't as quick as it might have been. The Yankees looked as though they were charging through seaweed. Slocum fired. The road cannon fired. Slocum fired twice more. When you killed the men in the front of a charge, you took some of the steam out of it, and three bluebellies had dropped into the brush, their long-barreled, long-bayoneted rifles useless now. The half dozen or so soldiers directly behind closed up together for comfort, and at the command of one of them—some private who didn't have the right to give the order but thought of himself as a "natural born leader"—the six fired harmlessly at enemies they couldn't see. Brought down one gunner too, by a piece of luck. The gunner turned loose of the vent before the ramrod handler had time to get the ramrod out. Some sparks burst into flame inside the barrel where they hadn't been cleaned out, and the gun fired when the rush of air got to it, freed by the gunner's dead finger. The ramrod went through the body of the man holding it, chased by the twelve-pound iron ball. The ramrod traveled through him, the ball liquefied him. Once it had hurtled three hundred yards, somewhere down the road the ramrod started flipping end for end. The ball, deflected by its passage through the handler's body, hit the center of the road, furrowed, skipped, and embedded itself harmlessly in the bank where the road took a turn. Once the ramrod lost a little velocity, it hit one end in the ground, sprang back into the air, and still whirling, cracked a Yankee officer's horse.

That officer commanded the detachment singled out for the follow-up attack. The officer, a captain, had his juniors gathered around him for last-minute orders. The captain was quite popular with his juniors because he was extremely courteous and wore a tailor-made uniform, cutting quite a figure in the officers' quadrilles. His horse went down all of a sudden, its spine broken by the errant ramrod, and took the captain with it. The horse pinned the captain, crushing him against the hard clay ground. With a single cry, the man was dead. The junior officers looked at each other, eyes wide with alarm, and then a kind of black fury came over those young faces, specific and communicable as a disease. The dead man's second-in-command forced his words out between gritted teeth: "Let's get us some of that rebel scum," and signaled for the bugler to sound the charge.

Mistake. His men piled down into the narrow road and rushed forward, pell-mell, with a mighty cheer, directly into the mouths of the Confederate guns, which were useful once again. They thundered into the wave of blue. Thundered again. The shot plowed through the dense ranks of men like a scythe. They went down. The survivors jumped for the roadsides, away from those terrible guns, to join their companions for the slower attack through the underbrush.

Slocum laid down his empty Henry, selected another tube of ammunition, dabbed his finger at the brass carrier button, and rammed it home. He rolled back into the stock of his gun and kept on shooting.

The old-timer across the road was working his Spencer. Slocum figured he'd take the bulk of the attack.

Varner had teamsters approaching the tails of the guns. The teamsters ran along crouched, tugging caissons and horses behind them, hoping they didn't lose a mount to Yankee bullets before they got hitched up and down the road. The cannons in the road had one round left and were loaded and ready to go except for the left gun, which was lacking a gunner and ramrod and slower than the other two. The cannons on the bank spoke—their deadly buckets of junk cutting down men and small saplings alike. The old-timer booted his jenny forward, his hand on the lashings of his ax. He eyed Slocum and raised his hand in a wave. Slocum lifted his slouch hat slightly before setting it back on his forehead. The major was firing his Dance. From time to time, Slocum let a Yankee in close enough so the major could use his Dance on them. The major always fired twice and he never hit his Yankees twice in the same part of their body, but they always went down, so Slocum didn't get critical of the major's marksmanship.

Slocum's Henry picked from the farthest ranks of blue figures—those untouched by the grapeshot.

The road guns fired again and maybe they did some damage down the road and maybe they didn't. The mist was too thick to tell and all the Yankees seemed to be on the road banks.

Varner was shouting. Nobody could hear. So many times had they executed this maneuver that there wasn't need for commands. The horses were attached to the tailpieces, the tailpieces lifted onto their caisson wheels, and the teamsters laid into them.

Slocum gripped the major's one arm. "Time we made ourselves scarce," he said. "The roadside guns will fire once more and then they'll pull out past us. Then we go. We're supposed to sting 'em a little."

The major cocked his head and then nodded his head in the manner of a man who doesn't understand but hopes to figure things out one step at a time.

The roadside guns slammed back against their aiming pegs and again buckets of lethal junk spun and tore through the woods. The teamsters hurried their teams forward without noting what damage the guns had done.

These men had confidence in grapeshot at close quarters. Slocum climbed out of his stump hole, slid down into the road, and ran for his horse. The horse wore blinders on both eyes, though he wasn't especially spooky. John Slocum had heard a horse will shy at flashes beside his face, and in a world where there wasn't much he could control, John Slocum could control that at least.

The major was getting onto his own horse. Slocum dismissed him: a man can't shoot and ride with one arm gone. Above the road the teamsters were cursing and wrestling the guns in the dense undergrowth. The Yankees were very much closer, coming as fast as they could run, and Slocum fired his Henry one full tube, another, and the breech got hot and the brass shell casings flew out past his ear. The teamsters howled with triumph and with a jerk the right roadside cannon was rolling.

The Yankees were very close to the final gun and the old-timer booted his jenny forward, swinging the double-bit ax in a glistening circle. Bullet hit him. He jerked as if he'd been hit with a bat. But the old-timer managed to get his ax in the air. His hands must have been getting numb because Slocum saw the gleam in the air when it fell.

The last gun was beginning to roll, and teamsters and gunners were jumping aboard and onto the horses and the gun captain had his arms around the wheel horse's neck as though it were salvation. Lurching and heaving, the gun crashed through the woods until the bank sloped easier and it could get down to the road.

Slocum had his Colts working now, with their steady hammer, their steady buck, the way they slammed back into his hands as his eyes roved the Union line picking his targets. Whenever he could, he put one round through two of them. Wherever he could, he brought a man down so he'd tangle the men behind him.

The old man toppled off his jenny and hit on his back in the road.

The one-armed major had reins in his teeth and the J. W. Dance firing in his one good hand.

Slocum kneed his horse and leaned over. The oldtimer had two bloody patches on his chest and one of them was just about over his heart. His eyes were already glazing and his mouth got loose. Slocum snatched the jenny's reins, nodded to the major, and they wheeled and made tracks; practically stood their horses on end.

Every Yankee rifle opened fire on the two fleeing men. Slocum was pressed flat, hanging on to his horse's side to present the least possible target. The major rode stiff backed as any huntmaster approaching the easiest jumps on a pleasant Sunday afternoon.

One bullet plucked at Slocum's sleeve and another cut a chunk of horsehair and hide off his big gray mare. Three fast jumps and they were in the fog, rushing through a world of damp whiteness. The crack of the Union balls passing by got muffled. Slocum dug his heels into his horse's side, but stayed low. Silly to die now. Silly.

The horse scrabbled around a bend in the road, and as if they'd been transported to another planet, the rain of Union gunfire stopped. Slocum slowed to a walk. His horse was puffing and blowing. In one smooth gliding motion he dismounted again.

The two men walked side by side. "Where'd you lose your arm?" Slocum asked.

"Cold Harbor," the major said shortly. He spat into the road. The major pulled a plug of roughcut chewing tobacco from his tunic pocket and offered it. Slocum nodded his no thanks.

"I was at Antietam," Slocum said. "Missed Cold Harbor though." He grinned but shut the grin off as quick as it came. "Christ, I was full of hellfire. Try anything once. Anything. Lucky I didn't get shot down; but they say God takes care of fools, babies, and drunks."

The major eyed the young man walking beside him. No more than twenty-five, he guessed.

Nothing on either side of them but the bare yellow earth of the road cut, and above that the forest. Not shot up like the forest they'd just left, but just as sparse. On their right they heard the steady rumble of artillery.

"Won't be good news," John Slocum said calmly.

The major looked his puzzlement.

"Back at headquarters," Slocum said. "I been called into headquarters three times. Twice to get bad news from home and once to transfer me from an outfit I liked into an outfit that wasn't worth a damn. Maybe you boys just picked me special to announce the war is over. That's it, ain't it?"

"No."

"Didn't think so."

The figures on the road ahead of them were Louisiana Tigers, set up here to hold the Yankees if they should come this far. The Tigers were dug in on both sides of the road and Varner's battery was two hundred yards farther on.

When Slocum saw the first picket he stopped and hollered who they were and that they were coming in slow. Stonewall Jackson had his arm shot off by one of his own pickets and John Slocum thought that was pure foolishness.

"The other sharpshooter?" the major asked.

"He was dead. I'll keep the mule. Maybe I can trade her off for some feed for this one. Wish I could have got his Spencer. You can trade for oats with a carbine."

"That sharpshooter did a fine job."

Slocum passed through the front ranks of the Louisiana Tigers. He didn't relax until he spotted familiar faces who knew him and waved.

"Yeah," Slocum said. "Everybody does fine. Why do they want me at headquarters?"

"I don't know."

At the battery, Slocum told Varner about his other sharpshooter and his orders to report to Lee.

"You leave me with no one to cover my withdrawals," Varner said. He was talking to Slocum but looking at the major. "I need two good men very quickly. Men with repeating rifles. Do you know how much damage my guns have done? How we've stung them and stung them again? Without this battery, the left flank could not hold. I don't have any more shot and only powder enough for two more firings." His eyes had dismissed Slocum and were making his case to the major from headquarters. "Do you understand I must have more ammunition?" he begged.

"I'll do what I can," the major said.

Varner spread his arms wide apart as though he were releasing all the birds in the world or his own responsibilities. Slocum asked him to care for his horse until he came back. The big jenny was in better condition.

The rain had quit. The sun was burning the mist off the road and more slowly out of the pockets in the woods. The mat of dead leaves gave off its faintly sour aroma. As they rode across a broad patch of sunlight, John Slocum stretched and perhaps five years fell off him as if he were too slippery to hold them. He thought he hadn't ever seen anything as beautiful as that patch of sunlight. He became aware of his smell—a man who'd been on the line for weeks without respite, who washed what he could when he could. The smell of gunpowder stuck to him too. He snorted to himself.

The right side of John Slocum's face was powder-stained from the Henry and both his hands were grimed from the Colts. He was muddy to the knees and his elbows and chest were muddy too in a long stripe that looked as though it had been painted on him.

The jenny had a good easy gait. It wouldn't be fast, but it could keep going all day. Maybe he'd swap the horse instead of the jenny. He needed endurance more than he needed speed.

The headquarters of the Army of Northern Virginia lay behind the center bulge of the line, held by its strongest corps. Corps headquarters was a sprawling affair and it wasn't more than a half hour's easy ride from the flanks. Roads and paths became numerous.

Files of Yankee prisoners being marched back to the adjutant. Some of the prisoners were badly wounded—others laughed and joked as they marched before a few Confederate guards. One old gray-clad trooper to guard fifty prisoners. No danger in that. Slocum and the major were forced off the road by one such column. As they passed by, Slocum took the gibes in silence.

"Hey, Johnny Reb! Just let me know where your girl is. I'll look her up for you."

"Hell! He'll do more than look her up!" Laughter.

These prisoners, taken just that morning, filled Slocum's heart with envy. For them, the war was over. Young recruits, they'd come to fight in the most terrible battle ever fought under the American sun and now they were laughing and joking because they'd been as lucky as a man can get. The adjutant would offer them the choice he offered every Yankee prisoner: sign a parole promising not to take up arms against the CSA or take the troop train south to Andersonville, the Confederate P.O.W. camp. Recruits are mighty foolish but it was easy to understand the correct choice. They'd sign the parole all right and they'd be hoofing their way home that very night.

Big double tents at Lee's headquarters held provisions, though the long line of wagons and officers outside those tents told their own sad story.

Ten percent. That was the rule today. If a requisition asked for a thousand cases of minié balls, the laboring soldiers were allowed to load a hundred. If a hundred, ten. And you couldn't fool these quartermasters. If you upped your order, some shrewd-faced quartermaster sergeant would say, "You're from the 14th Georgia, Captain? And you want fifty barrels of black powder. I don't know as if you've heard, Captain, but the Yankees have been striking at the center of our line and I can't let you have but two. It ain't been too hot on the left flank lately anyway."

Elaborately sandbagged hospital tents, where the surgeons worked until the limb bucket filled or their strength gave out. A steady trickle of wounded stumbled toward the field hospital on their comrades' arms. Always two wounded men supporting each other. They'd lost too many deserters when they'd allowed the healthy to carry the sick. One look at the bloody, lousy medical facilities was enough to drive the strongest hearts over the hill.

Outside the field hospital between a hundred fifty and two hundred soldiers sat down in the mud. Some lay in the mud and a very few had been propped up against tree stumps on stretchers. Two black orderlies carried the men into the tent. The batting average of the surgeons was about ten percent. Ninety percent of all seriously wounded died right here. The filth and horrible conditions saw to that.

Slocum wasn't interested. He'd seen it all before—the lines of men desperate for unavailable provisions—the wounded desperately seeking medical help. John Slocum didn't figure to live to the end of the war. His job didn't have much longevity to it. He hoped he died all at once rather than a bit at a time.

The major drew up before a small gray tent with a general's flag flying at the roof peak. A couple of sentries stood outside with muskets at parade rest. Both of them were very old: in their sixties, Slocum guessed. The major leaned over his horse's neck. "This man's to see the general," he announced. One of the oldsters nodded while the other came around briskly to take Slocum's reins. Slocum guessed they'd worked at some fancy hotel before the war, doing just this kind of work.

He relinquished the reins and swung down. "Don't forget the ammunition," he said to the major. He didn't turn to see if the major had heard. Reminding him was all he could do for Varner now.

One of the oldsters held back the tent flap. When Slocum obeyed the invitation, he realized his palms were sweating. Funny thing—to be frightened of your own general and contemptuous of the Yankees who tried to kill you.

It was dim inside the tent—dim enough to keep a kerosene lamp burning on the corner of a campaign desk and another on a tall old trunk in the far corner. A map hung from a tripod arrangement, and four officers were gathered around it, arguing about a road crossing. Slocum wondered if they knew about the crossing he'd just abandoned. Three of the officers were young; two majors and a captain. Like his guide, each of them had been wounded in some way and the captain had a wooden leg. The fourth officer was very quiet and the focus of all their attention.

He seemed awfully small. He seemed terribly old. His beard was the white of an old snowdrift and his cheeks were cold and pale. His uniform was clean and neat and the stars of his rank rode easily on his shoulder. He wore no sword or pistol. He wore shoes instead of boots. His eyes were at the bottom of deep pools of weariness and his eyebrows asked Slocum the question.

"John Slocum, sir. You wanted to talk to me."

And Slocum, who rarely threw any kind of a salute, did so, in honor of his general, Robert E. Lee.

"Mister Slocum." Lee's nod was quite casual. His face broke into a very faint smile. Without raising his voice, he said, "Gentlemen, why don't you get yourselves some nourishment. The lieutenant and I won't be long and it promises to be a tiring day."

One of the officers snarled, "Damn Grant," between his teeth.

"Yes," Lee said simply. He kept his eyes on Slocum's face and the curious half-smile on his lips, while his staff filed out behind him.

He wasn't a very tall man, not more than five and a half feet, but his carriage was flawless and he seemed taller.

"Ah," he said, "but I forget my manners, sir. You've just come off the line and I'm sure you can use a little refreshment." With his own hands he poured a wineglass full of something that looked like and smelled like and was, by God, fine Kentucky bourbon. It made Slocum suddenly dizzy. It had been a long time and he hadn't had a damn thing to eat that morning. He put one hand out to brace himself against the corner of Lee's desk. A flash of concern across the older man's parchment face. "Why don't you sit down."

"Thank you, sir." Slocum found a canvas stool. He didn't know what to do with his half-empty wineglass and set it on his knee.

Lee moved in front of his desk. He didn't lean or sit on it. "Tell me something about yourself, son," he said.

Slocum waited, hoping for more specific instructions. Lee smiled a slightly bigger smile. "I come from the Georgia mountains," Slocum said. "Livestock farm called Slocum's Stand. I was with Stonewall in the Valley. Got detached for a stint with Beauregard. Came back to General Jackson just a couple of weeks before he got killed. They made me a lieutenant 'cause there weren't many officers left. I'm no great shakes at officering. I'm a sharpshooter, with a 'shoot and skedaddle' battery attached to the Louisiana Tigers." Slocum stopped. Was this what Lee wanted to hear?

"Beauregard?"

"Yes, sir. I fought with him in Missouri, opposite the jayhawkers."

Lee wore his puzzlement plain. His drawl was very soft but perfectly audible—the voice of one who could permit himself no defects of speech or manner. "Why?"

"I was carryin' dispatches between the Valley Army and the Army of Northern Tennessee. Never figured it mattered where I was fightin'. It's all the same war."

Lee's laugh was soft. Later Slocum wondered if he'd imagined it. "Well, son," he said. "Do you know anybody in the Confederate legislature? Got any governors in your family?"

"No, sir," Slocum answered sturdily. "There was just me and my brother and Pa, and my brother died at Gettysburg and Pa took cholera last spring and he's buried too. We Slocums are some account to our neighbors and those who know us in Calhoun County, but I don't reckon we're related to any high officials." He wanted to ask Lee why all the questions, but for once, didn't mind leashing his curiosity. He didn't figure to be with this man very long or ever again and Slocum was enjoying the privilege.

Abruptly, the general turned to his field desk. "I have orders for you, Slocum," he said, unfolding a single piece of paper. "You're to return to Richmond on the best available transport—that'll be the Danville rail, which is still clear." He thrust the orders at Slocum.

Slocum stared at the official paper. "To report to the secretary of war?" he asked.

"That's correct. James Heddon." It was impossible to know what he thought of Heddon from his voice.

"I don't understand, sir."

Again that fleeting smile. "Nor do I, Lieutenant. Now if you were related to prudent and powerful relatives in Richmond, then I could understand. Some of our finer citizens, I regret to say, moved their young men to England in 1861 and hope to have them remain until this dreadful strife is concluded." He raised one hand to forestall Slocum's protest. "I do not believe you are such a man and I confess your orders are mysterious to me."

Slocum shook his head.

"When you return to this army," Lee said, as he reclaimed Slocum's orders and signed them, "I would like to hear what this was all about."

"Yes, sir." At the time, John Slocum meant to keep his promise, but as it turned out, there was no way in hell he could have.

2

Riders from Custer's unit of Sheridan's cavalry took pleasure cutting the Danville line and Mosby's Raiders liked to ambush them along the tracks and cut them down. The detachments were small—almost as though they were fighting a private war, only loosely connected to the greater war. They were fast to strike and counterstrike, and from day to day, Lee's quartermasters couldn't predict whether they'd have supply trains or not.

It wasn't a long run from Richmond, and it got shorter daily as Grant shoved the mass of the Army of the Potomac against Lee's army.

Grant never let Lee get loose. He never broke off contact. Every day the Danville railroad shortened. Sometimes by a hundred yards, sometimes a half mile, as more of it disappeared into Union hands.

Around the bend where the locomotive waited, Lee's infantry fought a delaying action.

Teamsters unloaded provisions from the train onto open wagons that'd haul them to the warehouses.

Locomotive, five flatcars, four boxcars, and two passenger cars. John Slocum stood beside the rear car, enjoying a quirly. He had his slicker tied around his shoulders like a blanket roll. Though he'd left his rifle with Varner and his extra pistols too, he carried a Colt on either hip and a full powder flask and plenty of spare bullets and primers in the leather pouch behind his gunbelt.

Though the fighting was only two hundred yards away and he could see the gray-clad backs of his fellow soldiers, John Slocum felt apart from the war.

The train crew was in the last boxcar now, helping the sweating teamsters to empty it. The engineer announced his plan to reverse the big driving wheels of the Baldwin 2-4-4-2 and push this train where it wasn't going to be shot to pieces.

The steam whistle blew, honk, honk, announcing the engineer's deadline. A new heavy volley of fire, and the Union troops started using mortars. Their first barrage—three rounds—burst fifty yards to the left of the train, and Slocum thought idly that that was pretty poor shooting even for bracketing rounds. A hail of loose metal fell on the train and some of it was hot and one nearly scorched the engineer's arm as he sat high in his cab. "Goddamn!" And he was hauling on the throttle even as his hand went to the whistle cord. His whistling now was shrill and continuous and he kept one eye on his gauge because he didn't want to lose his head of steam. He booted the trip lever on the firewall and the sandbox traps opened in front of the driving wheels dropping that badly needed extra bit of traction.

The flatcars, which had carried heavy goods up to Lee's army, were stacked with the bodies from that same army. Five high, eight deep, six wide, the pale yellow pine coffins were lashed down with cables.

The driving wheels spun, caught a grip on the sand and all the couplings clashed together. Teamsters and trainmen were jumping out of the last partly unloaded boxcar. Other trainmen were clamping the last holddowns on a load of coffins, and these men hurried alongside, still adjusting binders as the train picked up speed.

Slocum grabbed hold of the rear rail of the last car. The car passed two trainmen gasping beside the track. They'd hung on until their binders were taut.

Already the teamsters were moving out as the retreating infantry edged into the area where they'd been loading.

"Well," Slocum said to himself, "I guess that station's closed for good."

A gun car preceded the locomotive and ten slightly

wounded soldiers sat on kegs and boxes, hoping Custer's men wouldn't elect to derail and attack this train, because if he did, there wasn't too much, by God, they could do about it, and they'd be the first to fall.

The long pall of smoke puffed by over Slocum's head and dripped to the side of the tracks where it settled. Slocum entered one of those old-fashioned smoking cars, once, perhaps, the pride of the Danville R.R. and reserved for gentlemen of leisure.

Along the walls, the paneling was painted with chase scenes. Red-coated hunters bugling as they jumped improbable horses over impossibly high hedges. The chairs were all brown leather; heavy leather ottomans. Perhaps a dozen officers were sitting in the chairs. Most of them had parfleches at their sides. They were couriers. All of them wore clothing as tattered as his own.

Most of the other officers were seizing the chance for a little sleep. A couple captains were talking quietly in the corner, leaning over close so their words stayed private. John Slocum wandered around the smoking car to see what he might.

The carpet had been thick and new four years ago and even soldiers' boots hadn't been able to disguise its original magnificence. The woodwork was black walnut with beech for the paneling, and though it hadn't been washed since Sumter fell, it was quite handsome. Slocum bent to peer out the window. Not much to see but the other track.

He paced from one end of the car, nervous as a cat. He'd had to leave his jenny. Slocum always liked to command his own transportation. He'd been on trains before; they'd always made him jumpy. It worried him to have to put his life in a stranger's hands.

The Danville train wasn't making very much speed because it might round a bend and find a section where Yankees had torn up the tracks. So it poked along, making a five-hour journey of a four-hour trip, and soon the last of the officers in the train were asleep except for John Slocum, whose eyes never stopped moving.

Shacks beside the road. The forlorn look of ragged laundry on the line and a thin wisp of smoke coming out of a chimney made from a number ten tin can.

The towns they chugged through hadn't been destroyed—the Yankees hadn't been this far close to Richmond before—but they were singularly joyless. The folks Slocum saw were old, black, female, or very young.

Nobody waved at the train as it passed, not even the children. Sometimes the engineer hooted at crossings, but nobody ever waved back.

The train took an arc at Fredericksburg. They waited there for an hour while the caskets were unloaded and boxcars switched. None of the other officers woke to take note. Slocum stood on the back platform, smoking another quirly, curious about the huge marshaling yards. To the end, the Confederacy had plenty of rolling stock, but after Sheridan destroyed the Valley, very few provisions to put into them.

The train picked up speed from Fredericksburg, hurtling along at forty miles an hour as it roared by Spotsylvania.

Slocum stretched his feet on the ottoman and thought how foolish luxuries looked—how irrelevant—when life and death were too close together.

The sun was hanging low in the horizon as the train descended toward Richmond and the James. A few factories on the outskirts of the capital city, some belching smoke into the hazy dusk and now the tracks were six abreast instead of two. Slocum saw one other train. The locomotive roared straight through the signal blocks without a pause.

The Richmond station was a long red brick shed beside the James. The edge of the yard bordered the great wharves. The river side-wheelers were still busy, traveling to Lynchburg and Norfolk, but none of the great ocean-going schooners tied up there anymore. They rotted, sails furled and barnacle covered, at the mouth of the river. Trapped by the Union blockade, they were material for the sea worms.

No cabs. Outside the station, a couple blacks waited with buggy poles in their hands, like rickshaws. There weren't many horses in Richmond—if Longstreet didn't have them, Lee did.

In the great high-ceilinged shed Slocum asked a harried stationmaster for directions to the war office.

Slocum's orders told him to proceed to the secretary as soon as he arrived, but he was an old soldier and had other ideas. He'd skipped breakfast and lunch and now it was time for the last meal of the day, and he surely didn't intend to miss that one.

Halfway up the street, he found a sign, "The Tidewater Inn," which bore the pleasant emblem of a bowl of steaming something.

When the barmaid hurried over, he ordered a seafood supper with red potatoes because that's what they had. They also had some beer and some rum and water.

"Rum and water."

She turned to take his order to the kitchen, but paused and regarded him again. "Sir," she said, "I haven't seen you here before."

"I've never been in Richmond."

Her hands fluttered. "Well, I suppose I better tell you the Tidewater Inn doesn't accept any kind of scrip. Dinner is four bits in silver." She flounced away.

Slocum's grin was a little sour. "Funny thing when the capital of a country won't accept its own paper currency." It didn't bother him though; he had two dollars in silver and, hidden in his ammunition pouch, a gold double eagle. He'd won the coin in a poker game the year before, just before New Market. The men he'd played with were all dead now, so he figured it was his. Soldier's pay wasn't but twelve dollars a month and that was in scrip discounted ten to one when you could find someone who'd take it at all.

The Tidewater Inn was a big room with a serving counter outside the kitchen and eight good-sized tables.

You could sit just anywhere. The pine tables were scarred with initials, gouges, tobacco burns, and the scars where generations of hot platters had rested.

The air in the big room smelled musty and damp, and the fire in the huge fireplace couldn't warm a room this size.

"Mind if I sit?"

Tall, black-haired gent wearing a dark blue cloak and a swaggering kind of hat.

"Suit yourself," Slocum said.

Most of the other diners looked like legislators or merchants. Though a few men wore gray uniforms, their facings were quartermaster corps or judge advocate corps. No infantry or artillery officers here tonight. These officers seemed fairly well fed, which Slocum resented mightily.

New companion pulled an ivory toothpick out of a case and worried one of his molars. His eyes stayed on John Slocum. He'd noticed Slocum's twin Colts before he noted his face.

When the girl came back she smiled as she laid her platter down, but didn't take her hand off the lip of it until he dug in his pocket for four bits.

"The rum and water'll be another two bits," she said.

He thought that was awfully high and said so, but paid.

"I'll have a rum and water too," his companion said. The man had long hands, long eyebrows, long jaw, long mustaches—everything was long about him. Slocum dug into his fish.

The fish was sea trout, breaded in a batter and fried. It was real fine. Beside the trout was a mound of boiled turnips, a pile of boiled red potatoes, and some grits. Slocum ate it all and felt the warmth spreading through his entire body until it reached his ears, which glowed with prosperity.

His companion got his drink. "You from the front?" he asked.

"Yep." Slocum concentrated on the rest of his rum and water.

"How is it up there?" The man's voice cut into his enjoyment like an interrogator. He wasn't drinking his rum and water.

"More fun than a barrel of monkeys," Slocum said.

The man said, real quick, "Don't be impertinent with me, sir."

Slocum looked up. The man's hands were empty.

The man paused, waiting for Slocum's response, but Slocum figured he wouldn't like it when he got it and held off delivery. He worked on his rum and water.

Finally the long man said, "How do men in Lee's army feel about Lincoln?"

Slocum shrugged.

"Do they understand the perfidy of the man? He is the Antichrist."

Slocum didn't bother to shrug. He wished this fool would go somewhere else while he finished his drink.

"You wear weapons, sir. Would you like to dispatch the Antichrist?"

Slocum looked around for a napkin. Wasn't any. He drained his rum in one swallow. "Be seein' you," he said politely.

The fool half rose as though he meant to detain him, but Slocum cast off such an air of sudden danger that the long man backed off and slumped back into his chair. As Slocum settled his hat straight, the man introduced himself, "John Wilkes Booth, at your service, sir."

Though the sun still hung tangential with the dull red horizon, traffic wasn't heavy in the Richmond streets. A couple dozen beggars, some white, some black, intercepted the lanky young man as he made his way toward the Confederate War Department. Because he was full of food and feeling flush, he gave each of them a little money and stayed for each blessing that was offered before continuing on his way.

No guards outside the heavy bronze doors of the imposing marble building, but there was a reception desk, unoccupied, just inside.

A huge barnlike structure, it had been the Commonwealth of Virginia's office building before it got conscripted for the Confederacy.

It was after six. Nobody at the plain wooden desk. Halls branching off from the central rotunda and climbing to the upper floors, a wide marble staircase. Slocum scratched his head. Upstairs, somewhere, he heard a door slam and footsteps echoing on the hard marble floors. A tuneless whistle.

The man who came down the stairs carried a small leather satchel tucked under his arm. The tune he whistled was "Barbara Allen." He had the pale face of a man who spends all his time indoors and the sanguine countenance of a man looking forward to dinner with his family.

"Pardon me," Slocum said at the foot of the stairs. "I'm looking for the office of the secretary of war."

Curious eyes inspected him from head to foot. "Mr. Heddon?"

"Yep."

"Up the stairs, turn right. The next office past the double doors."

Slocum bounded up the steps. If this didn't take too long, he could take a good look at the town of Richmond tonight. Raise a little hell.

The upper corridor was lit by candles sconced twenty yards apart. The office doors had glass windows, frosted to admit light, and they seemed to John Slocum like so many faded eyes searching him and each other for meaning.

He rapped sharply at the door. SECRETARY OF WAR. Big black letters. He rapped again and tried the handle.

"Lieutenant Slocum," he announced himself as he stepped inside.

"Hold it right there," a voice said. The man behind the voice was well dressed and well armed and had a pistol pointed directly at John Slocum's forehead. The pistol was an old single-shot dueling pistol, and Slocum thought he might drop underneath the shot and come up spitting lead. The man lowered the pistol to his side. He eyed John Slocum hard, and Slocum returned the favor. He wasn't too awfully fond of men who threw down on him. "Lift that pistol again, friend," he said softly, "and it'll be the last thing you do."

The man wore a green frock coat trimmed with black fur. He wore his long brown hair tied back in an old-fashioned pigtail, and his boots were knee-high on his yellow britches. He seemed to have forgotten the pistol in his hand.

The room, in one quick scan: one door to an adjoining suite, closed; windows that looked out on the red faded cobblestones of the street below; heavy drapes, open; modest fire in an enormous fireplace.

"James Heddon, Lieutenant," the man said calmly, ignoring the threat. "At your service."

"I'm John Slocum. You sent for me." Slocum was still annoyed. The man had almost dumped them both in the soup.

Heddon uncocked his pistol and tossed it on the daybed. The lap robes folded neatly on the foot of the bed and a certain faint odor told Slocum that Heddon often slept right there. For some reason that let Slocum unbend. "I ain't accustomed to letting anybody draw on me," he said. Which was as much of an apology as he was ever likely to make.

Heddon smiled and the smile gleamed as though all his soul's light were gathered there. "Yes," he said. "Sorry. We can't spare troops for guard service here in Richmond and so I greet all my late visitors this way. Never know when some Union spy might decide to make his mark on the world."

Slocum's brow furrowed. "Is that a fact?" he asked.

"Yes. It is." Briskly the man poured hot water into a porcelain teapot. He hung the kettle back on the fireplace hook. "Tea, Slocum," he said. "Direct from England. Once in a while a blockade runner slips through, even now."

"Don't care for tea myself," Slocum said.

Heddon straightened and briskly rubbed his hands. "Ah, yes. You fighting men probably prefer rum, or bourbon."

"Yes, sir."

"Well," Heddon said, with a funny not-quite smile, "I wish I could help you, but I can't. Temperance man, myself."

"Yes," Slocum said. This was going a little too fast for him. "I don't care for tea," he said, because he knew that much for sure.

Heddon stepped suddenly to the windows. He stood to the side where the drapes would protect him from any curious eyes on the street. "Will we win?" he asked.

"What?"

"Our cause is just. Will it triumph?"

Slocum shrugged.

Heddon turned, his neck cocked back at a strange angle, so his eyes focused right over the top of Slocum's head. "I asked you a question, Lieutenant. As your superior in the armies of the Confederate States of America, I order you to answer. Will we win?"

"Oh, hell no," Slocum said. "We ain't got a chance in ten thousand. We'll need all the good cards we can get just to last through the winter, and Grant's never gonna let up. He's got four men to our two, three horses to our one, twelve rounds to our three. Why in God's name are you askin' me? It ain't my job to know those things, it's yours. You're the damn secretary of war!"

A faint smile rose on Heddon's pan. Vigorously, he shook his head. He loosened a few loose hairs from his head and his fingers tucked them in again. "Exactly," he said. "Exactly, Lieutenant."

He went into a desk drawer. Slocum hoped he'd produce a cigar or a plug, but it was just some papers, wrapped in a ribbon. Heddon leaned over to study them. Slocum pulled his pouch out of his pocket and sprinkled tobacco into a folded paper.

"Please don't smoke in here," Heddon said, without looking up.

Slocum carefully poured the tobacco back. He carefully replaced the paper with its mates. He waited. He let his eyes roam around the office. Two walls were covered with flags. Flags overlapping each other, stuck to the wall just like wallpaper. Another wall held a huge map of the Southern states at the beginning of the war. Someone had slashed the map with a red crayon near Vicksburg.

"You are admiring the flags," Heddon said, without lifting his head. "You may examine them."

Slocum did just that. walking around, peering at the flags, hands clasped loosely behind his back like a tourist in a museum. He saw flags from Rhode Island and Maine. He saw United States flags with thirty stars. He saw flags from famous Union regiments: New York Zouaves, Pennsylvania Blues. Many of the flags were tattered, a few half shot away. Some of them were brown speckled. the tint of old blood.

"Battle flags, Lieutenant. A few captured flags. We have fought well, sir. We have fought honorably."

Slocum figured he'd die under a flag very much like one of these and didn't see any point in going on about it. "Still fightin'," he said. Deliberately, he turned away. He'd seen enough trophies for one evening. He didn't want to count the dead men needed to win each flag.

"You're twenty-one years of age."

"Yes."

Now Heddon studied the young man. "You look older."

Slocum didn't feel a need to reply. He wished he were smoking a cigarette. He wished Heddon would get to the point.

"And you served in Missouri."

"That's where I got to be a sharpshooter."

"And you've been a sharpshooter for eighteen

months? Isn't that—well, isn't that pressing your luck? Junior lieutenants and sharpshooters have the highest casualty rates of all our troops."

"I'm no junior," Slocum said. "Bragg gave me a commission and I took it, though maybe I should have turned it down."

Heddon smiled. "I intend to promote you to captain."

Slocum thought that he could have done that by letter instead of dragging him all the way to Richmond, but he didn't say that. There was more to come.

"I see that doesn't excite you," Heddon said, still smiling.

"It's fewer letters on my tombstone," Slocum said.

"More pay?" Heddon's smile was unvarying. Scrip was worthless and many regiments didn't even bother to line up for the paymaster.

Slocum pulled his pouch out of his pocket and rolled a quirly.

"I asked you not to smoke," Heddon said. No cutting edge to his voice, only curiosity.

Slocum shrugged. "It's a condemned man's privilege. You pulled me off the line and promoted me and are meetin' me face to face in your fine office in Richmond. I figure you got something special for me to do." He lit his quirly and took a deep drag. "Maybe somethin' hazardous?" When he smiled, his smile was even more wolfish than the secretary of war's.

"I understand that you are the finest shot in the Army of Northern Virginia," Heddon said.

Slocum shrugged.

Heddon turned again to his papers. "June fourteen, '64: killed General Anderson at a distance of eight hundred yards during the battle of New Market. September thirteen: assaulted a Union patrol of eleven soldiers and slew them with pistols. August eighteen: covered the retreat of an entire company of infantry, accounting for twenty Union troops with rifle fire. . . ."

Slocum shrugged again. He felt his face burning. He'd done what he had to do at the time and most of it had been frightening and ugly and he didn't care to be reminded of any of it by strangers.

"Captain Slocum, you deny these deeds?"

"No." The quirly didn't taste so good, but damned if he was going to put it out.

"Might I examine your weapons, Slocum?"

"No, sir. They ain't CSA guns, they're guns I took myself off the Yankees and they respond fine to my handlin' but I'd hate to see somebody else toyin' with them."

Heddon had his hand out. Involuntarily, Slocum bent back at the waist. Heddon withdrew his hand.

"What weapons do you favor?"

Slocum felt funny giving the man even this much, as though he were risking more than he could win, but he told Heddon how he liked the Colt Navy revolvers and the Henry carbine.

"I see." He went into his drawer again for another piece of paper—looked like a letter—before he said, "What effect would a hundred men armed thus and mounted on fine horses have?"

His knowledge challenged, Slocum was finally drawn into the conversation. "They'd be unstoppable. Only thing meaner or more dangerous than a pistolero on horseback is another pistolero. If we made these Henrys and Colts, the war'd have turned out different, that's sure."

Slocum's heart leaped. Was Heddon going to ask him to organize a company of well-armed cavalry? His smile flourished.

Heddon didn't notice. He dropped the letter. Back to his desk for a newspaper. Though it was getting dim, Slocum could see it was a Northern paper, *The New York Times*. Heddon opened it to the editorials, marked one with his forefinger, and looked up. "What's going to happen when we lose the war?" he asked.

Slocum was startled. He'd never thought much past war's end because he'd never expected to survive.

Heddon thumped the paper with his hand. "The

Union senators, they're calling for treason trials, you know. All the Confederate officials, from President Davis on down. All the Confederate governors and the generals too, of course. Treason trials!"

Slocum waited.

"Robert Lee himself! Why, just yesterday," Heddon bent to the paper—Slocum thought he was paraphrasing—it was too dim to read: " 'If treason has any meaning, then these rebels are treasonous. If justice is to have any dignity, they must be tried.' That's Charles Sumner speaking in the Senate, sir."

"I guess I'll go out West," Slocum said. He hadn't meant to say that, it just sort of slipped out of him.

Heddon paid him no mind. "Do you know Colonel Mosby?" he asked.

"I know of him. The one who keeps the Danville train lines open?"

"Yes. The very same. I've asked him to disband his troop and disperse them among the regular CSA regiments."

Slocum was puzzled.

"Mosby is an irregular, you see. And if the Unionists can hold him up as an example, the whole lot of us are looking at treason trials."

Suddenly it all clicked in Slocum's mind. The questions about Missouri. The remarks about Mosby's irregulars. "No, sir," he said. "I'd rather be a damn lieutenant forever, and if you break me to private, I don't mind that either."

Heddon jerked his head up. Slocum couldn't make out his features, but there was a faint glow to his eyes. "What are you talking about?"

Slocum didn't want to say, for fear of having his suspicions confirmed. "I ain't gonna join Quantrill's guerrillas," he said stubbornly.

Heddon's voice was smooth as catsilk. "Slocum, do you have reservations about Quantrill?"

Still stubborn. "I've been in Missouri. I've seen what he does. I've seen the boys and the civilians strung up beside the road. I've seen folks turn their faces when regular Confederate army rode by because of what Quantrill's done. Him and Bloody Bill Anderson and the whole damn bunch. They're murderers plain and simple."

Angrily, Slocum stubbed out his quirly on the hearthstone where a tiny fire was doing its best, but that wasn't enough.

Heddon's teeth shone as brightly as his eyes. "You misunderstand me, Captain Slocum," he said. "I don't want you to join William Quantrill. I want you to kill him."

3

Osceola wasn't much of a town—a couple rows of wood houses under some bare elm trees. The more substantial houses were up on the bluff where they could get a view of the river. Their elms were bare too.

Slocum settled his knapsack across his shoulders. It was getting late; almost five o'clock by his reckoning, and he'd surely like to catch that ferry and be in Kansas in the morning. Missouri was Union, though it had more Confederate than Union sympathizers.

It was a clear, cold day and Slocum blessed his new boots. He was dressed better than he had been at the front, and armed worse.

He started down the last incline into Osceola. Though he'd started at dawn, he'd had luck and hitched a ride with a teamster hauling fresh pressed apple cider to the Yankee garrison at Sikeston. Generously, the teamster had offered Slocum all the damn cider he wanted to drink.

"Apple juice makes me trot," Slocum said by way of thanks. "Particularly when it's sparky."

"Well, won't the Yankees thank me for that?" the teamster had winked.

Because he was wearing a gray uniform, Slocum grinned back at him.

The teamster had been garrulous, but wasn't much of a conversationalist. His mouth hadn't stopped moving except when he had a pork chop in it at lunchtime, but fortunately, he didn't require much from his passenger except the odd grunt now and again. Thus, Slocum traveled a long way without trying out any opinions.

The Osage River was a glossy carpet below him, quite still and not very high. It had been a drought year upriver, and the mud flats extended way out into the channel. Below, Slocum could see where some of the wharves were high and dry, and their warehouses useless. Slocum had decided to cross here at Osceola because he didn't want to occasion any comment and the small ferry crossing would be less guarded than the bigger crossings.

But God, the drying mud stank. There'd been plenty of rain down this far and the stream had responded by getting big and then shrinking again, far more rapidly than usual, and leaving a quota of decaying fish carcasses on the shore every time the water receded. Slocum sniffed the ripe odor and his nose twitched.

He took long, ground-covering strides, in the manner of someone who'd been walking for a long time and had considerable distance yet to go.

He'd got his good boots in Richmond—along with the fairly newish gray uniform—the uniform of a sergeant of artillery. He'd been issued a new knapsack and in it he carried his worldly goods: one spare pair of long johns, a spare shirt and pants, his billy, some hard brown lye soap wrapped in a rag, a quarter pound of badly cured Kentucky burley, cut cigarette size, some lucifers in a tin. A smallish bowie knife, with a six-inch blade. A hone. A piece of silvered glass, irregularly shaped, that did for a shaving mirror. The bowie did for the blade. His two horse blankets he had rolled around the knapsack and his slicker was balled up in its own packet. The whole kit didn't make much weight. John Slocum had a pound of gold sewed into the padding at the edge of his blanket. The gold was U.S. government double eagles. Some of them from the Confederate vault at Richmond were quite old and bore the picture of a blowsy looking Liberty on the front and the edges were irregular from inferior milling.

He carried no weapons, except for the bowie, unless his stout walking stick could be counted. It was round, about the size of a woman's wrist and easily six feet long. It was seasoned ash. When Heddon had insisted he carry the money and no weapons, Slocum had observed that he'd rather have it the other way around, that a man with money and no protection was in considerable more danger than a man with guns and no money. Heddon didn't see it that way.

"You'll never get across the Mississippi with firearms, so you might as well get used to their absence," the secretary of war had ordered.

Slocum did carry the bowie and the stave though, just for peace of mind.

He'd been searched three times so far and had answered to as many different names. At the West Virginia border, his way had been blocked by irregulars who demanded to know where and how. "Goin' to Louisville," he'd said, truthfully enough. "I been paroled from Lee's army and I'm goin' home."

On the Louisville train he'd been "a paroled soldier from Bragg's army headin' for Missouri."

After lunch today he'd destroyed those papers and now he had his final set rolled tightly in the pocket of his uniform jacket.

The seagulls were flocking around something on the flats. Slocum was thinking that he'd never been anywhere near water without seagulls. He wondered if there'd be gulls out West. He supposed so.

Against the low hills on the other side of the river, the swallows arced and swooped, taking their fill of evening insects.

Slocum's low-heeled plainsman's boots were thin soled, and he could feel the sharp pebbles in the road.

The ferry would dock at a long wooden pier that jutted a good way out from the shore. A half dozen loungers waited for the flat-bottomed boat and there were two wagons and a couple of horsemen—Union soldiers.

The few stores Osceola boasted were closed for the day as Slocum passed them, all except one that announced CAFE and another that was ABBOT'S HOME BAKERY. The shop bell jingled as a lady came out Abbot's door. She had a wrapped parcel under her arm and Slocum supposed it was bread for the family supper. There were some smells in the air besides the stink of the riverbanks—the smells of a community preparing their supper, and for a moment, John Slocum felt terribly homesick. The young man settled his shoulders into his knapsack wth a sigh and his feet didn't falter. Time enough for home when this war was over.

A hundred times—a thousand times—he'd asked himself why he didn't just desert and go home. Hell, on the home place—Slocum's Stand—high in the mountains of Georgia, nobody would come looking for him, and plenty of other soldiers had taken the option of a self-granted early discharge. Slocum wasn't one of your patriots, no sir. He didn't care a damn about the causes that produced the war. And the usual bonds, loyalty to a regiment, to fellow soldiers, didn't mean much to him either. He didn't quit because he didn't know how to. It was that thoughtless and that simple. If he could have quit, he would have, but he didn't know how.

His boots echoed on the planks of the ferry dock. It was forty feet to the end and looked to be hinged, connected with gangways. Some of the sections of dock were floating.

The loafers were dressed roughly—farmers or roustabouts. One of the wagons carried cases of what was labeled medical supplies and bandages. Slocum figured it was bound for Sikeston. One wagon was a one-horse medicine show, with promises printed on the sides of the wagon, and a good many there were, too. If you were to believe the brightly painted slogans on the sides of the wagon, Dr. Brenner's Elixir would cure anything that ailed you. Since it contained "Genuine Tincture of Opium," it probably would. Slocum had known a few poor souls who got started on that kind of medicine. Most of them weren't much account after it got to be a habit.

One of the loafers gave Slocum a hard look as he leaned against the wheel of the good doctor's wagon.

The ferry was still tied to the opposite shore. Smoke from the ferryman's shack told the story: the Osceola ferry would run when the ferryman finished his dinner and not a moment before. Slocum didn't mind. It was a pleasant evening to enjoy.

The loafer wore a red-checked flannel shirt, blue flannel pants, and a long cavalry-style duster buttoned to the neck. His slouch hat slunk down over his ears as if it were abashed, and his boots were more suited to horseback than walking. The man was eyeing his uniform, and Slocum looked him straight back, right between the eyes.

The man was heavy set and his duster was a little too small for him and pulled at the button holes. His boot heels were indented from spurs. He was cleanshaven. High blank forehead that formed a level ground for a fine tough short crop of wheat-colored hair. Below his cheeks, his face narrowed quite alarmingly and his chin was sharp as a spike. Didn't leave him much room for his mouth, which was small, round, and packed with teeth. The blackened teeth looked like refuse thrown there after a serious fire. He nodded to Slocum like they were old friends. Slocum looked away.

One of the Union soldiers was complaining about the ferryman. He was side by side with the other Union soldier—a corporal—and was bitching a streak. "If we was those damn secessionists, he'd be over here. I been travelin' this pike in all sorts of weather, and I can count the kind words I ever got from that man on the fingers of one hand. He's with them damn guerrillas, that's what."

The corporal nodded his head in a way that left open whether he'd heard what the other had said.

High on the box of his medicine wagon, Dr. Brenner looked to be the worst possible advertisement for his own medicine. He sat absolutely still, dreaming with his eyes open. He was cadaverous, chalky faced, and enjoying scenes nobody else could see.

Slocum took a good pull on his smoke. The ferryman

came out of his shack and counted the crowd on the other side of the river before he started unlashing lines.

The ferry itself was an old flatboat minus the stern cabin. Propelled by sweeps or poles, they were numerous on the Osage. The ferryman stuck his pole into the bottom and commenced his march, bow to stern. The ferry was guided by a line from wharf to wharf and he had no rudder work. Wordlessly he pulled up to the wharf, wordlessly he tied up. When one lounger fastened a bow line for him, he examined it and retied it before allowing the wagons and horsemen aboard.

The planks had warped slightly and the flatboat wasn't entirely dry, so Slocum sat on the low wooden rail to keep his boots dry.

The ferryman went to each passenger to collect before he unfastened the lines. Two bits on foot, four bits for a horse, six bits for a wagon.

The doctor came out of his daze to complain. "I can buy a meal for that money," he whined.

"You can swim the river too," the ferryman replied.

The boat rode low and the current took it downstream, so the guideline formed a long bow. The ferryman marched back and forth with his long pole and the ferry slid across the water.

The banks were closer together here than upstream, and the current was swifter too, particularly in the main channel. The ferryman's muscles stood out like ropes, but he never complained and never asked for help either. When the ferry was on the other side, he tied up wordlessly and went back into his shack.

A group of men waited on the bank. They weren't waiting to cross. The Union soldiers glanced at them and continued their conversation. Dr. Brenner closed his eyes, the teamster with the medical supplies cracked his whip and rolled off the wharf, first in line.

The man in the duster stepped up next to John Slocum. "There's jayhawkers among 'em," he said. "Better watch your step." And he was gone as quickly as he'd come, his voice just a whisper in Slocum's mind.

The two Federals rode off the ferry. The younger bent to speak to one of the waiting party before the two men were on their way. It was the good doctor's turn next and he geed his horse forward.

Most of the bunch were uniformed soldiers. Fifteen bluebellies, mostly privates, though Slocum saw a few chevrons and the party was led by a young ensign.

The remaining five men were roughly dressed private citizens. Terrible clothes on their bodies, but they sat big graceful horses and the pistols in the saddle holsters were the latest type and manufacture.

Slocum was nervous but didn't let any of it show. He'd been stopped three times before and shook down.

"Where you takin' the wagon, Doc?" One of the civilians asked the questions. The Yankees backed him up, drawn across the road. The sides of the road were barren up to the tree line except for the ferryman's tin-roofed shack. No cover if a man had a notion to make a run for it. Through the windows of the shack, Slocum saw the ferryman pulling on a bottle. He passed before the window with the bottle to his mouth, and then he was gone. Suddenly Slocum knew how very bad it smelled inside that shack and how crazy the ferryman was in his misanthropy.

The medicine doctor mumbled his reply.

"Oh, goin' on to Fort Riley?" the jayhawker asked. "What you got back there that's good enough for the boys at the fort but too good for us?" His companions laughed at this sally.

Wearily, the doctor reached into the boot and tossed an unopened bottle of elixir to the jayhawker leader. The man pulled the cork from the pint bottle with his teeth, took a swallow, rolled it around in his mouth, and swallowed. He coughed. His eyes watered. Wordlessly he motioned to Dr. Brenner and the man clucked over his reins and his scarecrow horse started ahead. The jayhawker leader coughed again and wiped his eyes with his sleeve. He handed the bottle to the man behind him. His eyes were on the foot passengers:

couple young boys, not more than sixteen; John Slocum; and the man in the duster.

The jayhawker's eyes were hard and black as ironwood. His hands were short, stubby, and impatient. He put his hands on his hips, just above his pistols. "Get on up here," he said. "I ain't got all day."

Sent a shiver down Slocum's back, he did, though Slocum didn't know why.

"Not you, Johnny Reb. You ain't the main course, you're just the dessert." And the jayhawker crooked his finger and the two youngsters came forward, right smart.

"What's your name, boy?"

Both boys answered at once and a quiver of annoyance crossed the jayhawker's face. "I know your name —Keogh," and he pointed. "I know you got an uncle in Palmyra."

"Not Palmyra, sir. That must be some other Keogh. I'm from Springfield and all my uncles are up north in Illinois." The boy answered steadily enough, but licked his lips. The jayhawker looked him up and down and pulled the heavy Colt from his holster. It hung from his hand like an afterthought. The jayhawker's voice was full of menace. "I guess you didn't hear me good. You got an uncle in Palmyra named Jake Keogh."

"No, sir. Not to my knowledge. We don't claim kin with any Keoghs in Palmyra."

The jayhawker's thumb stroked the serrated hammer of his pistol. "What do you think of Palmyra, boy?" he asked.

"Sir, I've never been there," the boy replied.

"Well, I ain't been there either!" The jayhawker shouted these words and the shout was so loud that a couple of the horses got spooked and danced, and the Federal ensign looked like a man ready to interfere. He calmed as his horse calmed. "I suppose you ain't ever heard of Palmyra either," the jayhawker asked in an oddly hopeful voice.

"Yes, sir. I heard of it."

"How about you?" The sudden demand was punctuated with the pistol, which was pointing at the other boy like a schoolmaster's pointer.

"Oh, yes, sir. Most everybody's heard of Palmyra."

The jayhawker took a step forward. The second boy wanted to take a step back but didn't. Slocum shifted his weight from one foot to the other. He was thinking, rather philosophically, what a difference a good gun and fast horse can make in bad times.

The jayhawker leaned back on his heels and his pistol lay at his side. Once more in that harsh manner, he spoke. "And what have you heard about Palmyra, boy?" he barked.

As if he were going through a geography lesson, the second boy said, "Palmyra is on the Missouri, sir. North of Hannibal if I recollect. I don't have any kin in Palmyra either, though I've heard it's a lovely town." The boy spoke with his legs slightly apart and his head level in the manner of a recitation. His voice was very sincere.

"I heard Palmyra was an ugly damn town with mud in the streets so deep a horse couldn't walk." That was the man in the duster who spoke. He spoke angrily, impatiently, daring the jayhawker. The jayhawker just looked at him and his face lit up, briefly, with a grin. The man in the duster didn't return it. Once again the jayhawker raised his pistol. "Wait your turn, friend," he said softly. "You'll get your chance to talk."

Slocum grimaced, despite himself. The hatred between the two men was that strong.

Once more the jayhawker turned his attention to the first boy. "You know who's got a fort in Palmyra?" he asked.

"Yes, sir." The boy's voice was quite strong. Unfrightened.

"Well?"

The boy pointed at the Union soldiers. "It's them. They got a fort in Palmyra."

"They?"

"The Federals, sir."

"You mean the soldiers of your nation?"

The boy hesitated. In a much smaller voice he said, "Yes, sir."

"None of your secessionist scum. They may live in Palmyra, but they ain't got a fort there." He laughed at his own poor joke. Nobody, not even his own men, laughed with him, though one man showed his teeth in the routine soundless way a snake shows its fangs.

The jayhawker snapped his fingers. "Quick, boy, what happened in Palmyra?"

"Sir?"

"Tell me about the ten men Colonel Strachan strung up."

The boy started to say something, but changed his mind and shook his head. "I don't know anything about that," he said.

Mock surprise. "Never heard of it? Never heard of it?"

"I heard." The man in the duster again. He'd managed to get his duster unbuttoned. His hands were free to get inside pretty quick if that notion should strike him. The man stepped away from the other travelers, as though he needed elbow room. "I heard Strachan hung ten good men for no reason at all except he was drunk. I heard one of the men's wives came to him in the night sayin' that she'd do anything for her husband's release and old Strachan had her doin' almost anything through most of the night, until the poor woman was all sweaty and naked and covered with spunk and scratches and he kicked her out the front door in the morning looking that way. That's what I heard."

The Yankee troopers spread out casually along the road bank, the flankers curved inward like the tips of a longhorn, encircling the two men and two boys.

"Well, you're right about some of that," the jayhawker laughed. "I never heard about no woman, but I don't put it past ol' Strachan to take himself a piece of ass when the opportunity presented itself. But," he paused and raised his pistol in the air like an interjection, "you forgot the most important part of what happened at Palmyra, friend." He shot his fingers at Slocum, as if noticing him for the first time. "And what might that be, friend?"

"Couldn't say," Slocum replied mildly, keeping one eye on the flankers who were behind them now, closer to the river than they were, in case someone should take a notion the river was a lane of escape. "Never heard nothin' about Palmyra, until this very moment. Been away from Missouri for four years now and my family's all dead with nobody to write to me."

The jayhawker came up to Slocum's face so close he could see the blotches on the furious red skin and the wiry hairs growing from his nostrils. "I don't believe you," he said.

Slocum's shrug was modest and unassuming.

"I said, I don't believe you," the jayhawker repeated.

"I been in Tennessee," Slocum said, trying to keep it an explanation and not a plea, though the borderline was very fine.

The man pushed his hand under Slocum's nose and snapped his fingers, pop, pop. "Papers?" he demanded.

Slow as he could, John Slocum's hand went to his tunic pocket. As he unbuttoned the pocket he heard the too familiar snick, snick, snick, of a Colt being cocked and when he rested his eyes on the other jayhawkers, sure enough, three of them had guns drawn and one of those guns was cocked and centered directly over Slocum's heart. He took the parole between thumb and forefinger and presented it.

The jayhawker unfolded the paper and stared at it for a minute. "Ensign," he yelled, "why don't you come over here and take a look at this. I think it's a forgery."

For a man who'd made such a serious accusation, the jayhawker didn't seem very concerned, though Slocum surely was. One of the other jayhawkers jeered, "Hell, how could you tell, Bob? You can't read a goddamned word." He thought that was very funny and laughed quite a bit.

The ensign rode forward and collected Slocum's parole. Slocum had his eyes on the officer because this was a real sticky situation and somebody was likely to get killed. At such times, Slocum memorized men and terrain and anything else that might be of use. The ensign: short, blond haired. Rode like a plowboy and not much taste in horseflesh either. Wore his forage cap on the back of his head—again, like a farm boy. His single gold bars were tarnished so badly they were black and hard to see against the deep blue of his uniform. "It says this man surrendered to General Fremont. It says he promises not to bear arms against the Union anymore." The ensign folded the paper and stuck it in his own pocket. Slocum's heart fell. He wouldn't go far without that little piece of paper.

"Well, ain't that the damndest thing." The jayhawker was shaking his head in bewilderment. "A man goes and fights against the government. Takes up arms against it. Kills himself as many loyal Americans as he can and when he's caught square, he promises to stop killin' good Yankee soldiers and goes home where he can put up his feet in front of the fire and love the wives whose husbands are off fighting a dirty, miserable war."

"You've seen paroles before," Slocum said, terse.

Expansively, "Indeed I have. Indeed I have. Can't say I liked a single one of them."

Slocum eyed the ensign who still kept his parole in his pocket.

"Where'd you fight?" the jayhawker demanded.

"Lookout Mountain, Shiloh, Vicksburg, Five Points."

"Oh, my, you were a busy little bee, weren't you?" The jayhawker had his head cocked as though he were attending to a message only he could hear.

"No more than others," Slocum shrugged it off. "I'll need that parole, ensign. It's the only pass I got."

Without looking the ensign plucked the paper out

of his pocket and turned loose of it. It fluttered to the ground as he turned his horse and rode away, leaving all decisions behind him. Slocum bent over and picked it up. Dusted it off, too, before folding it.

"How'd you like to die?" the jayhawker asked.

"I ain't armed," Slocum said.

The man roared. "Now I didn't ask you that! Hell no! I asked you how you'd like to die."

Slocum didn't have an answer, so the jayhawker asked the boy Keogh the same question in a loud voice. "You, boy! How'd you like to die?"

The boy tried out a foolish smile, hoping the man was kidding. "Sir?"

The man stepped up too close. Perhaps the single word was offensive. "You heard me," he said. But this time, his voice trailed off like he was tiring of his own game.

"I'm going on to Springfield, where my home is," the boy said sturdily, setting the facts right. "It's a three-day trip and me and my friend hope to catch the coach at Sikeston. That stage leaves at five in the evening and we should be able to walk the twenty-three miles to Sikeston before the stage leaves, but not if we're held up too long."

At this minute show of defiance, the jayhawker's face went purple and he pushed his pistol to the boy's temple and cocked the hammer and asked, again, "You ready to die, boy?"

The boy went white as a pillow slip and swallowed. He opened his mouth. A dark stain appeared at his groin. One of the jayhawkers giggled. "You better back off there, Bob. Unless you want to get peed on." He hooted.

The disgusted jayhawker gave the boy a shove. The boy stumbled but caught himself and didn't go down. His face was white and scared and his trousers were soaked.

"Oh hell," the jayhawker said. "Now look what you've gone and done."

Slocum was thinking he'd made an awful mistake letting the secretary of war make him travel unarmed. If he'd had his wits with him, he could have predicted something like this. There'd be some man walking around just crying out with his need to be killed and there wouldn't be a damn way Slocum could help.

When the jayhawker pressed his pistol against Slocum's temple, the ring of metal had been warmed by the boy's head. The boy's friend began to cry. No sound. Just the tears chasing each other down his cheeks.

The jayhawker pressed his face close to Slocum's own. The jayhawker had some rot somewhere in his mouth or gut and Slocum smelled it. He wanted to pull his head back but didn't. "Since you-all are one of us now," he said, "I suppose you-all will want to fight for us too."

Slocum's head was tipped on his neck by the pressure of the pistol barrel and the sweat in his armpits was fresh. "Nope," he said. "Ain't gonna fight for anybody anymore."

The jayhawker started to laugh, but his laugh crackled and became something like a giggle. "Oh, I bet you're a real peace-loving gent. Take a look at this, boys. Don't he look like a peace-loving gent to you?"

He lowered the pistol, but only to press it hard into Slocum's stomach. "Drop the haversack, friend," he snapped. "We'll just see how peace-loving you are."

Slocum turned loose of his walking stick and it toppled into the road. He hitched the pack up off his shoulders and slipped his arm out. It dropped behind him.

"Well?" the jayhawker demanded. "Open the damn thing!"

Carefully, Slocum unfastened the top flap of his haversack. The jayhawker stood back a couple of paces and cocked his pistol again, and if Slocum had had a pistol, it wouldn't have been much use and the bowie was no use at all.

"Pull 'em out, Johnny Reb. Let's see all your possibles."

And Slocum pulled his clothing and his blanket out of the pack in a neat pile.

"Stand back. Keep your hands out front of you."

Slocum did as he was bid and the jayhawker rummaged through his things with a boot. "Nothin', nothin', nothin'," he said as his filthy boot marked Slocum's garb. As a little joke, he kicked at Slocum's long johns and they fluttered across the road like ghosts. The two boys stayed close to each other. The one who'd pissed his pants had his head bowed. The other had tears in his eyes but plenty of hatred too. The jayhawker had made himself two enemies this morning he didn't really need, but maybe that was the way they did things here.

James Heddon had told John Slocum about the Palmyra hangings. Though the Union general, General Lane, hadn't authorized the hangings, he was too drunk to object when his underling, Colonel Strachan, decided to make an example of Union vengeance. The men the colonel selected were from the general population of the Federal military prison. None were guerrillas. Several of them were paroled soldiers ready to go home until Strachan's finger picked them out of the line and measured them for a coffin. The night before the ten men were to be hanged, one woman, a Mrs. Thompson, reached General Lane in a rare moment of sobriety and extracted a pardon for her husband. Strachan was enraged. "Ten coffins to fill," he said. "By God, there'll be ten men to fill them." And he chose another soldier at random.

At dawn, Strachan walked out to the parade ground and had the men sit on the coffins, labeled with their names. When he was good and ready, he gave the order to fire.

His firing squad was sick at their duty and not very professional. Most of their bullets missed, or just wounded, the hostages, and two weren't touched by the bullets. A second volley improved the results slightly and a cursing Strachan walked through the wounded men dispatching them with his pistol.

"A terrible outrage," Heddon had said. "Just terrible. Bloody Bill Anderson and Quantrill were very quick with their own reprisals. Anderson himself shot twenty-one surrendered Federals at Sedelia; lined them up in a ditch and had his men bring him fresh pistols as he emptied them, one after another."

"Sounds like we're no better than them," Slocum had said.

"Worse," Heddon sighed. "I'm afraid that the horrors of Palmyra were small change compared with Bloody Bill and Quantrill. Quantrill had the audacity—oh, it was two years ago—to ride to Richmond and demand a colonel's commission. Of course we wouldn't give it to him. He met with me and Davis and raved about 'no quarter' and 'revenge' like they were coin of the realm. Jeff Davis was horrified. He's rather delicate, you know. He told that ruffian: 'There is no place in the nineteenth century for an army that rides under a black flag.' "

"Black flag?"

"That's correct. Quantrill's raiders ride under a black flag."

Slocum looked at the two frightened boys and read the hot anger in the one boy's stare, and thought this was how Quantrill got his recruits. No question about it.

The jayhawker came by Slocum, stepping on his clean shirt without paying the slightest attention. He approached the man in the duster as though he was the *pièce de résistance*. The duster was entirely unbuttoned now, though Slocum hadn't noticed hands working the buttons. The regular troops had drawn in so the travelers were encircled. The hammer of the jayhawker's Colt was drawn back to full cock and his stubby finger never left the trigger.

"And who might you be, bucko?" the jayhawker asked.

"Name's Smith."

"Not John Smith, by any chance?"

"You guessed it."

The jayhawker leveled his pistol at the other man's gut. "Where from, John Smith?"

"No place special."

"And where you going to?"

"Another place."

Sensing fresh meat, the other four jayhawkers nudged their horses near. One of them stopped beside Slocum. The jayhawker had his eyes fixed on the man in the duster who called himself Smith.

"God bless Abraham Lincoln," the jayhawker said quietly.

The man in the duster broke into a great brokentoothed grin. "Oh hell," he laughed. "Oh, goddamn it all to hell."

And his hands flashed at his duster and when they came out, each hand held a pistol.

Slocum was on his way to the ground at the first motion. It was going to get sticky here.

John Smith's guns spoke at a range of less than four feet and dumped the jayhawker back on the seat of his pants. He dropped one pistol and clasped his hands to his belly as if he could keep the precious blood from spilling through his fingers.

Slocum was flat on his belly and so the sustained roar of gunfire was just one sound to him. He didn't know who was doing what to whom.

The regular troops between John Smith and the river had their carbines working now but were too excited to make a hit. The jayhawkers' pistols were firing steadily and John Smith's right shoulder went red. His left hand was still working and his laugh rolled like the roar of water over a falls.

He blew one of the jayhawkers off his horse and ran for the animal himself. One of the Federals' bullets hit a boy.

Smith got one foot in the stirrup. While he was mounting, his pistol was quiet and a bullet took him low in the back. He arched in the stirrup and forgot whatever he'd planned. His teeth bared in a soundless snarl. He stepped down like he'd been planning to dismount and another jayhawker rushed behind him with pistol flaming. Slocum winced as one, two, three bullets smashed into John Smith's back. Then another rider joined the first and both men were firing and John Slocum lay still as could be because blood was up and it wouldn't take a whisker to create a general massacre.

Their bullets hammered Smith into the ground. A few Federals stepped forward to empty their carbines into the man's corpse.

The stray bullet had killed one of the boys. It struck him just in front of his left ear.

The jayhawkers hung John Smith's body from the ridgepole of the ferryman's shack. They hung the dead boy beside him, despite the protests of his friend.

Rebel Guerrillas—that's what the sign read they pinned to the shirtfronts of the bodies.

The jayhawkers were angry about the death of their leader and would have hanged Slocum and the other boy too. But Slocum's printed parole impressed the Yankee ensign and he told the two travelers to get on down the road or he wouldn't be responsible.

Slocum stuffed his clothes into his haversack and got. The boy didn't want to leave his dead friend, but Slocum hurried him away and out of sight.

"You're too damn easy to kill," he said.

4

"We were going to catch the Missouri packet," the boy said.

Because John Slocum didn't have anything better to do, he listened. Most of his attention was on the world around him—in specific, the hard clay road that wandered through the old pin oak forest, in no particular hurry to get where it was going. Slocum cocked his ear. A ruffed grouse flushed out of the branches and beat away. The boy didn't pay any attention. His face was drawn, quite white, and the pupils of his eyes weren't much bigger than gnats. He walked with his legs, not moving his arms or swinging his shoulders. "Fort Benton," the boy said.

Since Slocum had given room to similar thoughts, he asked, "What do they get for a ride upriver?"

"Thirty-five dollars," the boy said. "That's for steerage and you got to sleep with the cargo and bring your own shelter for rain and such. But me and Jimmy Keogh, we figured we could raise thirty-five dollars apiece. The army needs meat and there's so many buffalo in Kansas. You've never seen the like of it."

"You been to Kansas before?"

"No," the boy admitted. "Jimmy—he'd been there. It was his aunt we were gonna stay with. Do you know how to write?" The last words spoken furiously.

"I'm no great shakes at it," Slocum admitted, "but I did my McGuffey's and I can write a letter or read a newspaper."

Still furious, the boy asked, "Will you write a letter for me to Jimmy's Aunt Helen, telling how the damn jayhawkers killed him?"

"Sure."

The boy's eyes had got wider in his anger. The dead

boy had had the worst kind of bad luck, but the jayhawkers weren't particularly to blame except for clumsiness.

"I'm gonna join the guerrillas," the boy muttered.

"What about goin' upriver?"

"The hell with that. Upriver can wait. You know how long I knew Jimmy? I knew him five years, ever since him and me was in the schoolhouse in Cedar Bend."

"You know his folks?" Slocum paused—a slight movement next to the bole of a pin oak was only an old gray squirrel frozen against the bark. Damn, he was getting spooky. The sun was going and there was a nasty cutting chill in the air and Slocum considered unrolling his blanket for his shoulders. The hell with it. They couldn't be too far from Sallie Webster's place.

"I can't tell you very much about Miss Webster," the secretary of war had said. "Just that she's unmarried and one of the best agents we have in Kansas."

Slocum turned his gaze on the boy walking so silent beside him. "I believe I asked you a question," Slocum said mildly. No sense letting the boy go off like that. Not too far off, leastways.

"Jimmy's folks are dead. Mine too. We're both orphans." A touch of defiance in the boy's voice. And perhaps a touch of pride too. Slocum thought that probably the boy was lying, but the lie was of no account and so he let it by.

"I'm John Slocum," he said.

The boy hesitated. "Tommy," he said, finally. "Tommy McHale."

To ward off the chill, Slocum picked up the pace. The boy was wearing some kind of light leather jacket. He was more warmly dressed than Slocum himself, but the boy was feeling shock and would get colder quick.

The boy didn't ask any more questions. He just joined up, walking along, content to be going wherever Slocum was going. Slocum didn't mind the company either, to tell the truth.

The trees grew closer together here, and there were

fewer farm clearings. Most of the farms were deserted, abandoned when the men folk went to the wars. As usual, Slocum found himself thinking about his own place and wishing to see it.

The air smelled pretty good to him and it felt fine being on his own again, responsible only to himself. He'd scouted a little when he'd been with Bragg in Missouri before—good work. He was Richmond's dog, but he liked the work better on a long line.

The thud, thud, of boots against the hard clay road. The soft cry of a few lost whippoorwills.

"How come you surrendered?" the boy asked now. "How come you promised to stop fighting?"

"Figure that's my business," Slocum said, not varying his tone a single bit. "It's been a long war," he added for lack of anything better to say.

"We gonna stop for the night anytime soon?" the boy asked.

Slocum felt a mild annoyance. "You can do anything you damn well please," he said.

"Where are you goin'?" the boy asked.

Slocum stopped dead in the road. He waited until the boy faced him before he slapped him. It wasn't any love tap either. The blow was hard enough to lift the boy off his feet and drop him on his butt in the road.

"Son," Slocum said quietly. "I figure you aren't all growed up yet. If you want to get older, you better learn manners around men who ain't done you harm." And then Slocum walked on down the road, concealing the fact that the palm of his hand stung. He'd whacked that kid pretty damn hard.

Sounds of footsteps running behind him. Slocum didn't turn. The boy fell into step beside him. "Sorry," he said after a while. "I didn't mean anything by what I said, and I 'pologize."

"Accepted." Once again Slocum picked up the pace. It wasn't getting any warmer. Ahead, through a long lane of trees, he saw some kind of light, but damned if it didn't look like a red lantern, one of those lanterns whorehouses hang in their second-story windows.

They came into a wide space in the road. A building perched on the banks of some kind of little stream. Couldn't see it, but you could hear it all right. Unless Slocum was lost, it had to be Tuttle Creek.

He pushed through the gate and up the three wooden steps onto the porch. He removed his hat and the boy copied him. Slocum lifted the small iron knocker and rapped sharply.

Two small sounds inside. Slocum listened. The door swung open as fast as a gasp, and a woman pointed a tremendous Colt Dragoon dead center at his brain pan. "Welcome to the Light of Love," she said.

It was a credit to her that Slocum noticed her eyes at all. Remarkable. They were wide and bright yellow—the color of cat's eyes—and unblinking.

"Evenin', ma'am," Slocum said without moving. "Name's John Slocum, and I've come a fair piece and I'd appreciate what hospitality you have to offer."

"You a regular?" After her own quick glance at his uniform.

"Yes, ma'am."

When she withdrew the pistol, she pulled it straight back. When she uncocked it, the muzzle jerked slightly with her clumsy effort, and Slocum sweated. She dropped the gun into an embroidered reticule. Her hair was yellow as her eyes, almost the color of wedding ring gold or watch gold. And she was awful damn big, only an inch or two shorter than Slocum, who stood six foot two. The woman eyed John Slocum for a long time before she smiled. "And who's that boy you got with you?" she asked.

"McHale, ma'am. Tom McHale."

"Come on in, boys," she said expansively. "And don't call me ma'am. Most call me Sallie."

She ushered them into what had been her parlor in happier days.

There were great chunks blown out of the walls. Revolver slugs had chewed and split the planks and her fireplace had a perfect six-inch pockmark in the stone, like the blow from a miniature cannon. Two of the windows had been replaced with brand-spanking-new glass and frame. Sallie had paid a premium for that glass. The price was so steep the two rear windows were still covered with old patchwork quilts. On the outside, oiled butcher paper covered the space where the glass once had been.

Sallie had rugs scattered all over the floor because, try as she would, the blood had got down into the pores of that old pine and the only way she'd get it out was to have a carpenter work them over with a floor plane. Blankets and wraps disguised the holes in her overstuffed couch and the love seats.

Most of Sallie's doxies left the morning after the guerrilla attack. As one put it, "A looker like me can always find a crib in St. Louis and maybe the air ain't so clean, but there's fewer bullets in it." Jocko simply disappeared. The army undertakers came in an armed and nervous detachment to remove the bodies. Kin came for the dead jayhawkers.

The two women, Sallie and Roxie, waited, night after night, for customers who never came. Roxie, though still "ruined," had yet to take on her first customer. Sallie Webster drank a lot in the evenings. She still lit her red light, but it had become a vain summons.

The knock brought Sallie to her feet. The man standing before her seemed awfully damn dangerous and in that moment she almost pressed the trigger to send an ounce of lead into his brain. She ran her tongue over her teeth. His eyes were green; dark green like a jade stone she'd seen once, and flecked with something, just like that jade was flecked. He wore the Confederate uniform and she asked him if he was a regular. Noticed the boy standing beside him. Nothing but a kid, not more than sixteen and gangly too. He reminded her of the young man who'd posed as a woman to scout her place for the guerrillas. What was his name? Jesse

James? Except this lad was eyeing her breasts as though he'd never seen anything like them before. Gawk-eyed. Sallie Webster led them into her parlor. In the center of the room she threw her arms out wide like she'd done once in the opera house in Joplin during her brief singing career. "You wouldn't know it from looking around," she laughed, "but there's a war on."

"A war on whorehouses?" Slocum looked puzzled.

Sallie didn't enlighten him. Men came to the Light of Love to escape the war. "It's nothing," she said. "Let me take your hats," Sallie said. She blinked and widened her eyes and rubbed a knuckle into one of them. "I was asleep when you came," she said. Then she added, "Oops," and covered her mouth with her hand, which gave her a good chance to rub away a sleeper that glued her eyelashes together. She laughed at her own wit and then said, "That's probably what all the girls say to you," which wasn't the kind of thing that she'd say to every sport, but these two looked all right to her and the raven-haired man leaned back and roared his laughter, though apparently the kid didn't get the joke.

Ears turned red. He got it.

When the laugh died, she had a bottle in her hand and was pouring drinks. She owned two unshattered glasses. Her own drink she poured into a tin coffee cup. "Roxie, honey?" she asked. "You wanna join us?"

The girl's subdued yes set Sallie looking for the other big old tin cup. She found it in the washbasin with a couple days' dishes. Decorously, she shook it and a drop of something, coffee probably, ran out. She splashed a gold dollop of whiskey into the cup.

This was one of Sallie's two remaining bottles, but she poured generous measures, because if these two Charlies weren't good-time Charlies, she was out of luck anyway. So she poured as though her liquor were endless and smiled as if there were no tomorrow.

Roxie returned, dangling her slippers in her hand. Sallie laughed at the battered pumps and said, "You sure wouldn't want to go drinking champagne from them."

"No, ma'am," the boy said. His eyes fell. His ears began to glow again like the tip of a branding iron.

Sallie patted the sofa beside the girl's knitting and said, "Well, put down your things and sit a spell. How far did you come today?"

Neither man moved to put down his traveling gear, but both answered her question at the same moment. "Louisville," Slocum said. "Otter Creek," the boy said.

Slocum took a taste of his whiskey and raised his cup in a toast. "Thanks from some weary travelers, ma'am. Like I said, I'm John Slocum and this is Thomas McHale, known as Tom. We had a bad crossing at the Osage and a friend of his was killed, so you'll forgive him if he ain't the soul of jollity tonight."

Roxie raised her head then. She eyed the boy. She must have liked what she saw because she patted the sofa. Welcome. The boy sat down on the couch, on the extreme opposite end. Slocum faced away to hide his grin.

"Nice-lookin' house you got here, Sallie," he said. "Must have been something before it got shot up."

Sudden tears welled in Sallie's eyes. "Oh, it was. It was really something. Six girls and a black to cook. We ate cornbread for breakfast and ham and griddle cakes and sidemeat and stewed tomatoes, my goodness. On a Saturday night, you should have seen it." She waved her arm around conjuring, and the conjuring must have worked because Slocum could see it all right: Saturday night.

"You probably had all kinds of fancy folks stoppin' by here. Kings and presidents and such."

Sallie took him up on it. "How did you ever guess, honey? Robert E. Lee, Abraham Lincoln, Jeff Davis—they all been at the Light of Love."

Slocum made his guess. "Not to mention W. C. Quantrill," he said quietly.

She had been meaning to say something more about

kings and presidents, but choked on her words and coughed two or three times to clear her throat. Slocum slipped his shoulders from the webbing of his haversack. He leaned his heavy walking stick against the wall.

"Yeah," she said tiredly. She drank off her whiskey as though it were a restorative. "It was W. C. Quantrill came through here. That son of a bitch. Is there anything else you want to know, stranger?" she asked. "What do you want? The dinner costs fifty cents. We got possum stew and some turnips and carrots that I can fry up. You want to buy a bottle of whiskey that'll cost you two dollars. If you want one of us upstairs, it's three. All night is usually extra, but like you can see," she gestured at the shabby battered room, "we ain't doin' a thrivin' business just now."

Slocum gave his best grin. "This is as good a place to spend the night as any we could find, and your company would surely please me, Sallie. I expect my partner over there would be pleased too."

And Tom was too. Tongue-tied and pleased. Roxie looked at him and looked down at her handiwork. Her fingernails plucked at the edging where she thought she spied a fleck of lint. Tom loved the curve of her neck and the slope of her breasts. He thought he'd be seeing her soon without clothes and got embarrassingly hard, his penis bent and confined in his wool pants. In his possibles bag, he had sixteen dollars, six of it in scrip. It was part of his fare up river and he still hoped to travel west someday, after, of course, he killed himself a few jayhawkers, maybe five of them, to revenge his pal. So staying here would mean two-fifty, three dollars, and his half of the whiskey. He'd never had more than a couple of drinks of whiskey in his life, so he thought probably he'd only drink a fifth of that two-dollar bottle, which was, oh, the hell with it, his share of the evening couldn't come to four dollars no matter how you measured it.

"It'll cut into my travelin' money," he said to John Slocum.

Slocum's eyebrows climbed.

"I mean," the boy stammered, "I couldn't help seein' when they searched you that you didn't have cash. None at all, except for what you paid the ferryman."

Slocum cocked his head. "So you were lookin' through my gear same as those jayhawkers?"

"Sure." The boy was unabashed.

Slocum got angry, though he didn't quite know why. "Boy, somebody has surely neglected your education." He poured himself another drink from Sallie's bottle. He looked at her then. "I like your eyes," he said. "Don't worry about money. That little bastard's eyes ain't as good as he thinks they are."

"Good," Sallie said briskly. "Good. Why don't you all sit down and have a nice talk with Roxie while I get in the kitchen and get something cooking." She patted her belly happily and at that moment her gut grumbled. "Listen to me," she laughed. "Self-praise ain't no praise at all."

"I'll join you if I can," Slocum said. "Let's let these two get acquainted."

Sallie gave a little extra flounce to her hips to signal that Slocum was free to stroke her there if he cared to, which he did.

The kitchen had been spared the worst of Quantrill's attack. One window had been smashed out and the back door wouldn't close on its hinges anymore, but there hadn't been any gunplay in here. The platters and plates were undamaged, though her larder was awfully low because the guerrillas, indifferent to her crockery, were fascinated by the cured hams she had hanging in the pantry and the beef in the great brine crocks beside the stove. It was a good thing Sallie knew how to shoot, because they'd been hunting their meat ever since.

An opossum, shot this morning, was simmering on the coolest plate of her huge wood-coal stove. The stove had a deep firebox and Sallie figured that when winter got real cold, she and Roxie could move into the kitchen. Their beds could fit against the wall. Sallie had nexer enjoyed making love two to a room, but if that's what it took to hold body and soul together, then she'd begin to experiment with some of the sexual tricks she'd so far avoided.

Her hands were good and precise as she scraped and sliced her carrots. "Cut 'em the long way," she advised Slocum. "You get more of the carrot taste when you cut 'em that way."

"Uh-huh," he grunted. He leaned against the massive wooden table. It was big enough and heavy enough for butchering. "This must have been quite an establishment before the war," he noted.

"The Light of Love? You bet it was. Why, it was famous. Best fancy house between Cape Girardeau and Union City. Oh, folks used to come out here on Sundays, for picnics. All the young sports. And everybody runnin' for the legislature kicked off his campaign right here." Her voice lightened as she remembered happier days and her fingers slowed, working the carrots one at a time. "It was lovely," she said. She put some speed to her fingers. "But it's fallen on hard times now," she said.

"Were you here?"

"No. I used to work out of Plain Poll's in St. Louis. When the war came, the Yankees billeted thousands of troops in St. Louis. The armory's there. Well, I'm a Southerner by temperament and I didn't cotton to all those bluebellies, so I came downriver. When I felt I'd gone south enough, I stopped and bought the first and best operation I could find. The madam who had the place was eager to sell." Sallie shrugged. "I thought she was crazy. She couldn't wait to get out of here. Martha Canary. Her husband was a drinker and she wanted to get out West. Figured that way he'd take the cure." Sallie's expression was rueful. "I should call her crazy?" she laughed. She pumped cold water into the sink to wash her turnips. "At least the guerrillas didn't take the vegetables," she said.

In the other room, Tom McHale turned to the girl

Roxie, who had resumed her needlework when the other two left. "Where you from?" he asked.

Head lifted, she patted the couch. "My home's right here," she asserted. "Right here at the Light of Love."

He looked very young.

"How old are you?" she demanded.

"Old enough," he said. Under her not very well applied powder and rouge she was young but not, perhaps, as young as he was.

"Why I'll bet you're not a day older 'n sixteen," the girl said, pointing her finger.

"Eighteen," he mumbled.

"I'll just bet you are. Liar." Very grown-up, she marched to the side table where Sallie Webster had her second bottle of whiskey and tugged at the cork intending to pour herself a slug in a manner that would remind the boy of the way Sallie herself would have done it; and Sallie was really something, no question about that. Roxie couldn't pull the cork. She stuck the cork between her teeth and tugged sharply. The cork came out, and whiskey spilled on the front of her dress. "Oh," she said.

"I would have opened it for you," the boy said.

She poured her drink and took a tiny sip of it. It was harsh. She'd never get used to it. "You want to go upstairs?" she asked.

The boy got up as though he were spring powered. His hat hung in his hand. "Upstairs?" he squeaked. "You bet." He finished his own whiskey with one quick gulp, set his empty glass beside her full one, and took her hand. She preceded him up the stairs toward the back.

Sallie's bedroom was directly over the kitchen where a fire burned all day and most of the night, and a register let the heat rise from the cookstove. The two women slept in the once sumptuous bedroom.

Right at the door of the bedroom, Roxie had an attack of shyness and froze, her hand on the knob. She was very much aware of the boy's hand in hers. She was aware of the presence of his body behind her. When she turned the latch the click was very loud.

The register was in the center of the floor and the bedroom smelled of possum stew. The rich smell assailed their nostrils and Tom McHale's belly cramped. He licked his lips. "Somethin' smells good."

Though Roxie was hungry too, she chose to take offense. "Is that all you can think of? Your belly?" she asked.

"No. That ain't all I can think of. I just said it smelled good. You're an awful pretty girl."

She lay back on Sallie Webster's bed. Her own cot was too small and too maidenly for her right now. "No girl," she said. "I'm a woman. A ruined woman."

"Oh," he said. He put his hat on the chair. He started to sit on the hat but caught himself in time. "I knew a girl in my hometown," he said. "She was ruined too. She went away somewhere else to live."

"My mama and daddy are dead and only Miss Sallie cares for me," she said.

"I care for you." The words came out sounding a little funny.

With scorn: "How can you care for me? You only met me tonight. Tomorrow you'll leave and I'll never see you again. You're just here to use me." She threw her head back like the great Sarah Bernhardt. "Just like all the others."

The boy was grateful there had been a few others. That meant she had the experience he lacked. But he was deeply offended there had been others whom she had probably loved more than him. He mumbled, "I guess I better take my shirt off." He eyed the rug and as he unfastened his buttons, kept his eyes there. His ears were alert for any move she made. He heard the rustle as she unwound her scarf. He heard the almost inaudible pop of her buttons. When he had his shirt completely opened, he looked up and she had her dress unfastened top to bottom. She was lying on the bed, perpendicular to his gaze, with her dress closed over her nakedness. He stepped out of his socks. He skinned out of his trousers. His groin was heavy and taut with desire and burning with an unquenchable itch. His mouth was cotton dry as he padded across the floor to the bedside. He placed one knee on the bed. The girl kept her eyes closed—not as though she were asleep, as if she were a corpse. "Roxie?" he said.

Her eyes flew open. "Well now," she said.

His hands went to her dress and spread it open. Like a gift. The swell of her nipples, the slope of her breasts. The gradual childlike bulge of her belly. Her dark patch of hair. The loveliness of her thighs. The innocence of her knees. He stroked her, with a wondering hand. She caught his hand and pressed it hard against her belly flesh. "Harder," she said. "Don't tickle me."

"Oh sure."

And the smell rose up from her, warm, and filled his nostrils and he was so hard he hurt. He crawled over her knees. She spread her legs. He dropped his hips and hit something slippery and skidded again and again as he lunged.

"Here," she said. "Let me."

It was the greatest warmth he'd ever known. "Oh," he said, surprised.

Downstairs, Sallie's knife peeled turnips, slashed, and worked, and she talked as she cut, nonstop, because the vent was just above her head and without wishing to, anyone in the kitchen could hear everything that went on in Sallie Webster's bedroom. With the clamor of the bedsprings and the boy's "oh," Sallie got a little hot under the collar herself, blushing like a girl. It was a good thing her cook was gone, because if she hadn't been, in this moment, Sallie would have fired her. Upstairs, the springs set up a rhythmical squeak, like the squeak of a porch swing. Sallie ignored Slocum's broad grin and concentrated on her turnips.

"This'll make a mighty good stew," she asserted.

"Sure smells fine," Slocum said, partly to let her off the hook and partly because it was true, the good smells needed a bigger room than this kitchen to contain them. "I've always been partial to possum meat. Had plenty of it when I was a boy. During the bank panic of 1852 when so many of the farmers failed. Anything that walked on my daddy's place, hogs, sheep, cows, even the family milk cow, went under the hammer. Our bank closed, you see, and the man who took it over came after everybody who owed that bank one copper penny. We all had nothing to eat, me, my brother, and Ma, so Pa took to the woods. One thing about Pa, he was a crackerjack hunter. Just seemed to feel his way into the brain of the animal he was hunting. Well, he wasn't overfond of unadorned vegetables. 'I'm a meat-eatin' animal,' he used to say. He killed us some deer and some turkey and a black bear or two, just like they'd been eatin' when his granddaddy pioneered in those mountains. I am partial to wild meat, myself. It don't put fat on a man, except maybe bear meat, just the energy and the lean."

The springs upstairs were singing. Very loudly. Someone was grunting too, couldn't tell which one, but louder than a straining locomotive.

"So what?" Sallie asked, her spoon resting against the side of her pot.

"I got mighty tired of wild meat," Slocum said. "From autumn through winter and spring—hell, it was August before we had pig to slaughter and he wasn't a big one, couldn't have gone a hundred pounds. Only thing you could say in his favor was that he wasn't a possum."

The springs hurried into their crescendo, jingling together in the sound a waterfall makes.

When the springs quit, the two of them eyed each other. And Sallie dropped her wooden spoon in the stew and covered her mouth with the back of her hand and sat down, laughing into her hand, her eyes all red and tearing. Slocum had to look away or he would have started laughing too. His jaw muscles were set, and when she said, in a very weak voice, "You want to taste the stew?" he couldn't restrain himself, despite his intentions. He covered his mouth and his gusts of laughter sounded like a giant having hiccups. The sight of him swallowing his mirth got Sallie Webster going again and the big blonde's peal of laughter soared through the house.

As if in answer, above them the bedsprings jangled loudly again and the two of them laughed until they cried.

"My oh my," Sallie said, wiping the tears from her eyes.

Slocum took out his handkerchief and they both blew into it. Since she didn't trust herself with words, Sallie Webster pointed at the possum-turnip stew, and if he hadn't already laughed himself out, Sallie, pointing out their dinner like a birddog, would have started Slocum off again.

She scooped him a big helping and took nothing smaller herself. "Pour me a dram of that whiskey," she said. When he slid her glass to her, she added water to the booze, which she hadn't done often in the last two weeks. "Feels good to laugh," she said.

Slocum nodded his agreement. She'd put some kind of hot spice in the food, red pepper and maybe some ginger to boot. It worked with the possum's strong flavor and the blandness of the turnips. "Good," he said.

"Don't speak with your mouth full."

The warmth spread through Slocum's bones from his stomach outward to his fingertips and the tips of his toes. He luxuriated in the simple fact of the meal, drinking deep from his glass occasionally. When he was finished, he scooped more out of the pot and started his second helping with the same enthusiasm as the first. It was quiet upstairs. If you listened closely, you might have heard voices murmuring, but Slocum didn't listen closely. Sallie finished before he did and put her plate in the washbasin to soak. When he pushed his plate away, it scraped harshly against the rough table. He rolled a quick quirly and paused. "Smoke?"

When she nodded her yes, he tossed her the cigarette and rolled another for himself. "I was in Richmond three weeks ago," he spoke plainly. "Talking to a fellow by the name of Heddon. He says you know him."

Sallie froze. Suddenly she was alert as a sparrow.

Slocum waved one hand, a little awkwardly. He wasn't good at explaining himself and preferred not to. "Heddon's the secretary of war for the CSA. I was on the line outside of Richmond and his man came and got me."

"Go on." Absolutely noncommittal.

"I was in his office at the War Department. Heddon said the war was lost—which any damn fool can see—and once it's over, the Yankees will try the leading Confederates for treason. Every street in Richmond would be lined with gallows, which was maybe stretching the truth, but maybe not. Lee, Longstreet, Jeff Davis, even Heddon himself. The angrier the Yankees get, the greater likelihood of the treason trials. Somebody down here in Missouri is a greater threat to the lives of Confederate leaders than Grant, Heddon said."

She spoke very carefully. "You must be talking about William C. Quantrill."

"That was the name Heddon used. Indeed it was."

"But Quantrill's a Confederate, same as you and . . . uh, Heddon."

"Nope. He's fightin' and killin' Yankees, sure enough, but he's been ordered a hundred times to join up as a soldier under the regular flag and regular discipline. And he always said no. Hell, he don't ride under the stars and bars. He flies a damn black flag. Nothin' but his own name on it."

"I saw Quantrill once. He was here."

Slocum needed to know where this blond woman stood and how far she was willing to commit herself. "The secretary of war said you spied some," he said bluntly.

She wouldn't look at him. Her cigarette smoldered, forgotten between her fingers. "I had two brothers, once. My home was just outside St. Louis. It wasn't anything real grand. But it was stout and would have lasted somewhat longer if the damn jayhawkers hadn't put the torch to it."

"How do you get your information to Richmond?"

"New Orleans side-wheeler. New Orleans is a Yankee town now, but once the message gets there, it travels up the coast all right."

"Sounds slow."

"Usually is. But sometimes it surprises me. It didn't take long for my report of the attack here to reach Richmond."

Slocum didn't have the heart to tell her the decision on Quantrill had nothing to do with the Light of Love. "I'm to find Quantrill," he said quietly. He looked down at his hands.

"And then what?"

Slocum smiled. Smile came and went quick as a cat.

"I see."

"Where is he?"

Elaborate gesture of unknowing. "Hell, if I could answer that I'd have something the Federals would surely love to buy. Last I heard the offer for his whereabouts was a thousand dollars and the jayhawkers been scourin' the countryside hopin' to scare up sign."

Upstairs, the springs swung into rhythm again, slower this time.

"Hell, Quantrill ain't nothin'. He was a no-account nigger stealer before the war. And a low-grade holdup man. He never killed from the front and now he's ridin' with a hundred meaner than him. Ain't much short of a Federal fort that's safe from him in a pitched battle. No pitched battles for him. He hits and runs away. He dresses his men up as Federals and waylays other Federal troops who trust him."

The springs singing their song. Slocum took another drink of whiskey. "Nobody knows where he is," he said.

"Mostly he goes to ground south of Westport. Near the Sni River. It's rough country back in there. A few small homesteads his friends work and enough poor ground to hide three outfits like his. I don't know where he is now, but there's been some whispers about . . ."

"Whispers?"

"That he's plannin' some piece of meanness worse than anything he's done so far."

Slocum put his glass down with a thump. His stomach was full, he was content, he wanted her. "Where shall we go?" he asked.

"Upstairs?" she said. "I suppose it'll have to be upstairs. I'd rather lose modesty than freeze, and that room's the only heated bedroom in the house."

Like her young friend before her, Sallie Webster led her man up the narrow stairs. The two of them walked quietly down the hall and when they reached the door, Sallie put her ear against it. After a moment, she said, "They're just finishin' now." She kept her ear to the door for another moment and finally lifted away with a funny smile. "Kids," she said, though she wasn't more than twenty-four herself, and John Slocum was only twenty-one. "Let's give them a minute."

So John Slocum spent that minute kissing her. She tasted awfully damn good to him. Her lips, soft and fragrant under his, her body, bound up in whalebone constraints, pressing against him. He pulled away finally and scratched his head. "Whew," he said. He banged on the door. "You all done in there?" he bellowed.

Great silence. A tiny sound like a mouse scurrying around.

"If you're done in there," Slocum went on, "there's a good dinner waitin' for you in the kitchen and your elders and betters have need of this room."

No reply within. Sallie knocked on the door again and said, "Roxie, get your lazy ass out of bed. I didn't cook up all that good stew just to see it go to waste."

That brought a little commotion, and in a moment, the door opened. The boy stood in the doorway with his braces hanging at his sides and his shoes in his hands. He looked at Sallie Webster. He looked at John Slocum. His face was all blotchy from love and he must have been scratched pretty fierce on his forearm, since there was blood easing out under the cuff of his shirt.

"Don't say anything," Slocum advised him kindly. "You'll just sound foolish. Get yourself downstairs and get back of some grub."

For once Tom McHale followed good advice. He tried on an odd smile and hurried down the stairs.

The girl's eyes were downcast, but she wore a kind of sly smile and had the unmistakable odor of a happy woman when she murmured her way past them and followed the boy.

"Jesus H. Christ," Sallie Webster said, eyeing her bed. "Looks like a tornado hit in here."

"Nothing like following one rough weather with another," Slocum said, holding her from behind while he kicked the door shut, nibbling at her ear.

And very shortly the springs were singing one more time, deep and loud, and if there was laughter from the kitchen, just below, John Slocum certainly didn't hear it, nor did Sallie Webster.

5

His eyes flicked open. Ten minutes before, the dawn light had washed through the windows of the Light of Love. He didn't move a single muscle. He never did move until his body had gathered itself. One arm was underneath the yellow-eyed woman's head and the bed smelled rich and warm. Her breathing was soft and regular. He heard a raven cawing outside. The breathing in the other, smaller bed came from Roxie and Tom.

Somebody was groaning in their sleep. The boy. No lump of heavy metal under Slocum's head, just the pillow softness. Man could get used to sleeping on pillows.

In the field, he'd usually tucked his boots under his head and kept a Colt inside a boot. If it rained, he'd have five dry rounds anyway. The leather of his boots was stiff against the back of his neck and there's nothing soft about a Colt, but he'd be more comfortable with a boot and Colt than these soft pillows. Sallie Webster had said something about guns she'd taken off a dead jayhawker. Maybe he could buy up part of her armory. No sane man traveled unarmed in Missouri.

"Promise me," Heddon had said, "you won't carry arms until you get where you're going. Unarmed, it will be easier to bypass Union checkpoints."

Slocum had promised and made his journey and now he'd got where he was going, and he wanted some pistols again.

He padded naked to the window to pull the curtain aside. A faint gray stripe above the trees, all around the horizon. In the west, the evening star shone, fat and faint above the depths of the western forest.

He pulled on his clothes except for his boots and slipped noiselessly downstairs. The water in the boiler on top of the cookstove was filmed with ice, and cold made the iron stovetop greasy. Slocum set newspaper and kindling in the firebox, after he knocked the ashes down. When he had his fire alight, he rubbed his hands over the open flame. First thing was getting some hot tea inside of him and then he'd see if he could scout some grub.

He was sitting on the front porch with his cup of tea in his hand when the Federals rode in.

Slocum didn't drop his foot off the porch rail and didn't unclasp his hands from the hot tin cup when the first Yankee troopers rode by the front gate and into the yard around the side of the house as if they'd been there a hundred times before and maybe owned the place. The Federals dismounted quickly, and rifles in their hands, they searched the barn. Another small party was coming around the back of the house. They weren't saying anything, or calling out to each other. There were a few hundred of them—and a Dalgreen battery drawn up behind. Horses' hooves shook the earth, and the jingle of bridles and bits and O-rings was loud and continuous. Slocum could hear smaller sounds in the house as the three sleepers got up. The dew was heavy on the ground, muffling the dust. The sky had got itself into full gray, and in a few minutes, the sun was going to shove itself over the horizon.

Yankee officers stopped in front of the gate, a half dozen of them, with the guidon bearer and the troop sergeant too. A couple of men in civilian clothes. Black slouch hat on one of them and a duster. Slouch hat had been with the jayhawkers. The ones that killed the boy yesterday by mistake. One of the officers might have been the ensign from the same ford, but he was behind the others and Slocum couldn't see his face well. A troop sergeant opened the gate for a banty little officer, a major from his epaulets and hat braid. Slocum took a sip of tea. The jayhawker dismounted and followed the two regulars into the yard. The jayhawker left the gate open, Slocum noted.

The major wore what seemed to be a hand-tailored uniform. Pretty good tailor. The gold in his epaulets was polished so the metal shone dark in the gray light. The ends of his sleeves and shoulders glittered. He was sallow in the face and had dark hair, sunken cheeks, and a black mustache like a crayon mark across his face. Discounting his plume, he was about five foot six. The plume was white and a foot long and rather lacy. Slocum didn't know the bird that the plume had come from.

He took a sip of his tea. He listened to the sounds of the soldiers searching the loft of the barn and their footsteps on the kitchen steps. The tea was pretty good.

"G'mornin'," he said pleasantly as the Yankee trio mounted the porch. Slocum dropped his feet flat. Sometimes it doesn't pay to be too relaxed.

The major dipped his hat in what might have passed for a nod. His heels stopped not too far from where Slocum sat. The troop sergeant was drawing his sidearm as he stepped through the front door of the Light of Love. The jayhawker had his hanging loosely in his hand. Slocum eyed the officers over the lip of his cup. "Looks to be a warm day," he said quietly.

Apparently the major thought remarks about the weather were beneath him. He hardened his gaze and kept mum.

Slocum supposed that the short officer's stare was supposed to intimidate him. It did make him angry because it was a childish trick. They all heard the scuffle upstairs and the boy's curses. "What the hell do you mean, comin' up here . . . ! Leggo of me, you bastard." A blow. The splat of flesh against flesh. Murmuring, "That's all right, ma'am. I'll just get on out of here now and take this boy downstairs. Ma'am, I think it would be better if you returned to your bedclothes until we're gone."

A woman's voice—unintelligible. Another sound, a woman's shriek, perfectly clear. Sallie Webster's clear hard voice: "Get out of my bedroom, you sorry-looking son of a bitch, or you'll regret it until your dying day!"

"Yes, ma'am."

The major's voice was flat and without inflection. "Wipe that grin off your face, friend."

John Slocum did stand up. He didn't do anything threatening, but he got to his feet with the fluid grace of a snake uncoiling and it was so quick that the major took a half step backward before he stopped himself.

Slocum said mildly, "I expect you're lookin' for the Quantrill guerrillas. Well, I ain't one, and the boy upstairs ain't one either, and the two women your men are insultin' don't customarily ride under the black flag."

"Major Terrell," the major said. He didn't stick out his hand.

"John Slocum," Slocum said. He didn't stick out his hand either.

The six Federals inside the yard gate were drawn up in a loose line—if there were guerrillas inside the Light of Love, this bunch was prepared.

In one stride, Slocum bypassed the major, again a little too quickly for the little man's reflexes. He walked into the kitchen, though the major had come into the house behind him with one hand on his unbuttoned holster. John Slocum poured himself another cup of hot water and added fresh tea leaves to his cup. The sound of feet coming down the stairs. The clomp, clomp of soldiers' boots on the hardwood floors. When Slocum lifted his hand to his mouth, it was shaking, which surprised him. He thought he could control his anger better than that. Too much rapid travel can unsettle a man. The half-full whiskey bottle was on the dry sink. One shot would make his tea much tastier. He ignored the bottle and walked back into the front parlor of the house. The little major was examining the boy as if he were a dirty rifle. Hands on hips, face pushed slightly forward in a glare. "And that's your story? How old are you, boy?"

"Sixteen."

"Sixteen what?"

"Sixteen years." The boy's lips stuck out sullenly.

"Sixteen—sir!" the major reminded him.

McHale was naked except for a blanket around his shoulders. The troop sergeant held one arm and the jayhawker the other. The jayhawker was bored, but the troop sergeant seemed relieved. They might have caught a houseful of armed, dangerous guerrillas.

A ruckus coming down the stairs. Roxie rounded the corner and the next thing they knew, she was flying at the major. The jayhawker dropped the boy's arm. The boy turned on the troop sergeant, swinging.

Roxie was wearing a flannel nightdress, and her hair was unbound and her feet were bare. She was punching that Federal major all the same. Slocum leaned back against the door frame and enjoyed it. The major was getting the worst of it. With one sweep of her arm, Roxie knocked his plumed hat clean off his head. The troop sergeant was bent over sucking air into his lungs. They were giving a good account of themselves, that pair.

The jayhawker backed away from the tussle and lifted his Colt Dragoon. Without paying very much attention, he pulled the trigger. The heavy slug crashed into the plank wall—not six inches from Slocum's ear. The thunderclap in that small enclosure stopped everybody cold.

Sallie Webster had made her way downstairs. The single gunshot stopped her dead. She put her hands to her cheeks and fainted.

"Call 'em off," the jayhawker told Slocum.

"That's enough," Slocum said, barking his words. Somebody was going to get hurt bad and there wasn't anything here worth it.

Slocum's command brought results. Panting a little, the boy stepped back. The girl dropped her face in her hands and cried. The troop sergeant gasped his complaint, "You little bastard."

The diminutive major retrieved his hat. His hair was the same brilliant black as his mustache. Even thick hair grease hadn't been able to keep it flat and it looked like a fallen shed roof.

He patted his hair into place, restored his hat, and said, "I want Bloody Bill Anderson's head. Or William Quantrill's head. It doesn't matter which first. Whichever soonest meets the edge of my saber. I have a full squadron of the best regular troops in Missouri to make my boast good. I will break any man who stands between me and my object: total, merciless victory."

The jayhawker grinned over his black beard. His eyes laughed at John Slocum. He seemed to share some secret with Slocum—a secret appreciation only the two of them could enjoy.

"The likes of you will never get Bloody Bill," the boy said. "He'll cut you down like, like you was nothin', that's what he'll do."

The major's right eyebrow rose, but the left stayed right where it was.

The jayhawker said, "These two were at the ford when we killed that guerrilla." Using his pistol he pointed at Slocum. "He's some kind of paroled Rebel soldier. The boy ain't anyone special."

Roxie was kneeling beside her mistress, trying to wake her from her faint. Sallie Webster came to after a moment. Then, refusing more help, she sat upright.

"Sorry, ma'am," the major said stiffly. "Didn't mean to cause you distress."

Her wave was abrupt and angry as a shout would have been. She chopped him away as though he were dead wood.

"Paroled, eh?" The major stepped closer to John Slocum. "But sound, I see. No missing limbs. Are you deaf or blind?"

"No," Slocum said. He was being eyed by a recruiter.

"Frank James was paroled once. Did you know that?"

"Who's Frank James?"

"He's one of the murderers. I don't want his head. I want to hang him." A slightly dreamy expression crossed the major's face.

"Which murderers?" Slocum didn't follow.

"Those who ride with Quantrill." The major's voice got harsh as a rasp. "You fellows don't pay too much attention to a parole, do you?"

Since the major was asking him just what kind of double-gaited liar he was, Slocum kept mum. No sense fueling the flame.

"Frank James promised never to fight for the Rebels again if we turned him loose. He wasn't back in Missouri more than three weeks before he signed up with Quantrill. Is that what you intended?"

"Not exactly what I had in mind," Slocum said.

With Roxie's aid, Sallie Webster got up. Her face didn't have much color in it. She whispered, "What are you doing in my house, you miserable half-pint?"

"Major Terrell," he said, touching his hat brim.

"Why don't you get the hell out of here," she said.

"Of course," he said, and spun on his heel. "Troop sergeant, march the prisoners along."

The troop sergeant had recovered from the boy's blow, except for a slight quiver at his nostrils. "All right, you," he said, motioning the two outside.

The major's eyes examined his squadron as he drew on his black gauntlets. "How do you propose to demonstrate your loyalty?" the major said.

Slocum went into his shirt pocket for the parole. He offered the folded paper to the man. The major didn't take it.

"Speak up, man," the major said, irritated. "If you want to die here, I'll want to detail gravediggers."

On cue, two pistols were cocked. The jayhawker and the troop sergeant had weapons drawn.

The troop sergeant said, "Why don't you two step down from the porch onto the walk. These ladies have had plenty of blood shed on their property."

No choice. John Slocum went down into the yard.

The troops in front of him prudently moved their horses and quicker than you could wish for it, a firing lane had opened.

"Come on, man," the major jeered. "Surely you can think of some way you could demonstrate your new unswerving loyalty to the Union."

John Slocum knew what he had to do, but he didn't have to like it. "I suppose I could ride along with you."

"A volunteer?" The major's voice went flat again.

"Somethin' like that."

The boy couldn't contain himself. Though he was goose pimpled in the cold and wore only the blanket wrapped around him, he shouted, "The hell with you! I ain't gonna fight for no goddamned . . ."

The rest of his message was lost because John Slocum hit him very hard, just where the neck meets the skull, and the boy's knees lost all their strength and he fell straight down to the ground, his blanket fluttering with him.

"Boy's young," Slocum drawled. "He's young and he's dumb."

For the first time, the major smiled. It was an impersonal kind of smile without much warmth to it. "Boy's old enough," he said. He gestured behind him where Roxie had her head stuck outside the door. The girl had tears in her eyes, but she wasn't going to run outside in her nightdress. "He's had himself a woman. Time he learned how to kill and who his enemies are."

"Sometimes that takes a while to learn," Slocum said mildly enough. "I reckon I'll try and borrow a gun from these fine ladies back there," he said.

"Bring a weapon for the boy," the major insisted.

Slocum kept his tone jesting. "Hell. He's too damn young for this. He's just a pup. Let him go his way."

The major toed the prostrate form. "He'll kill somebody before the month is out," the little man said. "I'd prefer his victim to be a Rebel."

Slocum pushed the matter further, though he'd already lost the argument, "He's young, major. If you got any pity left . . ."

Slocum could see the sense. Once the major got the boy killing Confederates, it'd be a hard habit to break. That's how killing worked sometimes.

"Get that boy on his feet," the major said.

"Get some ammonia under his nose and get him dressed," Slocum said. "He'll be groggy, but he'll come 'round."

Slocum took Sallie Webster for a private confab. Sallie wasn't in the best shape. "I'd like to look over your guns," Slocum said. "Take a deep breath now, and hold it. Won't be any killin' here today."

The woman took a draught of air and shook her head as though she were trying to drive blood into all the chambers of her brain. She swallowed. "I'll be all right," she said. Then, steadied, she added, "I hate to see you leave."

Slocum grinned. "Got to get the work done," he said.

Maybe it wasn't the wisest thing he could have said, because she lost color and she didn't have much to spare. "Don't you think . . . ?" She put her hand on his arm.

"The guns?" he reminded her.

So she led him into the storeroom behind the kitchen where a heavy trunk contained the guns she'd removed from the dead jayhawker. She hadn't bothered to clean them before she'd put them away. Slocum could tell that when he looked down the first bore. It was spotted with the heavy residue of black powder. He winced. "How long ago was it that you put these sidearms away?" he asked, hoping it hadn't been long.

"I dunno," she shrugged. "Two weeks, three. If you don't want 'em, I can close this lid."

"Don't do that." He selected a Remington 1860 Army for himself and found a Dance revolver for the boy. The Remington was only slightly better than the Dance and had a groove in one grip from a bullet and the holster was thick with blackened blood that fell off in chunks. It'd do as well as some. He hurried upstairs for his haversack. There he popped a couple double eagles loose from his blanket and left them on the secretary. He was too vain to pay for a woman. He told himself he was paying for the guns.

He stuck the pistol into the black holster and buckled it around his waist. The rig's previous owner had been two sizes bigger than Slocum around the middle and the gunbelt hung funny.

The banty major was bellowing, "Squadron, prepare to mount!" He added, "John Slocum, get down here. I have a couple horses saddled for you and the boy."

Under his breath, Slocum muttered, "All right, all right. Keep your shirt on." He opened his Barlow, slashing the flap off the military holster and scooping a half round in the cup of the leather. The holster hung on the belt by two slots. He'd have to cut two new slots to cant the gun better. For the present, he set it on his left hip for a cross draw and stabbed a new buckle hole in the belt so it rode up high on his hip. He made two practice draws before he hurried down the stairs. He was clumsy with an unfamiliar rig and the Remington's trigger action was horrible, but the gun felt right to him, like finding a favorite that he thought he'd lost.

"One minute, Slocum," the major called the time.

Slocum gave Sallie Webster a peck on the cheek. It's not to his credit that he forgot her as soon as he saw his new horse. It was probably the poorest horse the Federals had. The draft horses pulling the gun caissons looked younger and sprightlier. The boy's horse was no better. His feet dragged off the stubby animal. The boy's head was bowed. Slocum hung the boy's new gun over his horse's cantle. The boy's eyes were still dazed. Slocum hoped he hadn't hit him too hard. He'd seen men who'd been hit too hard. "You all right?" he asked.

The boy didn't say anything, but deep behind his eyes something glowed. Hatred. Slocum nodded the recognition and mounted.

Fifteen-year-old horse with spiny backbone, slat

sides, and a wheeze in his breathing. Windbroken. "Major, I'm not gonna be too much use in a charge," Slocum said.

That small impersonal smile. "You won't run too far, either," he said. "If the notion should strike you. You know how you can get a better horse, don't you?"

The question was stupid. Slocum let it drop. He didn't look back at the two women watching from the Light of Love, because he didn't expect to see them again in his lifetime. He swung his horse into line between the jayhawker and the troop sergeant.

"Welcome, partner," the jayhawker laughed. "Always glad to see a new recruit." Then he snorted and wiped his nose on the back of his sleeve. He took a chew of tobacco and offered it to Slocum.

"Nope," Slocum said. "I only dip snuff when I'm workin' livestock."

The jayhawker introduced himself. He said his name was Devers and he wasn't a regular Federal soldier because he hated to ride in ranks. "I like to ride out front," he said. "Like an officer. Can't be an officer because I got no schooling."

Slocum said he was a jayhawker now by force of circumstances. The jayhawker thought that was pretty funny and laughed. Tears came to his eyes. "Force of circumstances," he said. "My, ain't you the one?"

Taking advantage of the affability, Slocum asked the jayhawker about the guerrillas. Devers spoke openly as the column wheeled into line and set off down the road. The sun was up now, hot, and the heat felt good on the back of Slocum's shoulders and promised to dry some of the mustiness from his clothes. The jayhawker said the guerrillas were broken up into three troops that generally fought separately, though sometimes they combined operations when the three captains agreed. "Captain Thrailkill, he's the best of them," the jayhawker said. He spat. "That ain't saying much. Sometimes he takes prisoners. Thrailkill's got a regular commission in the CSA." The jayhawker laughed. "Though that wouldn't slow me down none, should he happen into my sights."

Slocum showed his teeth in appreciation of the other's ferocity.

"Thrailkill ain't got much of a mob. No more than forty men. It's Quantrill and Bloody Bill Anderson who have the troops. Now Bloody Bill, he's a wonder. You heard about his cord?"

"Cord?"

Another rough laugh. "He keeps score. I suppose if he whittled notches like some do, there wouldn't be enough gunbutt left to get a grip on. By now, they'd be all whittled away."

Although he was on an awful horse with an untested gun on his hip, John Slocum began to feel pretty good. He was still a young man and the warmth spread down the back of his arms, and the grass smelled damp from the dew. As they passed a dense thicket a covey of quail jumped up in a terrific hurry. Slocum watched the birds until they settled down, some fifty yards off the trail. "If I had a scattergun, I'd get me some breakfast."

"Oh hell," the jayhawker said. "You mean you ain't fed?" In his saddlebags he found a chunk of stringy beef jerky. He took a hard bite and put the food back. "If you was free as one of them birds, you could eat," he said. "I expect the major'll give you somethin' by and by—scraps if nothin' else."

"Uh-huh."

Slocum watched the man's jaws move. To forget the saliva in his own mouth he faced away, backward. His practiced eyes evaluated the major's squadron. Most of the cavalrymen were young; corporals and sergeants, no more than twenty with only a few seasoned veterans, like the troop sergeant. Three hundred men and, of course, the Dalgreens. The Dalgreen had begun the war as a naval gun, but it was a quick-firing breech loader and popular with both sides. Unlike the cavalrymen, the gun crews looked old enough to have smelled powder smoke before. Like many Federal detachments in the

West, the squadron was made up of inexperienced men with only a few old hands for guidance. Under a good commander these Federals would fight. Under an indifferent one, they would break brittle as glass.

"Is the major serious? He really wants Bill Anderson's head?"

The jayhawker chomped down the last bite of meat. He was one of those men who couldn't stand the silence from his own company. "Oh, he's fierce, the major is. Used to own a dry-goods store in Ohio before the war. There's something about running a dry-goods place that brings out the meanness in a man."

At least while he was talking, he wasn't chewing his meal. Farms on both sides of the road. Most of them bore scars from the troubles. Half of them had been burned out completely. No bustle of farmers or farmhands when the column rode by. Slocum didn't see cows or pigs or horses or sheep. They'd been kept away from the main road to keep them from foragers. At that moment Slocum could have eaten half a pig by himself, or a couple of chickens anyway.

The road turned. Rock walls on both sides announced a more prosperous place. The bare elm branches overhead had been pruned and the dry wall had been carefully constructed and as carefully maintained. The jayhawker answered Slocum's unasked question. "Puffenbarger. He's a kraut. He's for the Union, too, him and his sons. They bought substitutes to do their fighting, or so I heard, and they been lining their pockets since the war began. One thing about a war, the man who's got produce to sell is going to do all right out of it."

Slocum knew his own home place would look more like the abandoned farms than this one.

The road entered a pasture where twenty black and white spotted cows grazed. Slocum had never seen cows like these before. From their udders, they looked to be milk cows, not beef. On a good strong horse, on the far side of the herd, a single rider watched the Federal column.

"That'll be one of the Puffenbarger boys," the jayhawker volunteered. "There's three of 'em, all of decent size."

The rider didn't leave his post, but watched the passage of the troops with impassive curiosity. The rifle across his saddlebow didn't move either.

The road dipped into a narrow creek bottom. The creek was no more than a trickle, this late in a dry fall. The deepest holes would fill a bucket or let a horse drink. No water now, just mud. The creek bottom was churned into a muddy swamp by the passage of hundreds of shod horses. The V-shaped banks were chewed up too, fifty feet on a side; the riders had left a watermark of their passing. Here a hoof had cut the turf, here an alder root had been exposed and then trampled and then cut. Though clean water was finding its way through the mud, the mud was the victor and Slocum didn't figure the riders were too far ahead of them.

The major detailed a patrol of men to follow the creek bed. He led the remainder up the brief rise on the opposite bank.

As they climbed, first the cupola then the roof of one, no two, no—by God—three barns showed themselves. Thick bushy elms surrounding the farmhouse.

Chickens aplenty, and Slocum could hear a pig squealing behind the barns. One of the barns was for tobacco, which surprised Slocum because he didn't know tobacco grew this far north.

Farmhands in the yard. This time of day you'd expect a man to be out in the fields shucking corn or in the woodlot cutting the winter's wood. Five blacks—free men from the looks of them. All carrying guns. Another dozen whites, standing around. These men held the bridles of their best riding horses and were also armed. The major lifted his hand and his NCOs echoed his order down the length of the column.

Slocum risked a glance at Tom McHale, but the

boy's eyes were still red with hatred and he kept his eyes on John Slocum like artillery commanding a prominence. It could have sent a shiver down Slocum's spine if he let it, which he didn't.

A portly farmer separated himself from his circle of friends. He wore his facial hair in sideburns and a short beard. No mustache. His round face looked like a plate with hair growing all around the rim. The man's eyebrows were invisible, they were so sparse and lightly colored. His eyes were the curious china blue of pig's eyes. His mouth was small and fleshy and set in a twist of discontent. The man's hands were the broad flattened hands of a man who'd used tools all his life. The stock of his rifle rested on the ground and he held it as he might have held a pitchfork. "I am Hiram Puffenbarger," he said. "This is mine." He flourished one hand briefly at the house, barns, everything. The flourish contained the other men standing with him, though Slocum didn't know how that could be. "I was robbed of cows," Hiram added. He spoke with relief in his voice, like a man finally talking to someone who can solve his problem.

"Where are the guerrillas?" the major asked.

"They come here yesterday just at six. There were many of them. Hundreds. Their leader was Quantrill who I saw many years ago in Kansas. He is not a big man, but his horse—I've never seen a bigger horse."

"What did he say?"

The farmer looked at his friends for a second for reassurance. "He said take the cows."

"Where?"

"They were two veal calves and a slaughter steer. We meant to butcher this Saturday. My wife told this to Quantrill."

"What did he say to you?"

"Nothing. It was my wife who talked to him. I . . ." The man dropped his gaze to the ground. When his face lifted it burned with shame. "I did nothing wrong. My sympathies are with Lincoln and the Union." The farmer paused. He repeated himself. "Lincoln and the Union!" And his neighbors picked up the cheer, the freed blacks cheering the loudest. They all waved their rifles and shotguns in the air, though they, like the farmer, had been somewhere else when the raiders rode into his barnyard.

"Your wife talked to him."

The man's face got red. "They said . . . I hear . . . none of the guerrillas will kill women." He paused and his face cleared up. "There were women riding with them. A dozen or more."

"Soiled doves?"

"They were no better than they were meant to be," the farmer gave the stock answer about prostitutes.

"Your wife . . ."

"While I and my sons were hiding she talked to Quantrill. He asked for me." His hand shot out, independent of his will, pointing at a door in the barn loft. "I was up there. I heard every word. My sons had ridden into the woods."

The major snapped, "Perhaps I should interview your wife, then, Mister Puffenbarger."

The farmer didn't understand the major's annoyance. "No. She is busy in the kitchen with her work. She is bottling out sweet cider. We keep our cider until haying time, Major, and she is too busy to talk to you."

Bit by bit, a picture emerged from the major's questions, like a daguerreotype finding its shades and shadows in silver solution. Quantrill's troop had quickly searched the house. When Puffenbarger's wife, in her most tremulous voice had said, "Hurray for Lee and the Confederacy!" Quantrill merely said, "Sorry, ma'am. That ain't what I heard," and turned his hunters loose. They looked long and hard, but had to be satisfied with the three cows in the home corral. Quantrill had told her that they'd go for now, but would certainly return the next week or so to "have a little chat with your husband." The wife nearly fainted but managed to keep herself from it by a grip on the porch rail she later described to her husband as a "deathgrip." The guerrillas rounded up the stock and disappeared into the creek bottom like wild Indians.

"I followed them," the farmer nodded his head. "You bet I did."

Farmer Puffenbarger didn't actually do the following personally. He detailed one of his farmhands to do the job—the hand Puffenbarger could most afford to lose. Lazy. No account. But he was of just enough account to track the two hundred men a couple miles where the creek bottom widened out into Puffenbarger's very best rye grass pasture. "I have my best bulls in that pasture," Puffenbarger said.

Caught up in the man's circuituous story, the major asked, "What difference does that make?"

"Major, I intend to send those forty bulls to Salt Lake City," Puffenbarger said.

The major didn't disguise his puzzlement.

Puffenbarger explained, beginning his explanation with a gasp of exasperation. "So I do not wish two hundred horses eating my grass," he said. "I fatten animals for the long trail to Salt Lake City in Utah Territory. The last sutler's train leaves Fort Selby in two weeks and my animals must be ready for the trip."

Concerned with his grass and annoyed at the loss of three animals, Puffenbarger had notified the Federals. Federal telegraph lines buzzed and two forces set out to converge on the guerrillas. Major Terrell's squadron from the east. Another Federal squadron, commanded by a career captain of cavalry who'd seen service against CSA regulars—including General Shelby—that force was riding in from the west.

"Have you kept watch on them?" the major asked.

Swelled up a little, proudly. "I have." His least important farmhands had. "He remains in my bottom pasture, below Shaw's Ridge. He maintains his campfires inside the woods."

Most of the major's command had dismounted now, stretching themselves, giving their horses a break. Maybe a couple of troopers meant to appropriate themselves a chicken or two, but farmer Puffenbarger's neighbors saw to it that the birds stayed well away.

The patrol he'd sent out earlier galloped back. The sergeant threw a salute. "They're a mile ahead, sir," he said. "They got all their horses in this big meadow. Most of the Rebs are in the woods."

Armed with the guerrillas' location, the major planned one decisive battle to destroy the guerrillas once and for all.

The column was turned on its axis in minutes. Experienced troopers checked the greenhorns' weapons. "Load 'em up, gentlemen. Five in the revolver. A full Spencer. No brass under the hammer, or you'll shoot yourself, sure as God made green apples."

The jayhawker didn't bother to check his pistols. Once in the morning would have to do. Slocum wished he could pull the caps and recharge his Remington.

Puffenbarger was lecturing the major, saying he should be very careful of the bulls in the field because they had been sold already to agents forwarding them west to Mormon farmers near Salt Lake. The major was too busy soldiering to listen. He ordered four men with the fastest horses directly west. After five miles or so, they were to arc south again, to intercept the second Union command. The two forces had been in messenger contact since dawn and Major Terrell hoped to bring the other group of Federals behind the guerrillas. "A nutcracker," he said.

"Don't let my animals get hurt," Puffenbarger said.

Slocum waited easily. The boy glowered at his back and Slocum would stay a foot or so behind him once shooting commenced. Slocum wished to avoid avoidable errors.

Failing to get reassurances about his livestock, Hiram Puffenbarger said, "I will accompany you." The first time he said this, it was below the hearing threshold, but the second time was louder. He asked each of his neighbors and some turned away, others set their hats more firmly and looked to their guns. Fifteen farmers, including Puffenbarger and his three sons, rode out with the Federal squadron.

The major ordered the troop sergeant to ride behind Slocum and the boy, "Until their loyalties have been proven." Slocum expected him to add, "with blood," but he didn't, though that was what he meant.

The muddy creek bottom twisted slightly, no more than a roll of the shoulders as it meandered along below the level of Puffenbarger's fields. The farmer rode on the hogback above in a black buckboard, drawn by a fine piece of horseflesh that Slocum admired. The horse had the exaggerated stride that marks the walking horse and his muscles surely did eat up the ground. Slocum's horse wheezed under him, and on the side slope, it stumbled twice and almost went down. If the major expected him to ride a charge on this animal, he was bound for disappointment.

The creek bottom opened up into the bottom pasture, the road dipped down the hogback and the farmer Puffenbarger passed in front of everyone.

The guerrillas had come into the pasture without closing the gate, and this fact annoyed the farmer more than the several hundred strange horses grazing his lush field. As he hefted the heavy wooden gate, he was muttering curses.

In silence, the major raised his hand. His NCOs joined him and they rode onto the pasture to reconnoiter.

The field dipped slightly to a scraggly oak forest on the other side. Curls of smoke rose from the woods and one campfire was visible, with men standing around it.

The guerrillas spotted the Yankees before the Federal officers could make any plans. A hubbub. Yells. Men running around the campfire and into the meadow. Already some were astride their horses, bareback, and the first bullets whooped through the air just over the officers' heads.

The bullets galvanized the major into action. "Form up a skirmish line! Troopers, form up!"

The Federals weren't completely experienced, but they weren't all green either, and the horsemen poured onto the edge of the pasture, summoned by the bugler's "Assembly."

The battery of Dalgreens didn't get into action. They pulled in behind the third troop of cavalry. Artillery wasn't useful in a fluid situation.

The bullets were getting faster now; most of the guerrillas were mounted. The major raised his arm and three hundred Federal riders piled across that pasture, outdistancing each other in their eagerness for the attack.

They got stung. The Federals thought a surprised guerrilla force wasn't anything to fear, but each of Quantrill's men was an army in himself, and bullets had taken their toll. Farmer Puffenbarger's neighbors held back at the edge of the meadow to encourage the soldiers. When Puffenbarger saw that his precious Holstein bulls were rushing to and fro, he rode forward resolutely. Disregarding the bullets, he attacked at a diagonal from the Federal troops and once his neighbors saw what he was doing, they hurried to help. They knew nothing of cavalry engagements nor did they wish to know. They knew animals were in danger and must be moved to safety.

While the Federals executed their charge across open ground, farmers rounded up the stock.

Slocum's horse was shuddering with effort, but each time Slocum slacked off to spare the animal, the troop sergeant yelled and waved his revolver around. Slocum's Remington stayed holstered. He'd wait until he had a target.

His horse swerved to avoid a downed horse. It jumped over another dead Yankee and maybe its rear hooves struck the man's body and maybe not.

The guerrillas formed a loose screen at the edge of the wood and their guns took a toll, hammering the

Yankees pretty badly, but the momentum of the charge was strong and the horsemen smashed into the underbrush and through it, firing as they came.

The guerrillas, outnumbered better than two to one, withdrew deeper into the woods, firing from their horses.

Every time the Federals closed, the men on the point died, blown off their horses, falling like tenpins.

Slocum stayed back. Not his fight.

He rode slowly into the woods and some of the corpses wore butternut brown. Slouch hats, heavy coats. Slocum dismounted beside a couple of dead guerrillas and searched them. He found a Colt Navy in a saddlebag and took it. Finally he'd lost the troop sergeant and the boy. Maybe they'd shoot each other. Meanwhile, Slocum stayed just behind the fighting front, hoping to pick up a good fast horse.

The sun stood cold and bright over the November woods. The black powder smoke rose through the low branches into the treetops. Gun blasts shivered the last leaves on the trees.

Messengers reached Major Terrell, in the heart of the fighting, and a moment later the bugle sounded the recall. Some troopers were weary and weak and frightened and more than willing to sink back into their saddles and holster their revolvers. The majority were confused—they had their blood up and wanted to tangle with the Rebs. Hadn't they already pushed them out of one stand at the edge of the meadow? Hadn't they pushed them halfway up the low limestone ridge?

Major Terrell was delighted. He checked his watch. Tomorrow morning would have to do. There was an hour left of light.

John Slocum had found a horse. It had been a guerrilla's horse that morning, but it was his horse now. He transferred the old McCormick saddle from his swaybacked animal and turned it loose. Firing diminished to the random noise of skirmishers exchanging messages.

Slocum ignored the dead men he passed. Now he had a good Colt and a good horse. There was nothing further he required of them. Slocum was three hundred yards below the fighting and plenty of trees between him and bullets. He kept his eyes peeled for the boy. If the boy had been forced to kill, no telling what he'd do. No telling what he'd do in any event. Slocum had to smile. The boy was a tough nut—tough as any.

Standing just at the edge of the meadow, Slocum could see a good distance up Shaw's Ridge almost to the top of it. Plenty of smoke, rising through the trees, and where it was thickest, the fighting was still nasty. A few shots from the top of the ridge too, where the second force of Federals had skirmishers out. The main body wouldn't arrive until nightfall, but skirmishers had the guerrillas caught in a vise.

The Federal battery pulled back into the meadow four hundred yards to get some elevation for their guns. They unhitched from their caissons and began to set up an ammo passing line. The gunlayer was laying up the blocks. Shaw's Ridge was steep, and at maximum elevation they'd need to bury the tongue to get the altitude they wanted.

Other Federal troops were filtering back down the hill now, most of them, like John Slocum, leading horses. Slocum didn't spy the boy, though he did look for him.

The Yankees had plenty of rations. Enough for the farmers guarding Puffenbarger's presold bulls across the big pasture and enough for John Slocum and the boy.

Occupied with a real enemy, Major Terrell had forgotten about Slocum and Tom McHale. The troop sergeant had accepted them into the ranks of the blooded troops. He joined his brother NCOs at their campfire and left Slocum and the boy in peace.

Slocum said, "You want to clear out, just wait until it gets dark and slip on down the hill. Go around the edge of the meadow until you hit that creek bottom. Follow that back to the road and good luck to you."

The boy hadn't spoken, though he'd fallen on the hardtack and beans Slocum had cooked up with nary a by-your-leave and now had his face around a tin coffee cup, and his ass beside the fire. Slocum meant to have that spot for himself. Already his shoulder blades were shivering, and if you leaned your head way back and looked at the sky, the stars were out, hard as pinpricks and not a cloud among them. That meant a bitter frost by morning and though the sun hadn't been gone two hours, the cold was settling right in. The Federals kept their horses in a central remuda, grazing quietly on the edge of the meadow. The artillerymen had their animals hobbled separately near their guns.

The boy looked up. "Hell, I wouldn't leave," he said. "Wouldn't want to miss the chance to play the traitor to my kin and my country."

Slocum grinned at the boy's attempted cynicism. "Yeah. I know what you mean."

The boy's glare withstood Slocum's green laughing eyes. "I wonder how it's gonna feel," he said deliberately. "To fire a shot into a gray uniform. I wonder how that'll be."

Slocum shrugged. "Never knew any man who had to kill anybody if he didn't want to."

"I was gonna kill you today," the boy said, stating the fact.

"So I figured. Pass me that coffeepot."

The boy's hand performed the service. "You bastard," he said.

Undeniably, if Slocum hadn't coldcocked the boy he'd be dead right now—buried in the backyard at the Light of Love. He didn't mention it. It rarely did much good pointing out what was in front of a man's face. If he wanted to notice, he could have done the job himself. "I ain't slow to anger, boy," he said softly, pouring his coffee.

The boy swallowed his reply. Slocum rolled himself

a quirly and scratched his lucifer into light. The smoke tasted good and the coffee had a touch of chicory in it. These Federals had picked up some Southern habits. The glow of the guerrilla campfires, about five hundred yards above them. On the ridgetop, the Federal troops had erected bonfires of blown down jackpines. Just below the top they sparked and flared and any guerrilla who wanted to slip through would burn to death for sure.

Slocum wondered.

Major Terrell and his NCOs sat by a campfire in the center of the position. The NCOs would sleep under the stars tonight, but the major had his own small tent, which functioned as his headquarters.

"Before dawn," Terrell ordered. "Give them a dozen volleys with the guns. When the troopers mount that ridge, they'll find nothing but scraps to contend with—or my name's not James Terrell."

And the listening Federals raised their canteen cups in a toast recognizing an official occasion when they saw one.

It was not to be.

6

Slocum was restless. He'd moved his bedroll twice before it got pitch dark and once afterward. Cold at the tail end of the year—it was worse than the chill of winter or early spring. The cold was absolute and the darkness swift. There was some light from the moon and the glare of the stars as he hiked across the meadow, leading his fine new horse toward the farmer's campfire.

John Slocum had plenty reason to move his soogans. No sense tempting the boy's knife.

Sometimes electrical tension in the air before a battle can keep everybody awake, worse than a swarm of mosquitoes. Nothing like that tonight. The small picket fires were low on the major's side. The bigger fires on the ridgetop were the other Federals. Most men slept.

From the guerrillas' position, no fires at all—nothing but the plaintive wail of an ocarina, playing "Rose of Alabama."

The words slipped into Slocum's mind as he listened to the tune.

Under his breath, John Slocum sang the words and the tune. His fine new horse stepping along behind him. The light washed the gentle contours of the pasture, and Slocum felt exposed, though he knew he'd be nothing more substantial than a shadow to watchers on the solid block of dark ridge behind him.

He was confused, maybe that was the trouble. When he'd fought outside Richmond, it was dangerous enough, and the food was infrequent and poor and he wasn't going to live through year's end. But he knew who he was fighting and had a simple reason why.

Now it was awfully hard to know who was in the right. With his own eyes he'd seen the Yankees committing murder and they didn't expect to take any prisoners tomorrow. When he saw W. C. Quantrill's body with his own eyes, his orders would be filled, and then John Slocum would face another choice. He didn't think he wanted to return to Richmond. No sense walking back into a death trap once you'd escaped it. But it wouldn't feel right either just to go home to Georgia. No, he'd signed on for the duration and he'd stick it out, once he figured what that meant.

John Slocum yawned hugely. The walk across the great moon-washed meadow was taking the last of the restlessness out of him. Maybe that was all he needed, just a little exercise.

Somebody else had the same idea—a shadow walking in front of him toward the farmer's bright bonfire. The bonfire held the black and white bulls, who were pretty spooky for good reason. Slocum wouldn't have spotted the other man if he hadn't got between him and that huge fire.

The other nightwalker wasn't leading a horse and Slocum wondered about that. A deserter would have a horse, for sure, to put as many miles as possible between himself and the deserter's punishment: the rope. Slocum wasn't especially nervy, but he moved to his horse's left as he came up behind the man, and his hand fell to the holster he'd made for the Remington this morning. Now it held the smaller Colt Navy he'd acquired. His hand unlatched the leather thong that held the hammer.

The other nightwalker wasn't running, but he was moving somewhat fast and Slocum had to stretch out to overtake him.

The other walker heard the horse and stopped and turned to wait for company. He wore an ancient buffalo coat thrown like a robe over his shoulders. Both his arms were inside.

He stood like a young man and wore a young man's flat-brimmed hat. No spurs on his boots. None that Slocum had heard, anyway. Without his willing it, John

Slocum's hand pulled the Colt Navy from the holster and laid it against the stirrup skirts of his horse. Most of Slocum was on the far side of the horse and his pistol was completely out of sight. He had no reason to draw. Instinct. A rationalist might argue that the absence of sound from the other, the invisibility of his arms, and his very stance were cues that alerted John Slocum. But it was predator's instinct, nothing more. Though relaxed, the nightwalker buzzed with tension and as he closed, John Slocum's nose flared. Muffling the sound with the web of his thumb, Slocum drew the hammer back to full cock.

"Evenin'," he said softly.

The nightwalker leaned way forward, exaggerating. "Is that a man behind that horse?" he asked. "I declare I see six feet over there and I do believe I heard a voice and I've heard of talking horses, but never met one, no six-legged one anyway." The nightwalker's voice was about Slocum's age and held some real humor. It was an attractive voice and John Slocum felt like stepping out and introducing himself. Instead, he dropped his Colt down below his horse's neck. No way the nightwalker could have seen it, not against the horse's mass, in this light.

"You have the advantage of me, friend," Slocum said vaguely. He clamped his grip on his animal's bit. The horse would stay put no matter what fireworks went off. "Suppose you tell me your name," Slocum said and the note of a threat was in his voice.

"I hate to talk to a man I can't see," the other replied, taking a couple steps toward Slocum and the horse.

"I hate to kill a man I don't know, but I will if you take another step nearer. My name's Slocum. John Slocum."

The other hesitated and when he mentioned his name it came out funny like maybe it should mean something. "Cole Younger," he said.

It didn't mean anything to John Slocum, but he

meant to shoot if the man came any closer. "Out for a stroll?" he said politely.

That huge buffaloskin coat billowed along the man's shoulders and above his waist. Neither of his hands appeared. Slocum's finger got warm and desirous, and he didn't buy the man's explanation—something about "Joining his friends and neighbors at Hiram Puffenbarger's campfire."

"Uh-huh," Slocum said. He didn't draw a bead. That isn't how you gunfight in the dark. You let your instinctive sense of space and motion take over, you never use your sights. "You're probably a dead man, Younger," Slocum said, no louder than before. "If you push both your hands straight up in the air, maybe you won't be."

Younger said, "What the hell?" and crouched down, but his hands stayed inside the robe.

"Have it your way," Slocum said.

"Wait!" Younger's hands shot up. Glitter of metal in each hand.

Now John Slocum moved his horse closer. Now they weren't twenty feet apart and Slocum saw the man was no older than his voice and had light-colored hair. Average height. Slight of build. "You carry some iron for a farmer," Slocum observed dryly.

"Can't tell who you might meet takin' a peaceable stroll after dinner," Younger replied.

"Suppose you might turn loose of those pistols," Slocum said.

Younger hesitated. But John Slocum was behind a two-thousand-pound flesh wall and Cole was stark in the open. "I'll put 'em down easy," Younger said. "They're accurate weapons and I wouldn't want them damaged."

"Just so your hands come up empty," Slocum said.

The nightwalker did as he was told. The bonfire behind him threw up a tower of sparks. Slocum came around his horse's neck. "Suppose you wouldn't mind tellin' me who you're ridin' for?" Slocum asked.

Pause. Then, hotly, "I'm ridin' for the Confederate States of America, you ignorant jayhawker."

Slocum could see the sweat beaded up on Younger's forehead. He'd got himself ready to die. Slocum sighed. "You and me both, brother," he said. And lowered his pistol.

7

One hour before dawn. The farmer's bonfire had died back. Only one fat oak log flamed from time to time. A deep bank of red coals pulsated along it.

The Confederates eyed that fire with longing. The tips of the grass blades were white with frost and their boots left dark prints every time they shuffled for a little warmth.

"Damn, where's that sun?" Cole Younger whispered. John Slocum didn't work up a reply. One of the others spat onto the frosted grass for his answer.

Four of them, all told. Three of Quantrill's riders, led by Coleman Younger. And John Slocum—whose orders came from far away.

The four men waited on the far side of the bull herd that'd finally settled down, their broad backs glistening with the same frost that whitened the grass. They moaned and farted and the young farmer riding nightwatch rode around them before ground-reining his horse. For half an hour he watched without moving, his horse's head dropped and dozing before he too dropped his own head. "Hell," one of the Confederates whispered, "that boy snores worse than the bulls do." Some smiles.

It had been Cole Younger's plan, and so he was the one to carry it out—him and his cousin Jim Younger and Jesse James. Jesse was just fifteen then and his brother Frank figured that he'd be better off outside the Federals—no matter what happened—than on the inside with the others.

"If Cole's plan don't work, Jesse," his brother had advised, "at least you'll have a chance."

Coleman Younger talked up his plan and Jesse thought it was as good as any.

Old Quantrill, he didn't care. He figured they'd outfight the Federals in the morning and ride right through them. Failing that, they'd die here, caught on the shaley ridge. It didn't matter very much to him which.

Coleman Younger didn't share Quantrill's turn of mind. Cole thought they could stampede the bulls through the Yankees and better the odds.

Bloody Bill had argued, "Hell, I hate to sneak away from any bunch of damn Federals without bleeding a few." Bloody Bill was twisting that silk cord of his, the way he did when he was nervous.

Cole said, "They got us caught fair up here. Tomorrow, we're gonna be hit with cannon fire and those Federals'll pile over the rim on top of us."

"There's only five hundred of them," Bloody Bill remarked. Sitting in the dark, the slight, dark-haired, dark-bearded figure looked like a troll. In broad daylight, Bloody Bill Anderson, with his bright red shirt and his uncut braided black beard and his hair black and full and long as a woman's, was pretty splendid. At night he looked like a troll. Talked like one too. "We got two hundred riders. We don't need fancy. Pass bottle. In the morning we ride as we rode in. Over Federals." He took the bottle.

He and Quantrill seemed completely indifferent to Cole's plan. Frank James thought it was a good idea because it might get brother Jesse out of the trap. When Cole and Jim and Jesse slipped out, after dark, Quantrill and Bloody Bill were settling down to get drunk.

The three guerrillas separated to slip past the Union pickets. It was early in the evening, and the full-bellied pickets were still remembering their dinner and not worrying about guerrillas. That'd be later, and then they'd be very alert.

Cole Younger's journey was slow—one time he took twenty minutes to get across an open space of less than thirty yards. No problems until he met the stranger behind the horse.

Right now, Cole Younger wished he had a cigarette.

Just the sweet curl of the smoke in his lungs and nostrils.

He also wished he had an apple or a pear. The apple season in Missouri and Kansas had been long this fall and a few pippins still hung high in the branches where a man on horseback could take them. Cole Younger longed for the sweetness and moisture in his mouth. It was a funny thing, how his mouth craved sweetness just before the fighting started. Every damn time.

Cole Younger stretched out of his hunker. "I suppose it's time," he said. "Jesse, you and Jim come up behind the cows and push them slow and easy. Just get 'em on the move. Me and John Slocum will ride the point."

The two younger men nodded and set off, leaving black tracks on the frostbitten earth.

Slocum said, "I'll get you a horse."

"Hoped you might," Cole Younger said and flashed a grin. Younger was missing two teeth in the top and the gap made him look funny, almost clownlike.

So John Slocum got himself up on his new horse's back and nudged him forward with his knees; nothing quick now, nothing abrupt. The soft thud of his horse's walk didn't disturb the nightwatch's horse whose head stayed as bent as its owner's. Slocum reversed the Colt and struck.

The shock traveled up his arm and the nighthawk grunted and his horse woke, ready to bolt, but Slocum had the reins even as the horse's rider slid forward out of the saddle.

The horse was a big plow horse. Cole Younger grinned when he saw it. "Wouldn't want to swap horses, would you?" he inquired. "I believe mine has more power than speed in his build."

Slocum grinned right back. "Well, the bulls will know him anyway."

Slocum rolled a quirly and tossed the makings. "Don't know why a nighthawk shouldn't smoke," he said. "Hell, the damn guerrillas are too far away to draw a good bead on a cigarette."

The ridge was invisible. The mist was climbing off the pasture as the soil gave up heat to the colder air, and their horizon was fifty feet away. They sat their horses and waited. They heard the bulls coming before they saw them, the moo of annoyed animals.

That's how they held those bulls, in the mist, smoking quietly—the two younger men, Jesse and Jim, just behind the herd, mounted now. The farmer's nighthawks had gone to their reward and more luck to them. Slocum and Cole Younger bottled the herd in front, waiting as the mist changed from sullen brown to gray, and finally, when the dawn light hit it, to white. The mist muffled sounds. There were plenty of Yankees on the other side of the pasture and they could hear them stirring around. Because the battery was well out in the pasture, artillery sounds were clearest. Slocum listened. The intent of all the commands was perfectly familiar to him. The clank of the closing breech, the cries of men straining at the bars to set the tailpiece, the clatter of the ramrod dropping into its circular iron holder. But the gun commander's voice wasn't anything like old Captain Varner's and he spent a lot of time encouraging his men, which old Varner never thought necessary.

Slocum drew his Colt and worked the action, raising the hammer and lowering it again with his thumb until the oil loosened very slightly. The mist lifted to a hundred, two hundred feet. They saw the battery. The Federal troops were ready. Shaw's Ridge was still wreathed in fog.

"YIP, YIP, YIP, YIP, AAYY." Coleman Younger hollered the shrill Rebel yell and the herd chasers lifted their own voices.

The bulls came awake at once. Holstein bulls are naturally skittish animals and they're big too, a ton or more each, and before they were completely awake, two hundred of them were hurtling toward the Federal troops, eyes opening as their hearts pumped hard. It was cold, so some of the younger ones got frisky and kicked up their heels, a ton of horned frolic.

For the first time in weeks, John Slocum was without confusion and the sudden clarity made him reel with joy. The Yankees were before him. Confederates rode at his side. How fine. His own voice joined the cry with the rest. He leaned forward in the saddle. He'd been right, the black mare had some real speed as she let the kinks out after a long peaceful night.

On his horse's heels, the first of the bulls thundered along, bug eyed with terror, tails straight up in the air. Holsteins have nasty hooked horns, which could gut a man or his horse in a second. Slocum wouldn't want to go down.

The ridge was clear now, but the Federal battery wasn't firing on it. The artillerymen who had rifles or pistols were firing them into the rolling mass of beef. One of the gun crews had got its tailpiece around so the gun was pointed at the herd, but the bulls careened into the gun before they could depress the elevation. A bull pushed the gunner off his feet and slammed him into his own gun and then other bulls were in the position and some of them were hooking with their horns. Slocum never got anyone to believe it afterward, but he did see a bull single out a fat ammunition carrier and race him for the safety of the caissons. The bull won, his horns vanishing into the man's back.

The Yankees in the woods didn't know what to do until the bulls rolled over the guns. Their rifles spoke in the faces of the animals and a good many bulls went down. Normally that would have been enough to turn them, but not this morning, not scared as they were. The leaders crashed into the brush gladly, and the rest of the herd was hot on their heels.

And with a howl the ridge erupted with guerrillas, crashing down on the distracted Yankees.

The Yankees had been waiting for the artillery to

do its work, had planned to climb the ridge once the guns were done and pick up the scraps.

The picket line was thick with Yankees beside their horses. The guerrillas rolled down on them, firing with both hands, the reins in their teeth.

The commander on top of Shaw's Ridge saw the whole thing. He groaned. He ordered his own troopers to mount up. Maybe he couldn't crush Quantrill's men, but perhaps he could catch them.

The gray-clad horsemen literally slid their horses through Federal lines, and the last thing many men saw that morning was the broad chest of a horse with legs stuck out front of it and its giant rider leaning forward, his six-guns blossoming fire.

The screams of the wounded, the shriek of hurt horses, the snap, snap, snap of Colts, the heavier crack of carbines.

Quantrill on the lead horse, laughing. Both guns holstered, he waved his men on. He was so drunk he could hardly sit his saddle. He lurched and a couple bullets parted the air where he'd been a moment before. He didn't notice, or care.

Bloody Bill was over his horse's neck, unbalancing him so the animal was trying to overrun its own hooves. With his black braided beard and his bright red shirt, Anderson was a striking target, but the Federals lost every instinct but flight, and most of the men he shot with his pistol only inches from the back of their heads.

And the scream. The shriek, the yell that set one's teeth on edge and made the hair stand up.

Frank James was hollering something. Frank was hollering that the Yankees were coming off the ridge behind them. "Ride!" he shouted. "Ride! Cut 'em down and ride!"

The edge of the pasture was like the chaos at the bottom of a waterfall. Anything was likely to turn up in the tumbling. The bulls bellowed and hooked, and the horses dying before their assaults were Confederate as well as Yankee.

Tom McHale's pistol was hot in his hand. He sat atop his unexcitable horse firing at the soldiers rushing through the mist and the black powder smoke. His eyes smarted and his teeth were coated black, but he was happy, no doubt about it. A gray-clad trooper busted by, his horse dropped and a bull appeared, intent on shortening the fallen rider's life span. The bull's head was lowered. The trooper was on his feet and the bull focused.

Bam. The blow didn't hurt the bull, though its vision seemed to be impaired. The second slug tore through its fist-sized brain and turned it into steak.

Tom McHale shoved out his hand and the other trooper, a boy no older than himself, grabbed at it and swung up behind. "Obliged," Jesse James said.

When Quantrill's fastest troops smashed through his front ranks, Major Terrell hollered with anger. He'd been outfought, no doubt about it. He yanked his white plume out of his hatband.

The first of the Confederate riders were out in the meadow, their horses stretching out. Bloody Bill raced past the ruined battery. The guns looked all right, though one was upended. Their gunners had been pounded into strange shapes by hooves. Bloody Bill jerked his horse onto its haunches and jumped down. Nearby riders followed his example because they were sworn to follow him anywhere, no matter what. Bloody Bill set his hands on his hips and eyed the ridge and his face drew back so his teeth glistened in what on another face would be a smile.

The Federal forces from the ridgetop had roared through the area the guerrillas had occupied the night before and crashed through the other Federals, collecting the disorganized remnants of Major Terrell's command as they came.

Jesse James was working both his pistols and Tommy McHale had his own hands full controlling the old horse who hated carrying double and wanted to lie down and shed his burdens. Each time Jesse's guns cracked, a man fell or threw his hands up to his face.

The two youngest guerrillas were last to exit the wood, their horse barely lumbering, Tommy's legs hammering its flanks. Ahead, the fleeing backs of their fellows and behind a howl of outrage as the Federal charge built up steam.

Though the combined attack had broken Terrell's command, the other Federals hadn't been scratched and, with the remnants they collected, they outnumbered the guerrillas three to two.

Bloody Bill Anderson was built on the lines of a hawser and he lifted one gun tail and leaned into it. It slid off the heavy elevation blocks and bounced, and the four-hundred-pound tailpiece kicked back. A couple of Bloody Bill's men laughed at him when he got knocked to one knee and he laughed too.

The guerrillas were swarming all over those guns and some of them had been regulars once upon a time and weren't likely to confuse a Dalgreen's muzzle with its breech. Men knelt before the guns working the elevation wheels, the barrels lowering ponderously as the twinkling brass elevation wheels spun in brilliant circles.

"Down! Down! Down, my boys! Oh, beauties!"

Slocum was sighting along the muzzle of one Dalgreen as the muzzle flattened out. "Come on down! Down!" he whispered.

The Federals burst out of the woods, many with sabers drawn. Two pistols are worth more than one pistol and one beats any long knife.

The Federals hollered their hurrah and sabered stragglers as they came.

Slocum's muzzle dropped so hat peaks were visible, those campaign hats the Federals wore. Down past their saber tips, their faces (empty blotches at such a distance), and farther down yet. A cannon spoke to his left. "Too early" went through Slocum's mind. Two guerrillas flogged by, riding double, and Slocum could have sworn one was the boy McHale, but couldn't look twice, because his sights were on the high arching necks of the charging horses and still the muzzle came down. He had the lanyard wrapped around his index finger. If he should fall in the next moment, the motion of his dying body would set the gun off and it'd do some good anyway. The shots cracked by like angry bees. The Federals were concentrating on the gunners, hoping to rattle them; kill them; make them miss.

The rest of the guerrilla force was wheeling its horses, coming around, and the front lines had changed so the cannons were the Confederate front. The Yankees weren't more than a hundred feet away when John Slocum yanked the lanyard and spun, bawling: "Loader!" praying there was one willing to serve his gun.

Sure enough a tobacco-chewing guerrilla slipped the catch as soon as the gun settled against its pegs and worked the breech open.

The first round crashed into the earth in front of the Federal charge. It was solid shot, not exploding shot or canister, but it hit a ground that was frozen, grazed bare, and shaley. The round exploded shale through the air and most of the pieces were no bigger than a pistol ball, and they slashed and slew men and horses alike. Slocum's crew jerked the tailpiece of the gun. A huge hole had opened in the Federals' line where it had been aimed and the second shot blew another great hole in the charge.

The guerrillas returned on a direct attack. There was nothing like them. Slocum had seen Early's cavalry at Shiloh and J. E. B. Stuart's at New Market and he'd never seen anything like this. The guerrillas came at the Federals like a family of killer apes on horseback.

8

In a way, Tommy HcHale was apologizing. "You should have told me last night. I looked for you. I meant to cut your throat when you were asleep."

It was hard to reconcile the boy's earnestness with the grim threat. Slocum didn't laugh. Why make enemies again? The boy had accepted him back into the CSA and he'd found himself a good-sized piece of smoked ham in Major Terrell's provisions, which he immediately identified as his own.

The major's saddlebags were slashed open and his packhorse was unburdened, and a gray-clad rider already had the major's headquarters tent bundled up, poles and all. He was strutting around, bragging on the comfort he intended to enjoy. "Oh, I'll be a damn king of the hill, that's what I'll be," he said.

Slocum offered McHale a chunk of the ham. The boy said no thanks, he had to be off, he'd met a real gunman during the battle and wanted to presume on his brief acquaintance. "I'll be a first-rate shot one day," he said, with the same earnestness. "And I'll kill me a few bastards."

"No doubt you will," Slocum said, smiling. The ham was pretty good and he washed it down with a canteen of captured water.

It wasn't noon, but the plain was quiet except for the shriek of the few dying horses that hadn't been put down and the low-grade rumble of gases starting to burble from the bellies of the dead, and the precise crack-crack of a revolver.

The guerrillas had destroyed the Federals with their lightning counterattack. Not many Federals regained the woods with its promise of safety. Later, a bunch of guerrillas rode into the woods looking for stragglers and when Slocum heard the muffled pop of their pistols, he figured they'd found some. Slocum didn't see the jayhawker anywhere. He'd been looking for him.

A delighted William Quantrill had found the major's spirit case. He sat down right away on a dead horse and with the spirit case beside him alternately drank from a decanter of brandy and a decanter of bourbon.

Some guerrillas were working the dead Federals' pockets.

"Don't you go pissin' on him, before I get through pickin' his pockets," one angry man squalled.

"I thought you was through with him. You already got his money and his watch."

"Some of these Federals carry gold lockets. Can't tell until you look everywhere. And now see what you've done. He's all wet!"

More pistol pops. The last of the wounded horses were done with their moaning. The entire meadow became a gassy plain: grumblings of dead stomachs, bodies giving up their heat, bodies attended by gray-clad scavengers. Men found new boots. One man discovered an engraved Colt. One scavenger unceremoniously approached the major and jerked his pockets inside out. "The hell you say," Major Terrell said. But he was looking away and his voice was so soft you could hardly hear it and the scavenger got his gold watch and the gold chain to boot.

The prisoners waited in a small group at the edge of the meadow. Thirty of them. From time to time, Bloody Bill Anderson walked out of the woods, whistling. He'd changed his shirt—another bright red one—and seemed quite the dandy in contrast with the Federal prisoners. The long silk cord lay across the palm of one hand, like a dead grass snake. One at a time, more picking than tying, Bloody Bill tied six knots in the cord. The knotted portion was very long and hung from his hand more than two feet. It was windless so the cord didn't sway at all, it just hung there. It seemed alive. The cord itself was braided black and white and might have served as piping on a lady's silk ballgown. He tied another knot, his eyes selecting more Yankees to accompany him on his little stroll in the woods.

"And now, Major," he said softly. "Why don't you come along with us this time. Somebody else will lead your men. Let's just take our stroll, like two brother officers."

The major's lip trembled and might have sought an excuse or a plea if either was possible. No chance at all. He nodded curtly. "Fall in," he snapped, and the five others pointed out by Anderson fell in under his command.

Major Terrell had never been any great shakes as a drill master and the cadence he counted for his little troop was pretty ragged. Hup, two, three. Hup, two, three. Silence. Some shots.

In a moment, Bloody Bill Anderson came down the path, whistling to himself. He whistled "The Cavaliers of Dixie" as he knotted the cord in his hand.

When the number of prisoners dwindled, Bloody Bill began taking smaller groups—diminishing at last to two prisoners at a time. Bloody Bill was a man who knew how to stretch his pleasure.

The looting was desultory at first, then systematic, and finally desperate as the Federal bodies gave up their treasures. Although they stole from the bodies of ordinary men, they expected their victims to have extraordinary possessions and many a soldier was roughly handled because he wouldn't give up a general's goods.

After he ate, Slocum found himself a nice spot in the woods to sleep. He wasn't much for these sorts of festivities. He put his back against the bole of a big old poplar and tipped his hat over his eyes. His duster made a good blanket and he pulled it across his lap and his Colt lay at his side, ready to hand. He slept for three hours, making up for what he'd lost the night before. The man who woke him nearly died for his trouble.

John Slocum came awake and alert all at once, the adrenaline surging through his veins like a flood through a two-inch pipe. His eyes stayed closed. His shoulders tingled, his hands gorged with blood, his ears cocked.

He heard boots on shale. He heard one man's easy breathing. Slocum grunted in his feigned sleep and his right hand fell, quite naturally, to the pistol at his side and his finger was through the square brass trigger guard. His eyes slid open, steady as a hawk's.

"Afternoon," Cole Younger said. He had a bottle in his right hand and another bottle sticking from the pouch on his hip. Slocum released the Colt Navy. "You don't like to let a man sleep," he said.

Cole Younger smiled in reply and hunkered down on his heels and thrust the bottle at Slocum.

Slocum licked his dry lips. "I don't generally roll out of bed right into the barroom," he said, still grouchy.

"Suit yourself," Younger said, taking a long pull on the bottle, his Adam's apple marking his swallows. "It's the best whiskey there is. Yankee whiskey. None sweeter to be found."

Slocum rubbed his eyes. He heard a couple men singing below. "Roll me over, in the clover."

"What time is it?" Slocum asked.

"Nearly dusk," Younger said. He glanced at the sky and nodded the way a slightly drunk man will to confirm some unimportant judgment. "Yep. Must be four-thirty, five o'clock. Not too much light left in that old sun now." Another swallow.

"So? Why'd you wake me?"

Younger reached out and slapped at Slocum's boot. "The women are due here any minute, man," he said.

"Women?"

"Kate Clarke and her girls. I don't know how ol' Kate keeps track of us, but she does. She's in love with Quantrill, but... that ain't exclusive." He winked broadly.

Slocum hadn't slept his tiredness out. He grunted.

"Besides, Bill Anderson and Quantrill want to talk to you."

Slocum opened his eyes wide.

"Oh no. Nothin' like that. They just like to say howdy to all our new recruits. They already talked to your ridin' partner, what's-his-name."

"McHale?"

"That's the one. Say, do you want a pull on this whiskey before you go on down the hill?"

"Yeah." And Slocum took a strong pull on the whiskey and the rawness rushed into his belly and woke him quick enough. When he got up, he gathered the duster under his arm and holstered the Colt Navy. Younger didn't miss the Navy or where it had been and gave him a little grin.

The interview with the guerrilla leaders was short. William C. Quantrill was passed out against a makeshift couch he'd built of the bodies of Union soldiers. He'd covered the bodies with their own greatcoats because dead flesh has a chill to it like no other. Quantrill snored happily through his open mouth.

Bloody Bill sat beside him, pretty drunk himself. His eyes were small and black and far back in their sockets. Like a bear's eyes.

He looked his inquiry at Younger and the stranger.

"This is the man I told you about," Younger said. "Name's John Slocum and he means to join up with us."

Anderson's head was swaying slightly. With an effort he held it still. The silk cord was out of sight. He tried to remember. "You was the judge's son?"

"Naw," Younger said, disgusted. "My daddy was a judge, Bill. I don't know who this hombre's daddy was."

"My daddy was a dentist," the drunken guerrilla said. "A painless toothpuller. House always smelled of alcohol."

Bill swayed but caught himself. Younger shouted for Frank James to come on over.

Frank James was built broad as Anderson but a little taller. He would have been handsome except for a nose that cut his face in two like the Great Divide. He was dead sober. Frank didn't believe in drink. He eyed John Slocum appraisingly. "Afternoon," he said.

Bill Anderson's hands, freed from all obligations, reached for the silk cord but couldn't find it.

"Frank, this man I ran into last night. He helped me run the bulls through the Federals this morning. Worked that Dalgreen, too."

Frank James's smile briefly overpowered the brooding quality his nose lent to his face. "That was a fine piece of work," he said. "The boy, what's his name? He's riding with you?"

"We met a couple days ago," Slocum said, noncommittal.

"Uh-huh. Well, my brother Jesse seems to think he can teach him a thing or two."

Slocum nodded. Probably he could.

"Slocum was paroled," Younger said. "Army of Tennessee."

"I was paroled myself," Frank James said. "Fought with the Trans-Mississippi under Kirby Smith until I got captured at Newtonia. Then I came back to Missouri where the good fightin' was." He laughed.

Slocum laughed too.

In the darkening plain, you could hardly see the women, but you could hear them well enough, hollering as they neared the guerrillas' fires. "Yoo-hoo, Bill Quantrill. . . . Where's that man of mine?"

Kate Clarke found the recumbent leader and didn't seem put out that he was passed out cold. She was a big blowsy woman with a pockmarked face. She sat beside Quantrill on his couch of corpses and took the whiskey from his grasp. "Here's how," she said. She coughed. "Confusion to our enemies." She drank again.

Two wagons filled with women. They'd come out for a good time and a little Yankee gold. It surprised Slocum they'd found the guerrillas so fast.

They were an ugly lot of women, too homely to make out in the whorehouses that catered to the Yankees. The fires roared all night long and men and women coupled on the bare ground. Some of them rolled Quantrill off his mound of dead so they could make love there and boast about it later. John Slocum found himself a bottle of good whiskey and drank it.

9

John Slocum had a few opportunities to kill Bill Quantrill in the next few weeks, but didn't take them.

The next morning, after the battle of Shaw's Ridge, Bloody Bill Anderson split his men away, some two hundred of them in all. It was a common enough habit—the guerrilla bands came together and dispersed in accord with the laws of wild things. Bloody Bill wanted to take his men west again, into Kansas.

"Tell Quantrill to meet me outside of Lawrence—in a month's time," he told Frank.

Frank was one of the few among Quantrill's fighters sober enough to talk. Cole Younger was down at the creek, trying to wash away a terrible hangover, and Quantrill was passed out, lying unconscious beside his couch. Kate Clarke and the rest of the whores meant to leave with Anderson. It had been wild and fun the night before, partying among the dead, but in the morning light, the corpses became less symbolic and more human and the whores were anxious to shake the dust of Shaw's Ridge from their heels. Some of them tried to pretty themselves up before they mounted the wagon. Others didn't. Kate's girls were anxious to leave this place while their bodices were noisy with gold. No telling what the guerrillas might decide to do once they recovered their wits.

Slocum stood beside the unconscious Quantrill. His sleeping face was innocent. Didn't mean much to Slocum. He'd killed downy-cheeked boys before. He'd never killed a man in his sleep.

Younger disturbed his contemplation of the man he'd come so far to kill. "Don't look like much now, does he?" Younger said.

Slocum shook his head.

Younger had his blue eyes squinted almost shut against the sunlight. The corpses didn't seem to bother him, but the whiskey sure enough did. "Wouldn't think he was the leader of the most feared guerrilla army west of the Mississippi," he said.

No comment that Slocum wanted to make.

Younger kicked Quantrill's boot. The leader retracted his foot and then let it slide back into its former place. He snorted and mumbled something.

"Sometimes when you kick him hard, he calls for his ma," Younger said helpfully.

Bloody Bill led his bunch out, the whores' wagons rattling along behind. Nobody waved or said good-bye. Slocum watched until they were out of sight, and when he turned again to Quantrill, the drunken sleeping man looked just the same. "Hell," Slocum muttered. He followed Cole Younger, who, despite his pain, was trying to scrounge up some breakfast.

"If the Federals ever hit us the morning after," Younger laughed, "they'd kill us all. We wouldn't stand a chance." He found the prospect pretty amusing.

In the weeks to come, Slocum had plenty of other opportunities to shoot Quantrill, but there seemed to be less and less sense to it. Quantrill was a vague man, who often wore a smile on his face, but never laughed. He was a pretty man, rather than a handsome one. Every week or ten days, Kate Clarke and her whores found the guerrilla band for a night of riot. The whores made love when the guerrillas were broke, but they seemed to know every time the men were flush and always collected their back wages. When Quantrill wasn't too drunk to function, he jumped on his inamorata, pumped away, indifferent to the men walking around them, and fired his salute. Then, often, he'd pass out.

On the trail he was almost always drunk and Frank James ran the troop. When they were looking for water, it was James who suggested directions. When they needed provisions, Frank James picked the isolated store or town small enough to intimidate, where they found what they needed. Plenty of folks in this part of the country were sympathetic to the South and many of them were helpful to the guerrilla band. As many as two thousand Federals scoured Missouri for Quantrill's hundred and fifty, and the hundred and fifty didn't lose any sleep over it.

The schemes came from Cole Younger. When a plan was necessary, often as not Cole Younger made it, submitting his ideas to the guerrilla leader, who always acquiesced with a wave.

It was hard for Slocum to understand why the band of guerrillas was called Quantrill's raiders and he said as much to Cole Younger one day. They were riding toward the tiny town of McDowell where they hoped to buy oats for their horses and get news of the pursuit.

As usual, Quantrill was drunk, leaning out of his saddle. But Quantrill rode at the head of the column, right beside the guidon bearer. The guidon bearer flew a solid black flag, the size of a battle flag, all black except for Quantrill's name, centered in gold.

"Why the hell do we follow this man?" Slocum asked. "He's nothin' but a damn drunk."

Younger grinned at him. "Yeah," he said. "But he's a real *mean* drunk."

Slocum spent quite a bit of time with Cole Younger, riding beside him almost every day. Though Tommy McHale didn't want to cut Slocum's throat anymore, he wasn't particularly friendly, preferring the company of Jesse James and his brother Frank.

They'd killed thirty Federals at an ambush near Christian's Creek and another eight at Duffy's sawmill where the Yankees had come to buy lumber.

They met two groups of soldiers on the road—half a dozen, and then three. They shot down the half dozen and hung the three. Tom McHale kicked the horse out from underneath each soldier. He seemed to take pleasure in it.

Quantrill's band had split up more, and now twenty

riders followed the black flag on a sunny Saturday morning, as they rode into McDowell.

The town was sympathetic and Quantrill's men had plenty of supporters. People came out of their neat houses and stood on their porches and waved as the guerrillas rode by. One man was clearing the last of the leaves off his front lawn as Quantrill rounded the turn. "Bill Quantrill, by God!" he shouted. "Good to see you, by God!"

And he ran to his picket fence. Quantrill's guidon bearer dipped the flag to the men. Younger gave the man a half wave, and even John Slocum politely dipped his head, but Bill Quantrill was too drunk and rode right on past, his glazed eyes fixed on the road ahead.

McDowell was a small farming town, halfway between Lawrence and Fort Riley, and since somebody was always driving livestock from Lawrence to the fort, McDowell had a hotel. Naturally it was called the Drover's Inn, though drummers who came to town gave it their custom too. It had a couple big columns holding up the second-story porch. The columns were ten-by-tens fitted together and they'd been last painted before the war but had been whitewashed since and when Slocum brushed against them, he collected a fine dusting of pure white.

Slocum had always been a livestock man. He liked the cows and sheep on his daddy's farm and loved the horses. The horse tied at the hitchrail behind him was one of the best. Back in Georgia, or even with General Lee, Slocum would have cared for the animal as best he could because this horse was big and fast and fine. When Quantrill unsteadily mounted the stairs, Slocum went to look for a good livery.

At first glance, Quantrill's officers looked very much alike. They wore gray coats, some of them, and a few wore gray trousers too. They dressed like bandits and soldiers, which they were. They bristled with guns. Each man carried two Colts, and Jesse James carried two more strapped to his chest. Many slung rifles under their arms—all repeaters—the others carried shotguns. A few favored the new Colt revolving shotgun, but most thought it too delicate and carried the more familiar side by side.

They walked with a heavy swagger, and they all walked alike. Their boots were better than most men had seen since the beginning of the war. All of them were officers' boots.

As they stamped up the porch steps, Cole Younger touched his slouch hat and said, "Afternoon, ma'am" to the woman who was old enough to be his mother, and she said, "Afternoon" right back, because she knew the guerrillas were exciting, and she thought they were patriots.

Jesse and Tommy McHale were joking as they followed their leaders into the Drover's Inn. The front door of the hotel was glass, for a wonder unbroken, and curtained with neat embroidered curtains, clean for a change. The hallway was sparkling surfaces of golden oak and the oak staircase bore a neat runner with a nice green nap. The barroom was off to the left of the small lobby. Because he was laughing, McHale passed the girl right by.

"Tommy?"

The barroom of the Drover's was as neat as the lobby. A single oak bar, not very long, and six square tables. The tables were covered with oilcloth and had salt cellars because they served dinners there too, every night except Monday.

He had some excuse for not recognizing the girl. Her hair was much shorter than it had been and the rouge and powder sat easier on her. She looked like any other whore.

McHale passed on. A second later he popped his head back out—something familiar. Maybe if he hadn't recognized her voice . . . "Jesus," he said. "Is that you, Roxie?"

And the dark-eyed girl smiled a tremulous smile. "Uh-huh. It's nice to see you again, Tommy."

For just a second, the boy's face flickered and in that instant his face lost the knowledge it had recently acquired, and the girl was glad to see the change. Her smiled firmed up.

"Why . . . how. . . . What are you doin' here?"

"Might ask you the same thing, stranger," she said and playfully pushed his chest with the heel of her hand. It was a light enough tap, almost a love tap, but he was a guerrilla now and rode with Quantrill and had hanged three men. "Don't touch me," he said in his new hard voice.

"Oh," she said. She was a little afraid, because his hands were flung out from his sides and he looked so dangerous. She put her hand up to her mouth and said, "Oh," again, dismayed.

He called to his pal. "Jesse. Come 'ere for a minute."

The bartender in the Drover's Inn was a large pink woman—the wife of the owner. Sometimes her sister helped clean the six rooms the Drover's boasted and sometimes she cooked the dinners for twenty people at once. The bartender had seen some fast drinkers in the Drover's on a Saturday night, but she'd never seen anything like this mob. Oh, they were polite enough and didn't use vulgar language, at least not in her hearing, and they seemed peaceable. They didn't look like they wanted to cause any property damage. Of course, just having them in her hotel made the poor woman nervous because there were Federal troops as near as Barkersville and that was just an hour away—Lord knows how many at Fort Riley, only eight hours from here on a slow horse. If the Drover's ever got shot up, she didn't know what she'd do. Business is business. And she was a loyal daughter of the Confederacy. When they first came in, she started as she always did. She went to the first table of four with her little towel over her arm and gave it a wipe and asked what they wanted, and it was "Whiskey," "Whiskey," "Whiskey," and "Whiskey." Well, she brought them each a glass of whiskey and passed on to the next table, but before she brought table #2's whiskeys, table #1 had finished theirs. The remaining tables hadn't been waited on and she called for her sister to come in and help, but even so, she was reduced to bringing each table its own bottle, which she hated to see at the Drover's because she felt that bottle whiskey lowered the tone of an establishment.

Jesse James waited at the oak serving bar because the older men had hogged all the tables. When Tommy McHale stuck his head in and called him, McHale sounded odd, gruffer and older than usual. No telling. Jesse got a bottle of whiskey before he answered McHale's worried summons.

Jesse James removed his hat when he saw the woman. He and his brother had plenty of kid cousins and a mother that ran the household with an iron hand. Jesse's sister had died when the Yankees pulled down the Johnson City jail on top of her and Jesse always had an exaggerated respect for womankind. Not Frank. Frank could take a woman or leave her alone. Jesse said, "Nice to meet you," and introduced himself.

"Roxie," the girl said with a blush. She'd come downstairs to meet Tom McHale, but right now she liked the looks of his friend better.

McHale wasn't blind. He got mad. "This is the woman who blooded me," he said, jerking his thumb. "She gave me one hell of a ride."

Her eyes narrowed and her mouth got tight. Roxie never did back down from a fight. "And I suppose you been with a whole lot of others since," she said.

McHale managed to look off, indifferent. He'd had two of Kate Clarke's whores. The second one had given him crabs, which he still had, though he'd painted his groin with oil of wintergreen just as Jesse suggested. It burned like hell, but it was supposed to kill the little varmints.

"I had me just about as many women as I could handle," he said. "Whooee!" His exclamation included some pretty hot women. "And they all had tits bigger than you got," he noted. His face got puzzled. Seemed to him he remembered Roxie being better . . . endowed. And her breasts had gotten smaller as they dried out. By now her baby was four months in its grave.

But she was insulted. "Nothin' wrong with my body," she snapped. "Least you didn't complain about it before."

Tom elbowed Jesse. "She was really somethin'," he said. He winked in case his message was lost on them. "Whooee!"

Since she'd been admitted into the pantheon of "hot women," Roxie grinned a whore's grin and flounced her hips.

Jesse licked his lips. "We might be here for a while," he said. "Shoppin'," he added vaguely.

Before she answered, John Slocum came in from the front. "Afternoon, Roxie," he said. And to McHale, "If you don't take care of your horse, he'll never take care of you." He turned back to Roxie and asked the same question the boy had, "What brings you to this neck of the woods?"

"Miss Sallie's upstairs," she said, answering the question he meant to ask next.

He nodded. He grinned at her. "Hope you been doin' well," he said politely. "Which room?"

"On the right at the head of the stairs."

Slocum said thank-you, and said something kind about the boy, because Roxie reminded him of their common past. He was starting up the stairs alone as Roxie started an explanation of her movements. "We lost the Light of Love . . . ," she began.

The door was very slightly ajar. Slocum rapped and pushed it open. Sallie Webster was lying on the bed in her chemise, her arm across her forehead. Her "Come in. It ain't locked," was curiously dispirited.

" 'Lo, Sallie," Slocum said softly.

She removed her arm and sat up. Her full breasts threatened the gathering of her chemise. "My God. It's John Slocum. You look different, but it's you all right." And she held up her hand to bring him closer—not as a whore beckons, but like a friend. He sat on the foot of the bed.

The bedroom was spare. One chair. One double bed with a plain white knobby coverlet and one dresser with a mirror. The chamberpot was underneath the dresser and a pitcher of water rested on top with a couple of glasses. Beside it, the towel rail held one faded towel and one washcloth. A kerosene lantern on the wall would provide light after the sun, and the blind could be pulled down over the window. The floor was the same golden oak, varnished and bare. It looked pretty uninviting for bare feet like Sallie's.

"Roxie said something about the Light of Love?" Slocum said quietly.

"The bastards."

Slocum knew to wait while she decided how she wanted to tell it.

"They burned me out," she said bitterly. "Set a torch to the wall and piled junk against it and she went up. Everything I owned went up in flames."

Slocum shrugged. He'd seen the Light of Love when it had already fallen on hard times but understood that in her mind's eye, she had lost the place in its best day.

"The damn Federals burned us out," she went on. "Said the place was a 'robbers' roost.' 'Dangerous,' they said. 'A violation of good order.' The Light of Love was a place to come when you wanted to have a little sport, that's what it was."

Slocum put his hand on her knee and squeezed. "I'm sorry to hear," he said. "What've you been doin' since?"

"On the road," she said. "Three days in this town and two in the next. Come into the barroom at night and work the customers from there. You can eat, but it's a hell of a life all right. A hell of a life!"

"I can see how it might be."

Her face changed. "John, you want to make love?"

Maybe his surprise showed because she continued right away. "For free. I mean it won't cost you anything."

His smile was warm enough but still curious. Suddenly, she turned away from him and stuck her face in the pillow. "I guess I gotta know I have *something* to give away," she said.

"Yeah," Slocum said. He reached over and gently rubbed her back through the flimsy chemise. Her back was fine and smooth and the chemise slid over her bare skin like a second skin. He liked the feel of her. "My pleasure," he said.

The trio tiptoed up the stairs past the closed door at the head as kids might in sharing a secret. None of them was seventeen yet, and right now they were children again, Tom and Roxie and Jesse.

Simultaneously they stopped just outside the door and grinned at each other foolishly.

They held their laughter until Roxie led them on into her own room. It was a duplicate of Sallie Webster's but faced down Main Street instead of across. Roxie's window looked out over the livery stable next door and she could see a long way down the street to where it became the road. She'd been one of the first ones to see Quantrill's raiders when they rode into town.

Roxie laughed breathlessly. "I guess Miss Sallie would raise her eyebrows at this."

Tom McHale removed his slouch hat to scratch his head. "Reckon she might." Then, more fiercely, "But it ain't no business of hers. I believe it ain't."

Roxie said, "Of course not," and sat on the bed. Her dress was fastened in front by a tie at the neck and a velvet rope at her waist. She kicked off her shoes, which looked too flimsy to wear on the street.

Jesse just smiled. He was a handsome lad, Jesse James, and Roxie's heart had melted when she first saw him.

Her hand went to the tie at her throat. She unknotted it with a practiced hand.

Jesse said, "I almost had your job, remember?"

The girl's eyebrows furrowed and her hand stopped its work. "Huh?"

"Back at the Light of Love."

Jesse thought it was self-explanatory. Roxie asked him for more information.

"I came in that mornin' dressed up like a girl, lookin' for a job of work."

Roxie gasped. "That was you?"

Jesse laughed out loud. "Oh yes. I came in there, lookin' for how we all could come back at night. Maybe get us some Yankees. Miss Kate Clarke—one of her girls loaned me a dress. Laugh? They was fit to be tied. None of the boys laughed though. It was Cole Younger's idea I should go. So I knocked at the door."

Jesse undid his shirt and pried at the heel of one boot with the other.

"Most men have hairy chests," Roxie said, as her robe fell open. "They scratch me."

Jesse touched his own hairless paps. "I reckon you have to get used to it. How 'bout you, Tommy?"

And Tommy McHale unbuttoned his own garment in a hurry. He was real excited. Never more so.

Jesse went on. "So I was inside the place followin' Miss Sallie around, askin' her all about the gents who came in, did they spend big, that kind of thing." He sat on the bed to remove his socks. He put his hand on Roxie's tan triangle and pushed. He bent to kiss her. He liked the feeling of her hair on his chest.

"What about me?" Tommy asked.

From somewhere deep in her throat, Roxie said, "You'll get your turn."

Down the hall, John Slocum and Sallie Webster lay face to face. He was inside her, motionless, and she had her leg over his.

"Why don't you just forget it, John," she said in her softest voice. "Just walk away from the guerrillas. You said it yourself. The damn war's over, anyway."

"I like it when you tremble inside like that," Slocum

said. He pressed himself another quarter inch deeper and she moaned.

"Forget Quantrill," she whispered. "Run. Oh damn you, run."

He said, "I like it when you roll your hips like that. Like you got me surrounded entire."

She pushed her breasts into him and said, "Don't change, John. I'm afraid you'll change."

He slipped out of her to the tip and slipped right back in. "Like that?" he asked.

Down the hall, Tommy HcHale was doing most of the talking. He said, "It's a good thing this is a warm day." He sat, naked except for socks, beside the bed in Roxie's room, and if it hadn't been a warm day for this time of the year, he would have been cold. As it was, sometimes the goose pimples hurried across his body anyway. He looked away and blushed beet red. Same color of red as the girl's lips. He wished he couldn't see. He wished he couldn't hear, even more. The steady ching, ching, ching of the springs. The wet noises. The muttered endearments.

After a bit he put his hand on Roxie's breast. Yep, it had gotten smaller. Considerately, Jesse kept his body arched up at the hips so Tom could have free play.

"Your damn hand's like ice," Roxie said, startled.

"Somethin' else ain't like ice," Tom said, smirking. He left his hand on her breast though her nipple shivered and got small.

Roxie ignored him. She swung her sweaty belly like a dancer. Jesse put his hands inside her hips and rolled her flesh. He lifted and came back, once, twice, three times.

"Don't know how you dressed up like a girl," Roxie said dreamily. "You surely ain't one."

10

The newspapermen followed the guerrillas by the fruit dangling from the roadside trees. The guerrillas made good copy, often the front page, and at one time, a dozen reporters tracked the three major bands of guerrillas: Thrailkill's, Bloody Bill's, and W. C. Quantrill's.

QUANTRILL SOMETIMES SPARES A LIFE—
Anderson never does.

St. Louis Post
November 14, 1864

"IF I CARED FOR MY LIFE I'D HAVE LOST IT LONG AGO," Guerrilla leader John Thrailkill asserts at ambush site.

Kansas City Ledger
November 21, 1864

At times, the guerrillas threatened to drive other war news from the front section of the papers. The news from the East wasn't very interesting, just the dull repetition of casualty lists as Grant pounded Lee, day after day. The guerrillas were only pushed to page three when the Yankees blew a mine in front of Petersburg because the reading public craves novelty and the thought of underground tunnels packed with gunpowder captured the imagination.

Once the great mine explosion paled, the steel engravings of the guerrillas in action began to reappear. John Slocum never earned himself a name. He never shot a man, though he fired in the heat of battle. His failure to kill Quantrill had stayed his killing arm.

They ambushed forty Federals and ten jayhawkers alongside the Kansas City Pike. They drew the Federals into the trap by posting a couple sharpshooters beside the road. Slocum was one. He took the hat off the Federal captain, but didn't scratch his hide. Of course, the column of Yankees chased the sharpshooters into the defile where a hundred rifles were waiting.

They rode into the defile gallantly. None rode out again.

The time Quantrill dressed twenty men up like Federals and joined up with as many genuine Federals, an augmented patrol from Fort Riley, the slaughter was quick and awful. Slocum didn't turn away, but he wouldn't kill anybody either.

Tommy McHale, under Jesse's tutelage, did his part and then some. He cut one man's throat and scalped another still-conscious victim before he put a tap just over his right eye.

Bloody Bill took the town of Bluefield and slaughtered fifty Yankees. The Yankees made the mistake of surrendering and Bloody Bill knotted his cord.

Thrailkill got himself chased by a militia major leading a column of volunteers. Thrailkill had a hundred men, the major twice that. When the guerrillas got tired of the chase they turned and rode the militiamen down. No survivors from that party either.

The guerrilla bands grew almost daily it seemed. And they drifted into Kansas because the pickings were richer, and there were more Union sympathizers and many of them were prosperous.

Lee surrendered Lynchburg to the Yankees. It snowed on the Kansas plains where the gentle rolling hills stretched onto the prairie. Many of those hills had been fenced and all of the fine bottomland by the riversides was under cultivation by men who'd never held slaves.

Rich pickings.

The guerrillas ate well and drank well, and Kate Clarke and her soiled doves followed them everywhere, campsite or town, it didn't make any difference. One night on the low slope of a hill in eastern Kansas, Bloody Bill Anderson smashed his beef bones with the butt of his revolver and sucked at the marrow. His shiny black beard was brilliant with grease. "What next?" he said. His tongue snaked out pale as a coral snake and took a meat scrap.

Dusk. The entire guerrilla force was camped on farmer Brown's back forty, farmer Brown having gone to his reward sometime earlier that day along with his two sons. The womenfolk had been locked in the barn and were still locked there as far as Quantrill knew or cared or could remember. Quantrill looked at Bloody Bill and said, "You are one disgusting animal, Bill."

"You ain't so fine yourself."

Quantrill acknowledged the compliment with a toast. He kept his flask at his side and pulled on it. That farmer this noon—what was his name? Beaver? Brown? —didn't have much horseflesh but he had a fine hogshead of whiskey. Most of the guerrillas were already drunk on it, but Quantrill was having one of those peculiar moments of great lucidity and nothing he drank today seemed to touch his sobriety. He smiled wolfishly. "We're gettin' too damn fat," he said. "We got to work off some of this fat." He burped and rubbed his own belly. "Lawrence," he said.

John Thrailkill had been a gentleman before the war. Tonight he sat on his folded saddle blanket and looked at the fine distant stars; he wished he were on one of them instead of on the muderous planet that had fallen to his fortune.

"Ten coffins made, ten coffins filled," Quantrill said and his eyes gleamed in the firelight.

Cole Younger and Frank James shared the leader's fire. Now Cole said, "I know. We all heard that story before. We don't need more reasons to kill Yankees."

"You know where that bastard Strachan is now?" Quantrill asked quietly.

"Nope." Frank James put down his tin coffee cup

and fired a cigar. He was enjoying himself this evening, enjoying the simple ordinariness of eating a meal (thanks to that farmer) and smoking. He didn't want to get mad or kill anybody. He wondered how his brother had got to be so damn fast with his guns. Sixteen years old and deadlier than most men twice his age. He wondered what they'd do this winter—whether the bands would break up or not. He wondered if his brother would live through the war. Sometimes he regretted signing him on, but he'd been so damn persistent.

"Lawrence," Quantrill said.

Bloody Bill threw the last of his beef bone into the darkness, wiped his mouth on his sleeve and his hands on his pant legs. "There's a lot of men in Lawrence," he said.

"Why do you think I asked for both of you?" Quantrill asked. He took another pull at his flask.

"Not because you admire our wit, I'd fancy," Thrailkill snapped. Thrailkill had ridden with General Jo Shelby and the regular Missouri cavalry and thought Quantrill's raiders were ruffians. But they could fight. He'd allow them that.

Once when Quantrill, Younger, and James were surrounded inside a brick house by Federal regulars, Quantrill issued one famous command: "Shotguns in front, rifles take up the rear." Seven guerrillas fought through a hundred Yankees and left twenty-seven of them dead.

"Troops in Lawrence," Thrailkill said quietly.

"Twenty raw recruits," Quantrill corrected happily. "Across the river there's a Federal encampment, but there's only one ferry and the river's too rough to swim and guess what side of the river they leave the ferry on at night?"

A chill climbed up John Thrailkill's spine. A violent urge to scratch something. He was holding his breath. "Which side?"

"Our side."

"That'd be the Lawrence side."

Quantrill was giggling now. The drink hit him and everything seemed very, very funny. "That's right. We'll burn the whole damn town and the Yankees won't be able to do anything but watch."

"Lawrence?" Frank James said.

"Strachan. Colonel Strachan makes his home in Lawrence. He got demoted on account of Palmyra. He's in command of the twenty recruits on the Lawrence side of the river. And there's a few other friends of ours over there too."

"I don't want Jesse in on this one," Frank James said quickly, some premonition of his. Frank was famous for them.

Thrailkill: "Why sure, Frank. We'll miss him though. He's a hellion, your brother."

"He's too young for this one," Frank said, and nobody said differently.

The news had spread through the camp during the night, and before the ashes of the breakfast campfires were cold, every guerrilla knew: Lawrence. The biggest prize they'd ever attempted. The largest guerrilla raid of the war. With Thrailkill's men and Bloody Bill's, Quantrill had three hundred fifty men riding under the black flag. Many a regular battalion didn't have so many and few of them would have matched the guerrillas' ferocity.

The chatter was quicker and happier that morning. Men who'd had arguments were busy patching their differences. Nothing mattered now, so much as the glorious prospect before them.

"No rape," Thrailkill said. And they shrugged and agreed. "No women killed." Thrailkill made the second of his two conditions for accompanying the band. And nobody cared too much about that condition either.

Tom McHale was thrilled. Jesse James was hurt and angry. He wouldn't speak to brother Frank. Jesse was ordered to stay with the remuda when the combined forces rode into town.

Tom McHale sat beside the guttering campfire, his

blanket wrapped around his bony shoulders, chewing on a strip of beef jerky. His strong teeth reduced the tough fibrous meat to mush before he swallowed. He spoke in grunts, between bites. "No cause to be angry with Frank," Tom said. "There'll be battles aplenty before this war is over," he said.

Jesse had his arms wrapped around his knees and his chin rested on them as he stared across the frost-bitten morning landscape. "Too goddamned young," he said in a monotone.

Perhaps Tom McHale wished he had somebody to say he was too young or too inexperienced, but like all young men, he wore his manhood stiff and unfaded and never took it off, not even among friends. "Yeah." He spat into the chip fire. "Pretty insulting, all right. How many you killed, Jesse?"

"I dunno." And the fact was, Jesse didn't know. How could you tell if a Federal who went off his horse in the middle of hot pursuit didn't ride again after you were miles away? "Enough," Jesse said.

Except for Bloody Bill, none of the guerrillas counted their kills.

The frost lay on the bare ground like a light coating of snow, ready to wet a man's boots or chill a horse's hoof. Tom McHale thought it looked like steam congealed. He wasn't much for wondering—he left the reflections to others, but now, beside his sullen pal he eyed the long white Kansas prairie in the distance and wondered if he'd ever get out West as he'd meant to months ago. He thought about Slocum.

Tom looked around, but didn't see the lanky dark-haired rider. Seemed as though he was around every time something unpleasant had to be done—gathering firewood, rounding up the remuda, building fires, riding nighthawk—but in the middle of all the action, the fighting and the killing, John Slocum hung back, as if he didn't want to get involved. Nobody cared what he did because to care would have been to invite a gunfight and one remark would have brought it on sooner. Slocum slept by himself, tethered his horse near his blanket roll, and lay his head down on one pistol and kept another always at his side. He exchanged no confidences, made few sociable remarks. Cole Younger liked him. But not even Younger could get more than a word or two out of him, though Cole was good at tickling fancies—he had that way about him.

Slocum was fully dressed, toasting a bit of beef on a stick. He'd picked up a good sheepskin and it kept his shoulders and back good and warm.

Like everybody else, he'd heard of the decision to sack Lawrence. Unlike the rest of the band he wasn't thrilled.

Younger came with the news and found Slocum graining his horse from a collapsible leather bucket.

Cole was his usual chipper self. "Mornin', John," he said. "I suppose you heard we're gonna make the newspapers again. We're doin' a darin' guerrilla raid." Slocum bent to lift his horse's forefoot. Fine horse. Best fed, fastest animal he'd had under him in his life. But the animal that should have been his most prized possession seemed inferior to him—disposable, stolen. Nothing wrong with the hoof though. He let it down gently. During the examination, the horse never stopped his chewing.

"Lawrence," Cole Younger said. "Ain't that a hell of a thing? We're just twenty miles outside Lawrence, Kansas, home of General Lane and Colonel Strachan, our good pals." Younger looked in the direction of Lawrence, but it was too far away and behind rolling hills.

Slocum faced the same direction and his eyes noted the frost on the ground and the frost on the bare sticks of sage grass. "Lawrence is a big town."

Younger laughed. Usually his laughter was light and cheerful. This morning it sounded like the cawing of a crow. "It'll be smaller once we're done with it." He stepped closer to Slocum to speak the secret known to everyone else in the hillside encampment. "We're gonna kill every man-thing in Lawrence."

"Man-thing?" Slocum's voice took on a stridency as harsh as Younger's. "Man-thing" is a harsh word.

"Any male big enough to shoot," Cole Younger said. "I guess that's what Bill means."

Despite himself, Slocum's face curled up in disgust. "Oh, Jesus Christ," he said.

"Lawrence is a jayhawker town, John. More jayhawkers in Lawrence than any three towns in Kansas. Our enemies, John. Or maybe you're forgettin' that." And Cole Younger stalked off, peeved.

Cole Younger's father had been a judge before the jayhawkers cut him down in the road outside his own courthouse. He became a dead judge. When Cole and his cousin Jim rode off to fight with the Confederates, the same bunch of jayhawkers rode to his family farm. Two winters ago, with six inches of snow on the ground, the jayhawker leader put a pistol to his mother's head while they torched the family home and its barns and outbuildings; the springhouse and the smokehouse and the tobacco sheds and even the woodshed. They left her then, to walk five miles in the snow to the next farm for shelter.

Despite Cole's jokes and his steady wit and his easygoing temperament, he was as fierce a fighter as any of Quantrill's men.

John Slocum sat down by the fire, his mind spinning. His thoughts were everywhere but on the piece of meat he had spitted for breakfast, blackening now, unattended in the fire.

John Slocum couldn't remember a time when killing had been difficult. The first man he'd shot had been a Union picket outside Manassas, just four years ago. He walked around the guerrilla encampment, bewildered. Groups of men clotted together, already speculating about the loot. Some men were arguing for torture of the jayhawkers, but these men were in the minority. Some men sat and cleaned their spotless guns, others put an edge on their razor-sharp bowies and checked their saddle straps. Bloody Bill Anderson was drunk. Quantrill too. Both of them reeling through the camp, accepting their men's congratulations for their audacious scheme.

"We ain't there yet, boys!" Anderson shouted.

"But we'll get there," his sidekick replied.

They repeated the remark and the response a half dozen times, and each time approval swelled and others began to repeat it and laugh and slap each other on the back.

"Every damn male-thing," Anderson said. His braided cord hung around his neck, like a string of pearls. The cord was one bump after another.

Slocum was a Confederate. He'd fought for his homeland—his own piece of earth—against men who were seeking to take it away from him. He'd fought so many battles he couldn't recall them all and he'd watched Union soldiers die before his guns and the guns of other Confederates.

This smelled different. It made Slocum sick. His hands were shaking ever so slightly and goose bumps chased each other up and down his spine. His sheepskin jacket wasn't doing any good, and Slocum wondered how he'd ever thought that it could.

"This morning we ride!" Bloody Bill howled and Quantrill grinned his agreement.

Informants were everywhere in the country they passed through. For every sympathizer there was another man who had cause to hate Quantrill. Once they decided on a course of action, the guerrillas moved faster than information about their plans. That's how it worked: last night the decision, this morning, they rode. Already some men were saddling up.

"What do you want?" Tom McHale asked.

Slocum had been wearing a brooding look on his face that gave Tom McHale a bad case of the creeps.

Slocum was startled. He looked around quickly, locating himself. "Cup of that coffee'd be fine," he said.

Jesse James got to his feet. He said, "I think I'm gonna talk to Frank again. Maybe get him to change his mind." He put his hands in his pockets. "Be seein' ya," he said.

The boy McHale made quite a business of getting ready to break camp. He folded his saddle blanket and rounded up his horse. He set the blanket just right—no crimps or creases that might sore the animal. He used his boot to push all the stored-up air out of his horse's gut. He packed up his possibles into the war bag that'd ride behind the saddle. He broke his pistols open, examined the chambers, and peered down the bright barrels. Like Slocum, he'd come to favor the Henry, and he unlatched the buttstock where he kept extra tubes of ammunition.

"You gonna want more of this?" he asked Slocum, holding up the coffeepot.

Slocum looked at his coffee with surprise. Full cup. He took a sip. It was cold. "No," he said.

The boy relented slightly. "What's the matter with you?" he asked. "You sick? If you're sick, maybe you should stay back with Jesse." It was kind enough, but the boy had been riding with Quantrill for two months now, so he couldn't help adding, "You can do the boy's work."

Slocum's face was white enough and he was sick all right, but he was sick at heart. He shook his head. He said, "What did you say?"

Sullenly. "You heard me." McHale poured the coffee into the fire, extinguishing it. He unbuttoned and drowned the coals further.

"That stinks," Slocum said. With a flip of the wrist, he emptied the cup and tossed it into the air. When the boy reached out to catch the tumbling tin cup, Slocum's hand dropped and returned. The muzzle of his Colt was suddenly just under the tip of the boy's chin, the front sight depressing the skin, and Slocum was saying in a soft voice, "I think you ain't too old to learn some manners, son."

The cup landed in the wet campfire with a clink.

"I ain't your son," the boy said. He was furious with resentment, because each time he started feeling like a man grown, Slocum came along to remind him that he was still a boy. "The hell with you," he added.

"It's probably hard for you to remember this," Slocum said, "but you're old enough to die. Your pal Jimmy back at the ferry wasn't any older than you, and he's dead, sure enough."

Tom HcHale hadn't thought about his friend in weeks. Quickly, moisture wet his eyes. "Yeah," he said. He reached up and moved Slocum's gun away from his chin. "It was the damn Federals who killed him," he said. "I ain't forgettin' that."

"Maybe you ought to help Jesse this afternoon," John Slocum said. He holstered his pistol.

McHale's brow got puzzled. "Stay with the horses?"

"It'd be wise. It's gonna be real bad this afternoon."

The boy spat. He packed the cup. He said, "Oh hell. We can take 'em. Scouts say there ain't but twenty Federal troops on the Lawrence side of the river. All we got to do is capture the ferry. Once the ferry's in our hands, we can do anythin' we want."

"That ain't what I meant," Slocum said. "If you go into Lawrence this afternoon, you're gonna wish you hadn't. I can tell you right now."

"Oh hell." The boy scuffed the ground with his foot. "That all you got to say? I'm gonna saddle up." And sticking his boot in the stirrup, he was as good as his word. Tom MacHale was a slight young man and his horse stood fourteen hands. Mounted, he seemed very far away.

The three guerrilla chieftains were hollering their morning commands. Anderson and Quantrill were holding each other up, and Quantrill still had a rye bottle in his hand, but they were shouting, "Mount up, you bunch of beauties! Now, we ride. Oh, we'll stick 'em and bleed 'em, we will!"

"Just a little tap over the right eye," Anderson roared.

With the smoothness of long practice, the guerrillas broke camp.

The men who usually rode as scouts formed their own party and trotted out front. They'd travel a couple miles ahead of the main column.

Since Thrailkill was more the gent than William Quantrill, his men took the next position, leading the column out across the frosty fields.

The roads through this part of the country were farm roads, narrow and dependable in good weather.

But the ground was frozen six inches by now and hard as macadam pavement. Riders formed five abreast and files rode out on both sides of the long column. There was no particular need for such precautions, but the guerrillas were men of habit. Slocum rode in the extreme left file, out from the main column. He rode behind the boy, trying to make up his mind. It didn't come easy.

When his horse drew up beside Tom McHale's, the kid kept his fierce eyes scanning the horizon. "We ain't out here to talk," he immediately volunteered. "We're here to spot danger."

"What's more dangerous than us?" Slocum asked soberly.

The boy took that differently than Slocum intended. His chest swelled out and his hands flipped his reins carelessly. "Nothin'," he said. "Not in this part of the country."

Slocum persisted. "How long you fought for the Confederate States of America?" he asked.

"Why, hell. You know the answer to that as good as I do," the boy said.

The point swept into the crossroads named Beulah. The sleepy storekeeper came right out in his apron and froze. Three hundred of the most dangerous men on earth rode by him. This storekeeper favored the South and had a son fighting outside Richmond, but these men scared him to death. His dog normally barked its fool head off at any horseman. The dog slunk back under the back steps and stayed there while they passed. It wasn't their armament—the storekeeper had seen men with more than one pistol or rifle before. Or their enormous horses. They rode by in silence, not noticing him; no jokes, no remarks about the weather, just the steady silent passage of hundreds of big, well-armed men.

He wished he had a telegraph to warn those on down the road. Several of the riders craned their necks, searching the rooftops of Beulah, and the storekeeper suddenly knew that once those eyes spotted a telegraph wire, nothing could save the telegrapher. He shuddered. He went inside and to his bedroom where he locked the door and sat trembling long after the last man passed.

The outriders crossed the ridges high above the tiny crossroads. The housetops looked like neat toys. The curl of smoke from the chimneys and the crossroads looked like one of those lithographs done by Mister Currier and Mister Ives. It made Slocum very homesick.

"I ain't sure you ever fought for the CSA," he told the boy.

The boy was disgusted at that stupid remark. He pointed at the troop. "And who the hell do you think they are?" he asked, his voice thick with contempt.

"Bandits," Slocum said.

The silent column snaked through the low valley beside a creek no more than six feet across. The slopes above the creek were lightly wooded and Slocum and the boy wove in and out of the trees.

Momentarily, the two rode stirrup to stirrup. "What the hell you tryin' to tell me?" the boy said. "Mister, just because we joined up with the same outfit on the same day don't mean you owe me anything. I don't fancy your warnin's about how terrible it's gonna be today. I ain't scared and you ain't gonna scare me. If I'm ridin' with bandits, I suppose that'd make me a bandit too. I ride with them of my own free choice."

"The Confederate government wants Quantrill killed," John Slocum said.

The boy was furious. "Oh, bullshit," he said. "You're a liar."

Slocum said, "Manners, son." He explained Heddon to the boy. The boy didn't believe a word of it.

Tom McHale opened his mouth to speak but something he saw in John Slocum's eyes persuaded him that this was not the moment for speeches. He wrenched his head, looking away. He saw his breath in the frozen morning air. Could see his horse's breath, too. Below, the column crossed the little creek, the horses' hooves ringing on the frozen gravel. "I'll keep your information in mind," he said. He meant his voice to sound menacing but it cracked like a kid's.

Slocum figured he'd done what he could and dropped back to ride alone.

The column of roughly dressed men passed the farmhouses that appeared now and again. Nobody came outside for a wave or a howdy. Once Slocum saw a curtain twitch, but that might have been illusion.

They rode through Tonganoxie, coming down toward Lawrence from the northeast. It was eight o'clock now. The roads got bigger and wider and the ground flattened out into prairie, interrupted by soft hollows.

Slocum scratched a lucifer against his saddle. In a very few minutes he had to make his play and he didn't see any good way to get away with it.

It wasn't a happy decision, but somebody had to warn Lawrence. With a few minutes' notice the town could put up some kind of defense, and without it John Slocum feared something unimaginable.

He had a fine horse and it felt good between his thighs. His guns were in good condition. He was as good with a Colt as any man riding with the guerrillas and more than their match as a rider. Three hundred fifty to one. Some trouble.

The flanker files rode in closer to the main column as it drew near Lawrence. The ground was almost perfectly flat as they came out onto the edge of the Great Plains. It was the finest form of glacier-scoured, buffalo-enriched bottomland here, and the German-Swiss immigrants who had settled here knew how to farm.

The barns were spacious—room for fifty cows at a time. They were two-story bank barns; ramps led to the upper floor, where haywagons could unload.

Farms on both sides of the road, fences crowding the column. Ahead of Slocum, the lead flanker pulled his horse onto the road rather than jump a fence. The next flanker joined the main column, too. Tom McHale slipped in with the rest.

Slocum kneed his horse and set his weight and the animal went back on his haunches and sailed neatly into the field beside the road.

A thin line of bare chestnuts were beside the road. The ten-acre field was corn stubble—from the looks of the ground, recently grazed by cows. The horse's hooves made a swishing noise against the high stubble. Slocum leaned back in his saddle, taking his ease, nothing in mind.

A rock pile was in the center of the field. No more than twenty feet high—the remnants of some ancient glacier, deposited here and too big to move. The farmer farmed around it.

Several other flankers followed Slocum's lead, jumping their horses into the field. They didn't follow him around the far side of the little hillock, however, and were puzzled by his move. He was the only flanker that far out. The other flankers guessed he'd seen something unusual when he came out the other side of the hillock, farther from the main body than he'd been before.

Tom HcHale didn't think so. He watched Slocum's moves and added things up.

Slocum jumped his horse over the fence at the other end of the stubble field, his horse at the canter now, no longer a walk.

"That son of a bitch!" the boy shouted. "He's a damn traitor! He's gonna warn Lawrence!"

And Slocum heard the shout and dug his heels into his startled horse and slung himself low and forward, just like a jockey.

The guerrillas reacted fast, but Tom HcHale and the other flankers had the advantage of a few seconds' notice. The boy jumped his horse into the field not more than two hundred yards behind Slocum and the other flankers followed, fifty yards behind. Riding hell-for-leather.

Slocum was widening the distance at every jump when the first rifle fire almost killed him. The nearest round took his hat clean off his head, one bullet plucked at the shirt billowing out from his side, and another cut his right rein. The guerrillas were good shots. They'd had practice.

His flankers depended on their horses. They were too far for a pistol and a man can't do well with a rifle from the back of a hurrying horse.

Slocum veered his horse to the nearest brush, the left hedgeline bordering the field. One jump, two, and then he booted his horse straight at the bushy tangle, hoping a low limb wouldn't take his head off, hoping his horse wouldn't impale itself on the stubs of old wood in any hedge, hoping it wouldn't break the horse's leg . . . hoping.

Something struck him a tremendous blow on the right arm as he crashed into the brushy tangle. The next second they were out the other side and his horse was going down in newly plowed ground and Slocum was standing up in the stirrups, back over its haunches helping the animal's balance as much as he could.

Slocum's mouth was wide open and he was yelling something. Even he didn't know what; some prayer? The horse caught its footing, and a moment later, its gait, and Slocum felt the pain in his right arm again. The upper arm hung funny and it was broken sure as hell, though it wasn't clear whether bullet or branch had broken it.

Slocum was almost free and clear. The guerrillas were formidable riders, but nobody wanted to follow him through the brushy menace where a man could get his guts hung up as easily as his horse could.

Only the boy. He crashed through the brush pile, right where Slocum had, thoughtless and excited. On the other side, he found a long plowed field, the dirt muddy, rocks lying on top of the ground like a crop.

Slocum was riding for the end of the field. Beyond that field were the farmhouse and the outbuildings and, though the boy didn't know it, the Lawrence road. Slocum was gaining.

"Oh hell," he shouted. He drew up, his horse stiff-legged and sliding in the soft ground. Slocum's horse was throwing up clods of earth behind its hooves. Slocum rode funny, favoring his right side.

The Henry fit snugly into the boy's shoulder and he held his breath. The dark splotch just above the tang of his front sight bobbled and weaved uncooperatively, but the boy wasn't really seeing the sight, he was seeing the man far out in front of him.

A couple of ravens were feeding on the seeds the plow had turned up. Slocum's pell-mell advance scared them up in front of the horse's hooves as the boy's Henry spoke once.

John Slocum dropped off the side of his horse like a sack of laundry. The boy felt a warm glow along his cheeks and the backs of his hands.

Slocum's body lay still.

The boy's voice cracked. His mouth was dry. "You never did know who the hell you were fightin' for," he said.

11

By nine o'clock the guerrillas were overtaking other travelers on the road. Most of them swerved off the road to the left or right, abandoning their rigs if they were in a tight place. Quantrill let these fugitives escape. "Can't have everything," he explained philosophically. "We won't give up the hog for the squeal."

Disregarding their official stations in the column, all the guerrilla leaders rode up front and Bloody Bill rode stirrup to stirrup with George Thrailkill, as if it were commonplace for a black-bearded, red-shirted, black-plumed ruffian to be cantering along beside a captain of Confederate cavalry in dress uniform with piping.

They didn't fly the stars and bars—the guerrillas unfurled their flag on the outskirts of Lawrence. A pitch black flag. Black as a moonless night. Black and stiff, it snapped and popped in the breeze and the name "Quantrill" seemed to dance and ripple like the scales of a snake.

The hoofbeats were very loud. Tom McHale felt the thunder in his blood. It was Tom who'd gunned down the turncoat and his boy's heart was full enough to burst.

He was the happiest man on earth, the newest hero in a band of heroes riding into blood combat boot-to-boot.

Tom McHale didn't think of his pal Jesse riding at the tail end of the column. Jesse had his orders—"Guard these spare horses."

So he did. It made him mad as hell, but Jesse James always did what his older brother wanted. Every time.

Tom McHale remembered that he hadn't recharged his Henry after dropping John Slocum—"Just one shot; and he must have been four hundred yards out if he was an inch, and on a running horse, going away fast. How's that for shooting?"

As McHale checked the Henry's chamber, Quantrill grinned at him. "Goddammit, boy, don't fidget so. You checked that rifle four times already now and it has been loaded every damn time you looked."

The blush started on the boy's neck and mounted to his ears as he jerked the rifle back into the scabbard.

Quantrill laughed and spittle flew out of his open mouth. The spit smelled like rye whiskey.

The guerrilla leader taunted Younger. Though Quantrill led the guerrilla troop, Younger supplied most of the ideas and Quantrill welcomed any chance to lessen his stature. "Cole, I guess we'd just as soon let General Lane recruit our new men, as you. Hah, hah!"

Younger shrugged. "He probably just wanted to desert."

The guerrilla leader hit Tom McHale on the back hard enough to drive the air out of him. "Bullshit," Quantrill said. "That son of a bitch was ridin' to warn Lawrence. He was settin' up an ambush against this company of brothers and only the boy's quick wits saved us."

Quantrill's red eyes were laughing and his mouth was laughing too. It was rare enough when Quantrill came out of his stupor, but when he did, he was a barrel of fun.

Lawrence had been settled by German-Swiss coreligionists twenty-eight years before. Their habits of austerity, thrift, and neatness had profited them; and the rich, never-plowed prairie sod hadn't hurt either. The railroad connected Lawrence to the rest of the country shortly before the war. Produce and livestock found its way via Lawrence to the great markets of the East. Its depots were filled with the skins of dead buffalo. Its merchants were shrewd, and contemptuous of those who didn't share their values.

Lawrence was firmly Union. Ten years ago, William Quantrill, then just a thief, passed through Lawrence.

He got in a drunken argument and a few of the townspeople beat him up and threw him in jail for three days. The jail was just as comfortable as any other structure in the stout town.

Quantrill never talked about the days he spent in that jail, but he never forgot Lawrence.

The guerrillas widened their front as they came past the edges of town. The north corner of the town square was the courthouse and Menger's hotel was on the south. The plain Pietist church faced the Farmers and Merchants Bank of Lawrence on the cross corners.

Three hundred men picked up the pace and now men on the boardwalk turned at the sound of a bad storm approaching fast.

"Oh, my God!"

The storekeeper who shouted that shout was the first man to die.

Quantrill's Colt spoke once and the man clutched at his throat, which blossomed and spurted as he toppled forward onto the street, which was still frosty but changing to slippery dark clay as the sun warmed it.

Quantrill yelled his yell, the Rebel yell, and hundreds of voices took it up at the same time.

"The ferry!" Younger bellowed and booted his horse and rushed toward the river where the only link to Federal forces was guarded by a platoon of green recruits, only half of them armed and those with single shot .69 Springfields.

Frank James peeled off after Cole and Jim Younger did too. About fifty men followed their lead.

Quantrill galloped his horse up the street, all thoughts of command lost in his very great desire to reach Colonel Strachan's home.

Thrailkill turned to his second in command. "Tell the men to spread out through the town. Don't give opposition a chance to get organized."

Racing horses—here two, here a dozen—galloped through the peaceful streets of Lawrence, knocking down neat picket fences, careening through barns, setting chicken coops awry. A man ran into his privy when a half dozen guerrillas rode into his backyard. Amused men surrounded the tall skinny outbuilding and fired into it, firing and firing and firing. Laughing at the holes their bullets made in the thin planks, laughing at how the dust bounced off the building and how it shuddered. "That'll move his bowels for him," someone shouted.

Colonel Strachan's house was at the far end of town. That fact and his immediate understanding of what the firing signified saved his life. The house abutted a twenty-acre wheatfield, gathered in the steeplelike shocks of harvest. Strachan threw open the back window of his study and without further question or pause, dropped into that field and ran as fast as he could for the first shock large enough to hide him. His wife watched his undignified flight with astonishment. She thought the rattle of gunfire was just the new recruits—lovely boys—practicing with their muskets. "Muskets" was what she thought, and couldn't dream why her husband bolted from the window that way. A terrific ruckus drumming and crashing outside her front yard sounded as if a dozen horses had come right into the flowerbeds. Mrs. Strachan wiped her hands on her apron. Still wondering about her husband, she opened the front door.

His pistol hung at the end of his hand like an extra set of fingers and he breathed whiskey fumes, but William Quantrill spoke politely enough. "Mornin', ma'am. Your husband at home?"

"No," she said. "He's in Wichita, but he'll be coming home later this evening if you gentlemen would care to come back then."

The recruits at the ferry heard the single shot as the storekeeper died, but paid it no attention. They had a neat row of tents set up next to the ferry slip. Though it was midmorning, only two of them were out of bed and both of those sat outside dozing. Their Springfields were lashed together in the military manner, forming a neat stack fifty yards from the nearest man. One recruit was taking a leak while the horsemen thundered down on his neat encampment. He must have thought they were drovers. He must have thought they were some kind of mistake, because he didn't raise his hands or warn his comrades and the bullets that hammered the life out of him didn't discover a single cry or moan. Several guerrillas rode their horses right over the recruits' tents. They converted dwellings into bundles of unshapely cloth, with live lumps moving around inside. One rider pulled up his horse beside the recruits' neat stack of Springfields and, with a kick of his boot, sent it crashing to the ground. He didn't value the Federal weapons enough to steal one.

Sportiveness overcame the guerrillas attacking the camp. Instead of emptying their guns into the masses of canvas, they looked for targets. "There's a bluebelly, Ralph. I saw it move." And a bullet would punctuate the words and sometimes a death tremor or blood leaking through the hole in the canvas verified the accuracy. They circled the tents firing steadily. Under the harsh weight of the canvas the recruits were crying out in confusion, anger, and fear, but the monotonous crack of the revolvers drowned out their cries and before very long they stilled. "Put the torch to 'em," Cole Younger cried. He meant to insure only that no Union soldiers escaped, but began what was a general conflagration.

Across the river on the easy slope, four Union troopers waited for the ferry tied up on the other side. They hollered to warn the recruits. The guerrillas never tried a shot at them though they were less than a hundred yards away, separated from the Lawrence encampment by the high river waters. The Federals cursed when the guerrillas began circling and firing. One man covered his eyes. One turned on his heels and ran as fast as he could for a horse. Other Union troops were nearby.

Cole leaned from his horse to cut the ferry rope. He sawed through the thick hawser and it flopped loose in the water trailing downstream. He lifted his hat to the Federals on the far bank. He could have killed them with his revolver but didn't.

They were off the killing floor.

Hot behind Quantrill, Tom McHale swept into Lawrence, his own Colts talking. Like the others, he cared where his bullets went. He put a couple bullets into the interior of the newspaper: Lawrence Gazette—Weekly—Custom Printing, but didn't kill anybody. A printer's devil already dangled half-out the window and the blood from his wounds ran over the ink-stained apron. Like the others, McHale fired into the frame houses that lined the street from sheer exuberance. He didn't mean to hit anybody, and didn't.

As a security precaution, Colonel Strachan had ordered all the firearms in Lawrence gathered up and put under lock and key at a central Federal armory. "We'll deny those guerrillas their guns," he said at the time.

The guerrillas surrounded the armory—a one-story brick building that also served as the town meeting hall. The front door was locked by a hasp padlock. Bloody Bill Anderson smiled and said, "Fire it. Those bluebellies won't need pistols in hell." Smoke from the burning tents had given him the idea.

Though a few men had defied the Federal colonel's orders and kept their sidearms ("Just something to protect the wife") most had complied with the order, and so, for all practical purposes, the prosperous town of Lawrence was unarmed.

The guerrillas hadn't known that fact when they rode into town, but understood soon enough that nobody was shooting back, that the only guns firing in Lawrence that fine morning were their own and that for the male citizens of Lawrence it was flight or death.

The largest mercantile in Lawrence had its front door locked, so they rode right through the front window displays. Hiding behind his yardgoods, the storekeeper fouled himself. He could have died from embarrassment and within fifty seconds somebody saved him the trouble. The guerrillas grabbed ax handles and maul handles from the open barrels and wrapped the tops with cloth dipped in kerosene. Whoop, whoop was the sound of the torches when the men swung them above their heads. The flames were almost invisible in the bright sunlight, but the smoke formed an oily plume. The first torches were tossed into the biggest mercantile in Lawrence.

A preacher (Methodist, as it happened) marched right down Main Street toward a group of men gathered around at the door of Wallace's Saloon. As the door went in, the preacher hurried, picking up the pace. "Stop that! In the name of God!"

Bloody Bill said, "You ain't him." One shot.

In Lawrence, only a few barflies made the rounds every morning, ignoring the steady pace of the town's commerce. Three old men, an Indian, and the bartender welcomed Bloody Bill into Wallace's Saloon. The barflies put their hands up, the Indian stared at the guerrilla's like he thought they were the DT's, and the bartender said, "Welcome to Wallace's."

A heartbeat later, Bill's guns replied, killing the barflies and the Indian. He holstered both pistols. He bellied up to the bar where the white-faced bartender was reeling. Bill said, "I hate the stink of gunpowder in a close place. Gives me a headache."

The bartender coughed, choked, rasped. "What . . . what'll it be?"

"The very best whiskey in the house."

Though Anderson's guns were at his side again, the five men with him had weapons drawn. Two of them hurried up the stairs at the back. Nothing on the second floor but the whore cribs and the owner's quarters. Mister Wallace himself. The men split up, one going one way, one the other. Crash after crash as one door after another gave up secrets. No girls up there this early but Mister Wallace would be in his quarters, putting the final touches on his toilette. The bartender gagged as he set out a bottle of Wallace's finest bourbon.

"What do I owe you?" Bloody Bill asked.

"Oh nothing. Nothing, sir. On the house."

"I got to pay you something. Never take nothin' for nothin'. That's always been my motto."

"Yes, sir."

"How much?"

"Two bits."

Bloody Bill shot him. Bill's hand moved so swiftly that the bartender didn't have time to prepare for the shock, and careened into the back bar, the bloody hole in his forehead like a third eye. Anderson snatched the bottle from his hand before he went down. "I seen 'em stand up for thirty seconds, sometimes," he said, to nobody in particular. "After they were dead as hell." He set the bottle down to knot his silken cord. A shot sounded upstairs where the searchers had found the proprietor. Bill didn't knot for Wallace. He never cheated.

Frank James and Quantrill had their eye on the main chance. They were the only living customers of the Farmers and Merchants Bank of Lawrence. Tom McHale was with them and not pleased about it.

On the marble floor under the high ceiling, all the male customers of the bank lay dead. The teller was inside his cage and Frank James stood on his body to rifle the till. The bank president lay beside the big safe, which he'd opened at W. C. Quantrill's request. In a rather undignified way, the president had begged for his life. Disgusted, Quantrill killed him with one shot instead of belly-shooting him and drawing it out.

"Take these bills, boy," Frank said, stuffing sheaves of currency into a bag and tossing it through the air. "This ain't military scrip, it's gold certificates." The bag wasn't heavy, but it had bulk.

Inside the safe, Quantrill was pulling drawers, letting most of the contents crash to the floor. The gold coin drawers he emptied into an open sack at his feet. "Ain't this fun?" he asked. He asked that question all morning and many of the men who rode with him that day recalled it later. At the very bloodiest heart of the action, William Quantrill wandered around, smoking pistol in his hand, repeating the remark, "Ain't this fun, boys? Ain't this fun?"

Per instructions, Tommy McHale lugged the canvas bag outdoors and fastened it behind Frank's saddle. Tommy guessed (correctly) that no other guerrilla would have done it for the band's leaders. He tapped his fingers on the saddle horn.

Shots rang out. Most of them single shots. Sometimes two or three at a time. Columns of smoke rose from the buildings already fired and ashes were falling through the air, and the air stank. In Wallace's, three guerrillas forced a hapless civilian down on his fingertips and one knee, just like a footracer. The three guerrillas made bets as their racer, a fat fortyish male, trembled in position. Tom McHale could see the sweat on his forehead.

McHale's eyes glazed with disinterest and he set off down the street. Nothing for him. Not the gold that Quantrill wanted or the whiskey Anderson sought. His revolver was holstered at his side. He made his way down the very middle of the deserted street, like a dare. If there were any Yankees behind the shot-out windows of Lawrence, he hoped they'd try something on him.

Behind him someone shouted "Go," and a moment later the fat man hurried past McHale, knees pumping, his hands clenched into fists and his lungs working like a bellows. It wasn't what McHale wanted, watching a fat rabbit run down the street. The first shot sounded after the man got a hundred yards away. It was a short contest. The first bullet broke him and he writhed around in the dirt like a grasshopper with a broken back.

Tom McHale meant to finish him when he got up close. The hurt man was very ugly. A guerrilla stepped out of the nearest house, fired, and went back inside.

At the riverbank, a few more Yankee soldiers had arrived and taken cover. Some of the more venturesome began shooting, but they didn't hit anybody, and the guerrillas didn't get mad. They abandoned the riverbank where the blood-spattered tents lay curiously still and distorted under the indifferent sky.

The Federals felt as if they were watching a theatrical performance like, say, *The Sack of Troy*. They were too few. They couldn't get across the river and so they watched with a certain detached appreciation.

Tom McHale was awfully restless. Something was wrong with him. He almost envied Jesse—back with the horses. Bodies stretched out here and there along Main Street, all of them civilians. The newspaper office was burning brightly now, blackening and bubbling the printer's body.

McHale had to do something. He drew his pistol (the same Colt Dragoon Jesse James favored) and rushed into the nearest shop. His feet bounced on the boardwalk and his hand hit the knob and he stepped into a barbershop.

It was a conventional barbershop with the big chair in the front, the array of barbering tools on a tray attached to the arm, and the various pomades, oils, and creams lined up below the mirror. The cylindrical stove held a teakettle full of boiling water and a towel rack extended to warm the towels. Just last week Tom had found a couple hairs growing on his chin. Jesse already had enough hair growing to start a realistic mustache, but he was darker than McHale.

The back room was for the bath, where a trail-weary cowhand or a dusty trooper could sluice off before a night on the town. Not that Lawrence was much of a town to have a night on. The bathroom was separated by a white and blue striped curtain that hung down not quite far enough to hide the barber's feet, which protruded into the doorway, far enough so the boy could see dark socks and the hair on his legs. Tom McHale thought the man's shins were ugly. He wished he'd got there first and asked the barber about chin hair before he was killed.

Impatiently, Tom McHale swept his pistol barrel against a milk white bottle of hair oil. It smashed on the tiled floor, and the preparation that oozed out was thick, yellow, and revolting.

Outside, the shots were as steady as ever. Every thirty seconds, some guerrilla unearthed a male citizen. Regular as clockwork.

Tom McHale came down the boardwalk, stepping over bodies. Guerrillas rushed back and forth in the street. Some of them already had loot. One man carried a parrot's cage strapped behind his saddle, though the bird had broken its neck the first corner the horse thundered around.

Bloody Bill Anderson waited in front of the hotel, his leg carelessly wrapped around his saddle horn, and his hands empty. "You all come out now," he called. "If I got to climb up into that hotel and drag you out of there, I'm gonna be awful damn upset. Come on out." His voice was impossibly smooth, slick as the underside of a slab. "Hell, you know me. You know I never hurt anybody who surrendered to me."

There were men in the hotel—some fifty of them had taken refuge behind its barricaded front doors. Two of the town's three pistols had found refuge inside the hotel, though the pistols hadn't been fired for fear of reprisals.

In his vivid red shirt, Bloody Bill was an astonishing target, but for that very reason, nobody made him one.

Bill was alone. Just himself, about twenty feet from the front of the hotel where men watched from upper windows and whispered among themselves. The boy stepped into the shadows, wanting to see what would happen, but unwilling to be a part of it. The door opened six inches, then closed again.

"Well, now," Bill said heartily, "somebody's bein' sensible. If you don't come out here and surrender to me, I won't be responsible. My men are getting wilder, the more they drink, and soon I won't be able to guarantee their behavior."

The squat man with the black plume looked like a statue. His hands sat easily on his reins. The door opened six inches again. One hand held the door open, the boy could see the fingertips, and when the civilian came onto the hotel porch, he came fast as though he'd just pulled away from someone. Nervously, he jerked his head.

"Mornin', pilgrim," Anderson said easily. "I don't suppose you'd tell me whether you're for the Union or for the Confederacy."

The man swallowed. "The Confederacy," he blurted. He ran his hands through his hair.

Bill nodded, calmly. "That's fine. Now you-all go down to the end of the porch and stand for a bit, will you? Make some room. What's your name?"

"Smithers."

"Well, then, fine, Smithers. You've surrendered to me. Now go stand down there." Bill returned his attention to the hotel. "Now, boys. I know you're in there. And there has to be some of you that is on the side we're on. Men who know the Confederacy has the right of the matter." He paused expectantly and the door opened again and another man slipped out. This one Anderson recognized with a nod, but didn't ask for his name or opinions.

As the boy watched, fascinated, Bloody Bill cajoled five men out of the front door of the hotel. He seemed to know when he should shop, when his honeyed pleadings would fail to get results, because his manner underwent a transformation. He got up in his saddle and sharply backed his horse away from the men on the porch. The men were young and old—from fifteen to eighty. As Anderson backed away, he passed McHale, and Tom could see Anderson's profile and the corner of his mouth working. Those citizens who owned hats had them in their hands, except for the oldest, who wore his narrow-brimmed Stetson as if it were part of his head.

"Boy," Anderson said to McHale.

The startled boy said, "Yes, sir," before he could help himself.

"Bring me your pistol, boy. Mine's shot out."

And the boy hurried into the street and held his own Colt dragoon up to the guerrilla leader who didn't thank him or remark how nice it balanced, but held it carelessly, ignoring McHale.

Strangely, the boy was ashamed to be here and he backed away like an actor onstage in the wrong scene.

"I suppose you're all Confederates," Bloody Bill said.

Most of the men nodded their answers. One said, "You bet I am."

The Colt spoke and the end man tumbled. It spoke again and he killed them up the line, one shot per man and a long interval between shots. When the last man fell, Bill stuck the Colt into his belt and said softly, "I don't believe you." He howled then, and yelled, "I don't believe you." A pistol fired at him from the second floor of the hotel, but Bill already had his horse crow-hopping down the street infected with his joy and his hoots of laughter.

Tom McHale ran too. He followed Bloody Bill down the street meaning to reclaim his firearm. He felt very naked.

Another rider intercepted Bill before McHale got up to him. They had a dozen men in an old tobacco barn behind the newspaper office. The rider wanted Bill to come along and throw the torch to the place.

Bill thought that sounded all right, and as McHale watched helplessly, the two rode away.

Tom McHale felt nine kinds of fool. Though the shots had steadily grown less regular, men were still shooting. Tom McHale couldn't imagine facing Jesse James without having killed one Yankee and having lost his pistol to boot.

He had a rifle strapped to his horse, but his horse was on the other side of town. He saw a better idea.

One of Thrailkill's bunch wobbled out of Wallace's saloon and he'd been hitting it pretty hard. One hand clutched the door frame and the other a half-full bottle. "Oh, Jesus," he yelled. "Jesus!"

McHale hurried across the street. The man recognized the boy for a guerrilla, that was all. He lurched for his horse. Helpfully, McHale made a cup of his hands and boosted the drunk aboard. The drunk lost his hat and wanted to get down to retrieve it, but McHale handed it to him. As if he had every right in the world, he unbuttoned the man's saddle holster and extracted a revolver. "Give it back to you tomorrow," he said cheerfully.

"Sure thing, pardner."

The gun seemed awfully damn dirty, but McHale wasn't choosey.

The boy ran down the street and turned onto another, lined with small one-family dwellings. Some of them were on fire. Many had had their front doors kicked in and Tom heard women wailing. Tom McHale was afraid he'd missed his main chance. He felt ill.

On impulse, McHale turned in at an undamaged bungalow, cocking the hammer of his pistol. The hammer was gritty and he looked down at it. Hell, no telling when it had last been charged and cleaned. He opened the cylinder and five were loaded. It would serve.

He pounded onto the front porch. Curtained glass window in the door. It was very clean and Tom could see his reflection. His hair was wild, his face dirty and smoke grimed, his mouth was drawn back over his teeth and his eyes glittered.

McHale liked what he saw so much he reversed his pistol and smashed the glass out rather than knocking.

Across the river, the Federals were firing seriously and twice a bugle sounded.

Down the main street, drunken guerrillas rode horses

loaded down with booty. Already Thrailkill was gathering his men together, looking worriedly off to the south where the Federals would come. Quantrill sat his horse like a stone, too drunk to care, and Bloody Bill didn't want to leave, swearing there were a bunch of damn male-things in the hotel and they could burn it if they didn't lack nerve.

A woman appeared inside the window McHale had broken.

"Lookin' for your husband, ma'am," McHale said.

The woman broke. Though it had only been half wood, the door had been some sort of protection. She raised her hand to her mouth and got pale and the boy grinned to reassure her.

"Doctor Johnson's not here," she squeaked.

"Mind if I look myself?" McHale said, holding his pistol partly concealed at his side. His hand came inside and opened the door.

"The others—the others who came—they trusted me," the woman said. "Won't you take my word?"

"Afraid I can't do that, ma'am," the boy said, with a fine surge of confidence. The woman backed away toward her parlor, keeping two feet between them.

A man's voice. "That's enough, Mag. I can't hide behind your skirts any longer."

The man came out of the parlor and stepped past his wife and there wasn't room for the three of them in the narrow hall. The boy backed up for room to breathe, his pistol in front of him like a buddy. "Stop," he ordered.

The man was in his thirties. Rich curly head of brown hair and thick high eyebrows. The little ridge across his nose showed the mark where his glasses usually sat. He was dressed in vest and matching dark trousers. His celluloid collar was higher than usual and he smelled faintly of soap.

His eyes were quite calm. "I shan't welcome you to my house," he said.

To his shame, it was the boy's voice that quavered.

"Who you for?" he asked. "You for the damn Unionists?"

And the man looked at him steadily and said, "Of course I am."

The words hung there and there wasn't room in the hall for those words. Outside, a rider raced past. "Mount up. Everybody mount up. We got what we came for!" The last words slurred.

Tom McHale looked into the man's calm brown eyes and blinked and worried. He twisted his face into a snarl, shoved his pistol at the man and let the hammer fall. It clicked on a dud cap. He cocked again and banged another dud.

"Get out of my home before I throw you out," the man said quietly.

As he advanced, the boy retreated. With the pressure of his own deliberate body, Dr. Johnson pushed him out the front door and backed him right off the porch. "We'll catch up with you," he said. Contemptuously, he turned to go back inside. He presented his back and though Tom McHale's eyes were tearing awfully, he lifted the Colt and aimed right between his shoulder blades and let the hammer fall with a click.

"Oh," he cried. He cried like a man who's been kicked too hard. He dropped the pistol and scurried out of the yard and ran like a hunted man toward Main Street where his brothers might be found. Not so many still looting. Most of them were already gathered at the edge of town, ready to move out.

The boy found his horse and mounted up. In the saddle, he underwent a transformation. His horse. His own gun. Under his breath, he muttered the lesson he'd learned, "A man's got to use his own weapons."

All the riders were hurrying south; he rode north.

Several shouted warnings. "Better move, boy. We done all our business here and we better make tracks." The boy neither acknowledged nor returned their warnings.

A lone man on horseback rode up to the hotel and

stopped, just where Anderson's horse had stood twenty minutes before. Tom McHale extracted his Henry and rested it across his saddlebow.

The bodies lay in a sloppy row across the front porch. The door was open now. The boy was calm. It had come to this necessity and he was ready for it.

In the distance, some of the guerrillas were hollering. The fires were the loudest thing in Lawrence, Kansas, just now.

When Tom spoke, his voice was smooth as the slick side of a razor strop. "You all can come out now. All the others are gone. It's just me and I ain't gonna hurt you."

He waited for a moment, intending to speak again if he must, but he didn't. One man came onto the porch, a nondescript man. The boy smiled and nodded. The nondescript man lifted one hand and shot the boy right through the heart.

Quantrill's men killed one hundred eighty-nine men in Lawrence, Kansas. Some were ancients. Some were babes in arms. Quantrill was heard to remark, "Hell, it ain't nothin'. Boys and babies are easy to kill."

The next morning, survivors dragged Tom McHale's body out of town and dropped it into a brush-filled ravine. They never did bother to bury it.

12

A natural human mistake created John Slocum's recovery. The farmer who found the wounded man in his newly opened ryefield surmised Slocum was a victim of the guerrillas. A guerrilla would have lived until the farmer located a stout limb.

Lawrence, Kansas willed him to live.

McHale's bullet caught him high in the back, collapsing one lung flat as a buckskin bag, and the fall from his running horse had smashed his ribs and his arm was broken. His skin color had a definite blue tinge to it and his breathing was shallow, urgent, and short.

When they rolled him onto the wagon, he opened his eyes. He kept his eyes open as they bundled him for the ride into town, but he didn't say anything.

Both of his Colts had bounced loose from his holsters when he fell and one buried itself in the farmer's soft dirt and was lost until the field was plowed again. His horse had no loyalty to John Slocum and continued in a vaguely westerly direction until it was caught square by a half-breed on the banks of the Red River. The horse still carried Slocum's saddle gear: one Henry rifle, two revolvers, and a canteen. Behind the saddle a horse blanket was tied whose folded edges were stuffed with gold. The half-breed thought he was lucky capturing the horse until he saw the guns. He knelt and gave thanks. Later, he found the gold and knelt again. He did not know why he had been so favored.

Quantrill's raiders hadn't left many wounded. Most of the ones they shot, they shot fatally. Jimmy Hooker was wounded. He'd been burned in the newspaper office fire trying to rescue his father. And Leo Lockridge, the town assessor, who'd been winged inside the county courthouse, but had the good sense to lock himself deep downstairs among his files before he passed out. And John Slocum. Young Jimmy died of his burns within twenty-four hours and it was a pitiful sight to see how he cried out in his pain. The hopes of the community of Lawrence settled on Leo and John Slocum, whom the Kansas City newspapers called "an unfortunate wayfarer." He carried no other identification, so that's what they named him.

Leo's wound wasn't too bad—a severed tendon in his shoulder, which would impair movement until his dying day. Leo rather enjoyed playing the wounded hero and was quite disappointed when he was turned out of the makeshift hospital in the back of Dr. Johnson's home. Dr. Johnson had wanted to keep the pistol he found in his front yard as a memento, but his wife firmly vetoed any such macabre idea, so Johnson reluctantly parted with it. It became the property of Colonel Strachan who made quite a collection of artifacts from "the Day."

Slocum lay between death and life so long many gave up hope for him. Johnson kept his wound clean and his body cool and that was the extent of his practice. This man would have to heal or die.

His condition was part of the daily news in Lawrence, Kansas.

Within days, the town transformed itself into an armed camp. Union troops established a nine o'clock curfew and one citizen too drunk to remember was gunned down by a trigger-happy patrol. Order and discipline had never been so rigorously maintained and hourly patrols traveled Main Street and those patrols were armed with the newest repeating carbines.

Other Kansas towns awaited Quantrill's attack. No Union town was unarmed or unprepared and many of them had central fortified blockhouses thrown up, just as in the bad old Indian days before Andy Jackson pushed the hostile tribes west.

Confederate towns armed themselves too. Fear of

jayhawkers' reprisals—and, some said, fear that Quantrill wasn't able to distinguish friends from enemies.

Ten thousand militiamen were detailed from St. Louis into the border country and they rode in bunches of five hundred, throwing up a dust cloud you could spot for ten miles on a windless day.

In Lawrence, a mass grave was dug hastily and the bodies of the town's citizens were piled into it and quicklimed. Nobody remembered Tom McHale's corpse, or if they did, they didn't say anything about it.

The newspapers were delighted. The Lawrence raid was the sort of stuff that sells papers. Before the last of the damage had been cleared up, newspaper reporters were arriving and they so monopolized the telegraph that the military finally restricted it.

Dozens of writers roved the town, interviewing almost everybody because everybody had been there and everybody had a story to tell. The goriest information found its way to the front page and steel engraving portraits of the three more prominent guerrillas were printed.

Even Kate Clarke was tracked down and interviewed: "Bill Quantrill is Gallant and Romantic, says Inamorata."

Slocum opened his eyes in the middle of the night. He had been attended around the clock by nurses and now one got up from her chair beside his bed and moistened his lips and whispered, "Don't talk."

As Slocum drifted off, he thought with some irritation that he hadn't meant to talk and where the hell was he anyway? If he was in hell, shouldn't he know it?

The very next morning reporters gathered outside the doctor's home, hoping for an interview. The window glass had been replaced and the curtains changed and the woman blocked the reporters in her hall more easily than she had guerrillas. "When the traveler is well, you may interview him and not a moment before," she said.

Two resolute reporters camped out in the yard all

night hoping for the first words from the traveler's lips, but Slocum's lips stayed closed.

The first few days men picked through the burned buildings for possessions and bodies. On the third day, the military commander ordered the burned structures razed. He feared typhoid in Lawrence's water supply from unburied corpses.

The guerrillas had been seen here and there and everywhere. Information about them was scarce and reliable information more so.

It was easy enough to trace them out of Lawrence. Their path was marked with discarded trophies: one parrot cage; one hall clock, grandmother model; an empty five-gallon hogshead that had held whiskey; canvas money bags bearing labels from the Farmers and Merchants. Some of these items eventually found their way back into the hands of their owners, but most were kept by the curious.

The news pushed other war news out of the papers. Grant's titanic battle with Lee was old news by now. Every day, the Union lines shifted a few hundred yards nearer to Richmond. Every day, the newspapers printed the casualty list.

LAWRENCE, KANSAS SACKED! That was how the staid *New York Daily Sun* put it. Questions were asked in Congress. Men of all political persuasions deplored the raid. In Richmond, the *Times-Dispatch* announced the deed in rather more restrained terms, underplaying the number of dead and overplaying the uniformed troops Quantrill killed. "Important Union Center Burned." That's how they saw it in Richmond.

The secretary of war groaned aloud when he heard— he searched the casualty lists, fearing to read John Slocum's name. At least there was nothing in writing to connect the CSA with Quantrill. Thanks be to heaven for that.

The reporters stayed in Lawrence as long as the Federal troops. None of them interviewed John Slocum because when the wounded man started to knit, he lay in his room staring at the ceiling. Oh, he could talk if he wanted to—"Bring me more tea" or "I need the bedpan." That kind of talk. That sort of speech doesn't sell papers and the reporters gave up on him. As soon as he could sit up unaided, the nurse staff quit and at the last, only Dr. Johnson and his wife cared for the wounded man.

Healing took forever. The infection passed out of his chest but he had to stay immobile for months while his broken ribs and arm came together.

The wife wanted Slocum moved to the hotel, but Dr. Johnson thought not. When they put the matter to the pale taciturn man, he indicated no preference. Since they needed his room for a treatment room, Slocum was moved to a much smaller back room, once it was cleared of stored family possessions.

This room was wallpapered white with tiny rows of blue flowers. Iron bed with white counterpane, reading chair, one table, one kerosene lamp. The window overlooked the Johnson's backyard where the snow lay and wouldn't melt for the rest of the winter. When the wind blew, it banked up against the picket fence. It got to be Christmas. The Johnsons had friends and family into the parlor where they had a tree and gave modest gifts to each other. Because of the raid, festivities were muted, no louder than the sound of green grass trying to grow. Mrs. Johnson invited Slocum out of his room for eggnog and holiday cheer. He declined.

His only interest was reading the newspapers and his exercise program. He was as single-minded as a narcissist and worked every muscle every day. He used a set of iron scrap from the woodshed to put more strain on his legs during the sit-ups, and tossed the iron scraps to strengthen his arms.

Dr. Johnson asked him what he did for a living.

"I've been a farmer," Slocum said, neglecting to update the picture.

The good doctor asked him if he could supplement his newspaper reading with books. Slocum said yes, and the doctor brought Shakespeare, some histories and geographies, and the practical treatises on mechanics no Victorian household was without. John Slocum read the Shakespeare and the Bible.

Grant pushed Lee around Richmond like a stubborn child shoves a plaything. The Confederate government removed itself to Danville. Slocum studied the war maps and dreamed of the places the maps signified and what they must look like right now.

The three guerrilla bands broke up shortly after the raid. They ran across Kansas and Missouri pursued by Federals. One morning, the *Lawrence Democrat* (founded 1845—refounded 1865) carried a story that fascinated John Slocum: Bloody Bill Anderson was dead.

A certain Federal command of regulars and jayhawkers had ambushed the guerrillas on a road outside of Bridgewater, Missouri. Bill was out in front of his men—only twenty of them now. Without a word of warning, the ambushers opened fire. Many rifles cracked as one. The guerrillas charged and three more died trying to reach their fallen leader. They were beaten off. The Federals cut off Bloody Bill's head and carried it into the nearest town where they mounted it on the highest iron picket fence they could find.

Toward the end of March, the ground started to thaw and John Slocum took to the outdoors, taking long, long walks after dark when he wouldn't be likely to meet people. Slocum went to work for the Johnsons as a handyman, repairing the warped cellar door, reroofing the woodshed, relining the well. He ate in the kitchen with the family now, as laconic as ever. One evening, April 14, the grass was just starting to green in the yard and the crocuses were well along when Johnson shoved the front door open with a bang. "It's over," he shouted, happily. "By God, it's over!"

The news had come on the telegraph. The telegram was dated "Appomattox Crossroads." Lee's broken Army of Northern Virginia had surrendered to Ulysses

S. Grant. Surrendered unconditionally. While the nation held its breath, Grant and his commander-in-chief planned the terms. Was it to be trials for the Rebels? There were plenty of men calling for trials.

Dr. Johnson was beside himself with excitement. "Slocum. It's over. Grant let Lee's men go home—including Lee himself. Asked them to swear to fight no more and let 'em keep their weapons and swords and even their horses. Can you beat that?"

Slocum sat quite still. "I don't believe I can beat that," he said softly.

The doctor had long since guessed his guest's Southern sympathies—Johnson was a delicate man by inclination. "I'm so damn glad this war is over," he said fervently, a smile spread across his face.

And John Slocum said, "Yes," though he wasn't sure the war was over.

A few days later, Abraham Lincoln was shot. Man named Booth did it. Slocum wondered if it was the same man he'd met in Richmond and decided it could have been. The newspapers carried news of a price on Booth's head. A hundred thousand dollars. President Jefferson Davis had a hundred thousand on his head too. He'd fled from Danville, hurrying west where Kirby Smith's Army of the Trans-Mississippi still bore arms. Lincoln's death raised new cries for treason trials and Quantrill's Lawrence raid was mentioned again in Congress and the newspapers as justification for hanging every ex-Confederate, even Lee himself.

Slocum's young body was almost mended. His breathing was good, his ribs healed and his arm, which was the slowest to mend, gave him trouble only at the end of a day. He painted the Johnsons' house the day Booth was surrounded and killed somewhere in Maryland.

The next morning he rose early and went out behind the woodshed. For the first time, he wore the Colt revolver. He emptied the chambers but left the caps in place because the hammer of a revolver should never strike hard metal and no man should draw and fire without pulling the trigger. It should be one decision, not two.

While lying there, that was one of the things he'd worked out.

That night, over dinner, Dr. Johnson said, "I think you're quite healed."

"I meant to leave in the morning," John Slocum said.

"I can't have a man fooling with a Colt in the backyard of my home," Dr. Johnson said. "You understand."

"Make me up a bill tonight," Slocum said. "I don't know how quick I'll pay you, but I'll pay you for all of it, and I'd take it as a kindness if you charge me fair, less the work I've done for you."

The doctor took him at his word, and when John Slocum walked out of his house in the morning, he carried one Colt revolver, the clothes on his back, and Dr. Johnson's bill for four hundred twelve dollars. Slocum thought it was little enough.

Wallace's saloon had done a much improved business since the raid. The new owners didn't know why, but welcomed the trade.

It could get rough on a Saturday night, which is why John Slocum got hired. He sat on a high stool against the back wall and watched for trouble. He could circulate through the crowd, but usually he sat there, every night, until the place closed.

There never was any trouble inside the Wallace saloon after he was hired, not so much as a broken chair or a bullet hole or a fist fight. Troublemakers always subsided and took their trouble elsewhere. Always. John Slocum never had to use the Colt revolver he wore stuck in his belt. It shone with a light coating of gun oil.

For his work, they paid him two dollars a day and his dinner.

He didn't talk much, but he did listen. Whenever someone came in with news about the guerrillas, Slocum heard it. Since Lawrence was Lawrence, every move or rumor about Quantrill was hot news and Slocum listened to all of it. Thrailkill had joined with General Shelby who had taken a party south into Mexico. Frank and Jesse James returned home to Missouri where their attempts to maintain the family's hardscrabble farm met with incredulous hatred from the Jameses' jayhawker neighbors. Cole Younger and Jim went home too. Jim was ambushed and killed on the road by men with long memories. The James house was shot up a time or two. Quantrill himself was in St. Louis, or Kansas City, or Westonia. He'd taken a steamer up to Montana Territory. He'd gone to Utah to the Mormons. Slocum heard it all.

One dollar of every two went to Dr. Johnson. He saved what he could. When he had fifty dollars he walked down to the livery stable and looked the animals over. Some fine horses, some lame horses, some old horses, some half-broke horses, and some mean horses. He bought fifty dollars' worth of mean horse. The horse was young and fast and big, but he was mean as hell too. Every afternoon Slocum worked with the horse, rebreaking him. He used a borrowed battered doubletree saddle for the job. Slocum worked that horse until he and the animal understood each other, which was no small feat. He made no friends. After watching him break the horse, the liveryman became an admirer.

Saturday, the 4th of July, 1865, was the first official festivity Lawrence had allowed itself. It was a fairly strange celebration, because from time to time citizens broke into tears, but the basic tone was cheerful. They had a parade with Uncle Sam leading it and all the farm machinery owners drove their implements down Main Street. There was a hay mower and one of Cyrus McCormick's new reapers. A steam tractor hissed along, its brass gleaming and its engineer hooting as loudly as his steam whistle.

In the afternoon they had horse races and the crowd swelled with sports and swells from miles around. The fancy ladies made a point of stopping in Lawrence that day because there was money to be made. Wallace's saloon had a small tent on the race course and John Slocum sat inside on his high stool. He watched the races but kept his eye on the customers too.

A bay mare was showing her heels to everything on the track and the crowd was standing and shouting encouragement when John Slocum plucked at one whore's sleeve.

She turned with her automatic smile. She was a little older than her competition and more heavily painted, and she wouldn't start to make her rent money until it got dark late in the day. "Howdy there, sport," she said.

" 'Lo, Sallie," Slocum said softly.

Her jaw dropped and her eyes opened up wide. "My God," she breathed. "Is it really you?"

Sallie's clothes weren't too good and her shoes were run down some. Her coat was a light summer one, and bright red, but a little frayed at the cuffs, and her dress was red with a black edge of piping at the bottom. She looked as though she'd been dressed in someone's living room drapes. She said, "I can't believe it. I just can't believe it." Her smile was younger than she was and cracked the paint at the sides of her mouth.

Slocum yelled for the bartender to bring him and the lady a beer. The bartender had never seen his laconic bouncer say more than three words to any woman. He hastened to bring them their foaming schooners. The owner-bartender made beer from the recipes that had come over from the old country. He kept his barrels in a cellar where the temperature was about twenty degrees cooler than the day outside, and they stayed cool until he served them.

Her yellow eyes sparkled at him and she said, "God, John, it's been forever. I thought you were a dead man for sure."

Slocum smiled. "Just lucky, I guess," he said.

The beer was awfully good and Slocum thought it

felt a lot like summer. "You look fine, Sallie," he noted diplomatically.

She made a face. She had a terrifically mobile face, her thoughts chased each other across it in hot pursuit. "I'm too damn old for the game, John. I'm competin' with sixteen-year-old girls for the barroom trade. I'm followin' the race circuit and I suppose I'll do the country fairs before the end of the season."

"You're still a beautiful woman," Slocum said.

She was pleased. She looked down the table and said her thank you. She asked him about his plans. He said he didn't really have any plans.

"What about your farm? You talked about goin' back home after the war was over."

He shrugged. Slocum felt changed, completely changed. Going back to Georgia would just be a new man putting on an old man's clothes and habits. He almost said as much, but didn't.

"I see you're carryin' a gun," she said.

"That's my line of work."

"You ever have to use it?"

"If you're good enough, you don't have to use it," he said.

She waved at the tent where the race crowd drank happily. "Is this your only line of work or do you moonlight?"

"You mean, do I do killin' for hire?"

She looked away. She said she cared about him. She said, yes, that's what she meant.

"No. I'll never kill anybody for hire again. I don't need any man tellin' me who or what to kill. Never again. Don't need Confederates tellin' me to kill Yankees and don't need Heddon telling me to kill Rebs. Ain't on the block. No more."

She took his hand and gave it a small squeeze. She took a drink of beer. She said, "I suppose you ain't heard that whores make the best wives. They know how to please a man."

"I've heard," he said. "I ain't gettin' married."

She nodded. She'd known that already but wanted to check.

"I was in Missouri. St. Louis," she said, to change the subject. "I saw an old ridin' partner of yours."

Slocum looked his question.

"Kate Clarke. She's got her own place now. With some of the prettiest girls in St. Louis. She said she wouldn't take me on. 'There's no room for sentiment in the love business,' she said."

"Where's Quantrill?" There was nothing particular in Slocum's voice to send the ice down her neck, but she felt cold. She hesitated for a second. She felt him pulling at her, though he didn't touch her. "Headed for Louisville," she said. "Kate said he was just outside Louisville."

13

He was just another drifter on roads clogged with drifters. A tall young man—early twenties at a guess—traveling east across Missouri toward the big river. His hair was black. Black as pitch; black as a raven's brilliant wing—he wore it longish, frontier-style.

He rode with the tireless poise of a natural horseman. It was a sunny, fine July. Spring rain had been plentiful and the grass was sharp green and the trees stretched their limbs and, from the road, he could see the vegetable gardens clustered near houses and shacks.

Most of the other drifters were black. Hundreds and thousands of black families were uprooted savagely and completely during the war. They were free. This was the day of Jubilo.

Missouri had no work for them and no food. As the occupying forces moved south, these blacks followed in their wake; begging food, scraps of clothing; their dead horses. At night, they camped where dark found them: just beside the road in burned-over fields or abandoned, gutted farmhouses. They managed to bury their dead. From kindness and love, they managed that much: they didn't leave their dead in the ditch.

Bit by bit, they abandoned the forlorn familiar countryside and gravitated toward the cities. Some of the boldest dared to take up plots on their former massa's land, understanding that food would be in short supply in this first year of their freedom.

These squatters sought the remotest, least productive sections of land for their 20 x 50 foot gardens, their shanties, and the little piece of corn they grew for their donkey or their chickens or a sow.

The sow was precious. Her litters meant cured meat, fresh meat, sausage, and plenty of leaf and ordinary lard. Lard to cook the wild greens and chitterlings. Lard to make the buckwheat cakes stick together. A family with plenty of lard wasn't too bad off.

The Federals delivered food to the cities. And the Reconstruction officials made sure some of the stores were unloaded and some of the unloaded stores were distributed to the starving.

"Reconstruction," the Federals called it. "Occupation" was the Southern term.

It wasn't so long since they'd defeated the very men who now lorded it over them. That's how Nathan B. Forrest, ex-general of cavalry, thought when he agreed to become the first Grand Cyclops of the newly formed Ku Klux Klan. The Klan was founded by some college boys with a taste for the melodramatic and was soon out of hand.

After dark, blacks moved in close to their fires. Nobody went out—except for a few young men, brave enough for courting. Too often they'd be found hanged with a cardboard placard tacked to their chest. "BROKE CURFEW. K.K.K."

Some Confederate veterans went home. For those who'd come from Richmond, Petersburg, Atlanta, and Chattanooga, home was free-standing ruins, inhabited by beggars, federal troops, and blacks. So, they took to the road. Many of them belonged to the invalid brigade—wooden legs, pinned-up sleeves; many were blind.

Slocum had one kind of work offered to him. In a country full of hard men, he was harder than most. No road was safe. Merchants who did cash business had an armed man on the premises. Riders were hired by the big farms to patrol the field edges at night. Robbers worked singly, in twos, and packs. Honest men feared.

John Slocum was hired to guard a bullion shipment from West Frankfort to Paducah. Three other ex-Confederates rode out with the two wagons carrying the shipment. The dispatcher hadn't liked the looks of Slocum's horse and had him riding shotgun on the first wagon. So, Slocum rode in comfort with a Greener between his knees. He smoked his roll-your-owns and made conversation with the driver. The driver was a regular employee with status mere temporaries didn't possess. The driver was just Slocum's age but avuncular and full of himself. He advised Slocum to go West where there was land enough for anybody and the lowest sort of man could find work. Slocum took the crack about "the lowest sort of man" to be directed at him but didn't care. He'd been promised three dollars for one day's work. "You heard anything of Quantrill?" he asked casually.

The driver hadn't heard anything and didn't think the guerrilla leader was in Kentucky. "Quantrill's out West with the riffraff."

This time Slocum took offense and spoke to the driver. The driver fell silent the rest of the way to Paducah.

At the terminal, Slocum traded one dollar of his wages for a money order that he mailed to Dr. Johnson. He figured to pay one-third of everything he made until his debt was paid off.

Next, he was hired for teamster's work. It paid better than baby-sitting bullion—four dollars a day—but Slocum didn't mean to make a career out of it. Five days on bad roads from Paducah to Bowling Green. Twenty dollars. No strain on his riding horse, which was tied behind the wagon. And no call to use his Colts, which he kept behind the wagon box out of sight. His cargo was forty short kegs of black powder. Because powder was valuable, the kegs were marked as "nails." If someone took a notion to steal a wagonload of nails there wasn't much Slocum meant to do about it and if somebody decided to shoot up his cargo—why there wasn't much he'd do about that either.

Slocum camped in unlikely campsites. He didn't want to trouble anyone.

His journey was nervous but uneventful, and not ten minutes after he'd been paid off in Bowling Green, he began to hear rumors about Quantrill. Quantrill had kin in Louisville. Cousins. Quantrill was in the hills above Louisville. Quantrill was this, Quantrill was that. All the rumors said he had only a few men for company. Slocum rode his mean ugly horse out of Bowling Green that same morning.

Kentucky hadn't been hurt so bad by the war and the famous bluegrass pastures stretched out from the Louisville Pike as far as he could see. The pastures were lush and good and men were making a second cutting of hay. The year 1865 was a good growing season and many preachers thanked God for it.

Slocum passed the lines of men with their scythes, cutting next winter's forage, and his farmer's eye noted every detail. A good hay crew could cut or pitch or rick three times as fast as a poor one and it was easy to see by their rhythm which farms would prosper and which welter in their own confusion. These farms had never quartered invading troops. They were neat, whitewashed or painted, and many of the fences were in good repair. Though successive Confederate levies had taken most of the young horses off the bluegrass farms, they hadn't taken the brood stock, and young colts gamboled near their too old mothers.

A fine warm day. Slocum rode in shirt-sleeves with his vest tied behind his saddle. His Colt rested on his left side. His holster was smooth and soft and angled nicely for the crossdraw.

This country didn't look one bit like the sharp V-shaped valleys and rocky ridges of mountain Georgia, but the land caused Slocum's mind to wander in a way it hadn't for a spell. A neat Kentucky springhouse made him remember his own springhouse and what repairs it had needed four years ago. A new sill. It had wanted a new sill then and Lord knew if it was still standing. An enormous stone barn reminded Slocum of his own smaller chestnut barn. Chestnut was impervious to the weather so long as the water didn't stand on it. The nail holes gave way first.

At noon, he drew up where a single span wooden bridge crossed a nice little stream. The banks were grassy to the water's edge and Slocum saw fish dart away from his shadow. It was late in the season for cress but Slocum looked for it anyway.

This side of the bridge was in shadow. He could see miles down the pike. Sounds: his horse munching the deep grass; a field chant in a distant field where they were gathering the hay into ricks. The hayricks looked like beehives and the poles laid across them looked like knitting needles. He drew. As his Colt lifted, his thumb —outthrust like a trip lever—caught the hammer and as the gun cleared leather it was at full cock. Slocum's feet were set wide apart—less like a fencer than a wrestler—as the hammer fell.

The hammer clicked on a used cap. His eyes were glued to a particular round stone—half-dollar sized— in the bridge foundation. If there'd been powder fired, his bullet would have gone there. As the hammer fell, his thumb opened, ready to hitch it back for the second shot. With the Colt Navy, the first shot was always quicker than the second. It took some character to pause that tiny fraction of a second needed to send the first one home.

Slocum spent an hour exercising. The field hands chanted, "Ho, won't you cut it. Ho, won't you lift it. Ho, won't you toss it." And their words came to Slocum like a distant dream. The heat shimmered golden off the deserted pike. The hay crew bent and moved like grass. Slocum's motions were like the snap of a whip.

John Slocum had been a gunfighter for years. He was refining a skill worn smooth by practice and his moves seemed fluid and simple. They were not. The quickdraw is a complicated combination, and though his muscles never hesitated from first move to recocking the hammer, his face glistened with sweat and the backs of his hands did too.

He started with his body in the most awkward positions. Draw and fire and recock while sitting down, one hand on the toe of his boot. Draw while falling. Draw, fire, spin, fire to the rear. The click click of the hammer hitting the expended caps. Draw-fire-cock. Do it again.

As he worked, he imagined the shock of bullets hitting him. How he could finish if hit in the chest—if a bullet broke his femur—if it shattered his wrist. He practiced the hand-to-hand border shift and the border shift recovery.

When the hay crew broke for lunch, they stopped chanting and John Slocum went to his saddlebags for his own grub. Before he unwrapped the ham bone he'd bought in Bowling Green, he loaded his Colt with new caps, powder, and ball.

That afternoon, he pressed through Upton, Kentucky. Abraham Lincoln had been born near Upton or so they said.

When he rode into Elizabethtown, it was six o'clock. It wouldn't get dark until eight, but the men Slocum was looking for had stopped work hours ago.

Elizabethtown was a crossroads town but the important road was the Louisville Pike which was Front Street too. Slocum passed by the farmers' saloons and the businessmen's saloons with their fine free lunchs. He rode by the sheriff's office and the sheriff—under the awning, picking his teeth. Slocum nodded politely and the sheriff grudgingly nodded back.

Slocum found his place—a low-down saloon by the railroad yards. The stockyards were near enough to smell. Beef came in from Texas these days—when it came in at all—and the yards were empty and dirty.

The saloon didn't have a name or tables. It had a bar with a rail, a wall to lean against, if that's what you favored, and the cheapest whiskey this side of Louisville.

The saloon loafers stared at Slocum wondering if he might turn out to be entertainment or, failing that, something they could rob or eat.

Slocum greeted the bunch of them with a nice chilly smile. He headed for the bar as if he meant it, and men parted for him. Slocum didn't care for this kind of hard game, but sometimes, it saved time. His two bits rang on the bar. "Whiskey." He tasted the whiskey and said it was all right. The bartender said that it was all there was and asked where Slocum was from.

"Back there."

"And you're goin' further on?"

"You guessed it."

Since he'd made his point, Slocum backed away from the position he'd commandeered and took a place by the wall. The saloon was full of the lazy, the inept, the greedy, and the murderous. This was a place you could find someone to burn your neighbor's barn or hire a man to kill your rival. If you wanted a few hearties to take a bank, you might look here. If you meant to form a society of ex-guerrillas, this would be a great place to hand out membership cards.

It was sleepy just now. Some slow drinking. A few very private conversations. A desultory game of dice for pennies.

As soon as the man walked in, Slocum recognized him. His two companions were strangers. The familiar face belonged to the jayhawker Slocum first met months ago at the Osage River ford. The jayhawker had his arms around his companions' shoulders and they had no more trouble clearing space for themselves at the bar than John Slocum had had.

The jayhawker's companions were in their late twenties. Their shirts and pants were civilian but they wore military boots and the spurs on their heels were U.S. Army issue. That's how they carried themselves too—stiff backed, with the slight swagger of cavalrymen. The jayhawker bought the drinks and raised his own glass. "Confusion to our enemies," he said as he tossed it off. His pals followed suit.

Though plenty of eyes were on them, the three men paid no particular attention to their surroundings. In a tenderfoot that would have been real dangerous.

The jayhawker spun and stepped right up to John

Slocum and planted himself there, with his hand on his gunbutt. His two pals spread out along the bar and they were ready too. "I know you from someplace," the jayhawker said.

Slocum didn't blink. "St. Louis?" he said, speaking with a burr in his voice that wasn't usually there.

The man lifted a finger like he meant to poke Slocum in the chest, but he thought better of the idea. "Naw. It wasn't St. Louis. Least, I don't think so." His puzzled eyes roved all over Slocum's features but couldn't link this calm dangerous man to a man he thought died in the general massacre at Shaw's Ridge, months ago. "What side you on?" he demanded.

"My side." Slocum's voice was so quiet a man had to strain to hear.

As quick as he'd braced Slocum, the jayhawker gave it up and downed his drink and growled, "My mistake, friend. No 'fense."

The trio finished their drinks and left the saloon. The bartender caught Slocum's eyes. "Hard nuts," he observed.

"Uh-huh." Slocum put a question mark in his voice and the bartender answered readily enough.

"Guerrilla chasers. They think Quantrill is nearby. If they asked me, I'd say, 'Look nearer Louisville,' but they ain't asked and I wouldn't tell them the truth if they did." He showed his teeth in a laugh. Slocum showed his teeth too and stepped to the door after the three-man party rode past. He noted their horses and the direction they took. He went out into the roadway and knelt beside the hoofprints.

When he came back inside, the bartender was curious. "Lose something?"

"The war," Slocum said, helpfully. He was feeling good and took a second slow whiskey before he quit the place. The jayhawker's horse had a T-shaped nick in the off-rear shoe and Slocum knew it.

Guided by sign, he rode slowly through Elizabethtown and north along the pike. He met a few travelers on the pike and nodded affably and said good afternoon. He was smiling, though he didn't know it. His smile looked okay from a distance but strange close up.

Every few miles, he examined the road for the distinctive mark and always found it. He enjoyed the scenery. It was good to be alive. It had been too long since he thought that.

When the sun went down, he rode on. The half-moon shed plenty of light on the white ribbon of the road. Honest men had made camp and wouldn't welcome strangers now. More frequently, Slocum checked the sign and dismounted to be sure.

Slocum was on the lookout for the jayhawker's fire and spotted it before his horse could exchange greetings with theirs.

The three men slept comfortably beside their fire and had a nice breakfast and set off after dawn. Slocum spent a cold night wrapped up in his soogans, was mounted at first light, chewing on cold beef jerky as he waited.

Slocum rode a couple miles behind. When he overshot their turnoff, he had to retrace his steps, scouring each sideroad until he found the T-shaped mark.

Above the sideroad, a battered signpost announced that this was the road to "Highgrove—5 mi." and Slocum supposed that's where they were going. The road climbed into the low hills. The farms got poorer and farther apart. Slocum passed a farmer with a wagonload of fresh-cut locust posts and a fellow dressed as a circuit rider, but there were few travelers and not many fresh tracks until another broad sideroad connected and Slocum counted the prints of twenty or thirty horses overlapping and concealing the tracks he followed.

Slocum checked every exit from this road for the T-shaped mark. Slocum stopped for an hour when the sun was hottest to let his horse graze and drink his fill of spring water. High in the hills, the air smelled good and the freshets were everywhere.

Slocum walked his horse up the narrowing road.

When the shadows grew longer, he pulled on his vest. Later, he put on his coat but didn't button it.

As the road climbed, the farmhouses beside it lost color, size, length, and number of stories. The barns got simpler—two nails to a siding plank instead of four.

The camp lay on a long slope that dropped to connect with the road at the valley bottom. Slocum came on the camp from above. Thirty men had four nice fires burning. Their horses grazed nearby, all of them hobbled. Two men sat with the horses—rifles across their knees. They weren't terribly alert and Slocum managed to get in pretty close. The horses wore USA brands and the two men carried issue carbines but wore civilian clothes. The guards were hard men but sloppy and Slocum eased by them on foot. His own horse was tied back in the woods.

The jayhawker had joined a circle of men at the main campfire. From his gestures and the other men's attention, Slocum figured him to be a figure of some importance.

The clatter of mess tins reminded Slocum that his last hot meal had been in Paducah. With real annoyance, he chewed beef jerky as they cooked their dinner. One campfire produced biscuits for the hungry men and Slocum wished the damn biscuits would fall in the fire but no such luck.

After dinner, while one detail cleaned up the pots and another grained the horses, the jayhawker sat down for some serious conversation around the big fire. Slocum would have given his eyeteeth to eavesdrop.

One of the sentries they set out passed not twenty feet above John Slocum to set up his post. Slocum lay still on the cold ground until the sentry was relieved, four hours later. The relief stepped fifty yards downwind to take a piss and stayed there. If he'd wanted to, John Slocum could have slipped into the camp then, but everyone was asleep. Cold and shivering, he returned upslope, to his own soogans and another night without a fire.

Though John Slocum promised himself a long hot bath once all this was over, the promise didn't warm his cold feet or shoulders and he was awfully glad to see the sky get light. When the sentries came in, they headed directly for the big enamel coffeepots that had rested beside the fire all night long. Slocum could have used a cup of that coffee.

The camp was in no particular hurry. It was eight o'clock before patrols started riding out. Three heavily armed men in each patrol. Yesterday's patrols straggled in. Each reported to the jayhawker but none caused any kind of stir. Sometime later, a farmer's buckboard rattled up the slope. He was stopped by a sentry but allowed to pass into the camp itself. The farmer's son rode beside him, one hand clutched to his cap.

The farmer didn't climb down, he just leaned over to deliver his message. The jayhawker started yelling. "He's found, boys! He's found! And he's not an hour away!"

Slocum jumped for his horse and he wasn't the only one. The camp exploded with running men. They left their bedrolls, their possibles and the big coffeepots in their hurry to mount up. They poured out of the camp, whooping, as the farmer finally got off his buckboard. The farmer and the boy started looting the camp.

Slocum was above the riders and half a mile behind. Despite his horsemanship, he rode a fifty-dollar horse and was already falling behind before he reached the main road. On the easier surface of the road, the others made a mile to Slocum's three-quarters, though he booted his horse unmercifully and spoke to it too, making promises and threats. The ugly horse poured out its heart for him, but the USA horses were younger and better fed. They took the curves wide, leaned into the banks and roared down the straights, their riders hollering like the hounds of hell.

John Slocum was furious. He'd come so far for this prize.

The road dipped into a broad valley, formed by the

tiny creek that bubbled along on one side and then the other. The horsemen thundered across a timbered bridge and the road climbed onto a hogback where they drew up by the farmer's front gate. It was a six-board gate, unpainted and sagging on its hinges.

Above them, the sky was one of its lighter shades of blue and the clouds were fluffy and impassive. Below, in the farmer's yard, four big horses grazed peacefully.

As the jayhawker's men struggled with the gate, the horses' owners boiled out of the barn in a terrific hurry. The jayhawker screamed with joy. The four wore butternut brown but none had a complete uniform. Their horses were recently stolen and not very tame.

The jayhawker produced a long-barreled pistol and fired and a couple others fired too. When Quantrill grabbed the reins of his animal, it exploded, bucking, twisting, throwing him around like a crack-the-whip.

As the band got through the gate, Slocum caught up with them and came through too. The jayhawker's spurs were red with blood and his horse was screaming as loud as he was. The butternut men were firing back but weren't coming close.

Afterward, Slocum wondered about that—why the guerrillas' deadly pistols missed on this particular day. He decided their time had come—it was simple as that. One of the guerrillas' horses went down, its heart shot out. Quantrill's animal was still pulling away from him and he was cursing it to hell and beyond. "Goddamn it! Hold still!"

The two successfully mounted guerrillas broke. One was flagging his horse with his hat and the other rode Indian style, slung along his animal's neck. The dismounted guerrilla had lost his pistols when his horse dropped and he was on his hands and knees looking for them. The back of his shirt puffed when the bullets hit it and something flew off with each shot: a chunk of blasted flesh.

Slocum's Colt was in his hand. He rode beside the jayhawker.

"Son of a bitch!" Quantrill let go his reins and drew and fired both pistols into his horse's body, point blank. The horse didn't die, but crashed against the rails of the corral.

Quantrill's last man was in the dust, barely moving. Thirty men bore down on him and William Quantrill laughed. His Colts barked.

John Slocum shot him twice. Neither bullet killed him but they knocked him flat and the pistols fell from his hands.

In a flurry of dust, the jayhawker dismounted. The crash of bullets and dust spouts among the horse droppings—it was amazing. Quantrill's man got to his knees and his feet and lurched toward the jayhawker and didn't stop, though the jayhawker was pounding slugs into him. He had his hand raised above his head with something glinting in his hand. John Slocum shot him in the head. He fell. He curled up like a sleeping baby.

William Quantrill lay on his back. His gray intestines peeked around the hands he was using to keep them inside his belly. His eyes were wide.

No more shots. The noise stopped as if someone had turned off a tap.

Slocum heard a raven cawing angrily at the disturbance. Cautiously, the jayhawker approached the man who'd nearly killed him and kicked at the arm. It opened. "A pocketknife," the jayhawker said, something like awe in his voice. "Boys! These guerrillas are really something!" He was happy they were really something. Slocum nudged his horse backward through the mob. Men parted for him hoping to see William Quantrill, in the flesh.

The jayhawker caught the movement and faced Slocum directly. "I know where I saw you," he howled. "I know."

Slocum didn't twitch a muscle but meant to kill that man in a moment.

The jayhawker relaxed. He pointed at the body at

his feet. "I reckon I owe you a service," he said. "I reckon we can forget it."

Though the jayhawker's men examined Slocum with some curiosity, William Quantrill was the main attraction and they crowded near.

The jayhawker stood by the guerrilla leader's feet. "I guess I got you, William Quantrill."

Quantrill looked at the scudding clouds and held his tongue.

"I didn't get in on hunting Bloody Bill, but I done hunted you. And I caught you too. Just me." For the purpose of his boast, he ignored the thirty men crowding around. Some of them carried the dying man into the farmhouse. The owner was absent or he might have objected to a gutshot man laid down on his best coverlet on his best bed.

Nobody pursued the two guerrillas who'd escaped. In the space of two minutes, they'd become ex-guerrillas and could make what they wanted of that.

A few worthies dragged the dead guerrilla to the barn where they pulled a couple siding boards loose and laid the man on them. They stuck his open pocketknife into the plank beside his head and tore the front of his shirt out so they could see his wounds plain.

Someone pulled Quantrill's boots off. Somebody else kept them. Some lucky man found Quantrill's pistols and rubbed them in the bloody patch where he'd been lying, soaking the ebony grips with his blood. Quantrill's horse was down by his forelegs and moaning. A man who meant to put it to sleep missed with the first shot and the hurt horse flung its head around until the second bullet found the mark. Though a couple men turned Quantrill's saddlebags out, they never found the black flag. They found forty dollars in gold, three watches, and some spare ammunition. At the end, William Quantrill didn't own a change of clothes.

The slugs in Quantrill's belly created a truce, though it wasn't clear how long the truce would last. The jayhawker's riders were interested in Slocum but let him be. The war was over. Everybody said so.

The guerrilla leader had been in this country before. He had friends here and kinsmen too. The jayhawker got generous and let Quantrill have all the visitors he could handle.

Within the hour they started trickling in. Hill folk with their slouch hats and their underfed wives and silent children. Some carried flintlocks their granddaddies had used.

The trickle grew—became a flood. They came to see the man who'd defied the government—an act beyond politics and maybe beyond right and wrong. Quantrill had stood up—that's what mattered. The men formed quiet lines outside the house and removed their hats when it was their turn inside. Slocum hunkered by a corner of the horsebarn. He had no place to get to tonight and didn't expect to see anything like this again.

In the yard, the women gathered around the better wagons for gossip. The kids were slipping away with infrequently seen friends.

A small crowd lingered near the body on the plank. Somebody said he'd been from Tennessee.

It was three hours before the ambulance came, which was good time, considering. Like the horses, the ambulance was an army model.

The jayhawker was conferring with the attendants when the two riders rode back in. "Hssst!" The men nearest the body backed away—as though they had nothing to do with it. Men kept their hands in plain sight.

The two men were the butternut men who'd been with Quantrill when he was alive. They were heavily armed but they kept their hands high on the reins, demonstrating their peaceable intentions. One spoke. "We wanted to see him," he said, loudly. The men in the yard separated into two groups: those who'd come to see the bodies and those who'd provided them. Slocum stayed put.

The jayhawker could have said anything.

"Bill's dying," the guerrilla said. "We're here peaceable."

The jayhawker's head described a short nod. Men parted before the guerrillas' horses like water before the prow of a ship.

They drew up before the man laid out on the plank. The man's mouth was open, his chest wounds exposed. One eye was gone where Slocum's bullet had struck. The guerrillas removed their hats. They murmured something that nobody heard. Then, louder, "His name was Raleigh Williams and he was from Tennessee."

The jayhawker stayed on the porch when they went inside. When they returned their faces were no softer than before. They gestured at the man on the board. "He was a soldier to the end," one said. "Bill Quantrill said he should be buried like a soldier." The two galloped their horses out of the yard, afraid the truce might end abruptly.

The jayhawker found plenty of volunteers to carry Quantrill to the ambulance. When his men returned to Ohio, or wherever they'd come from, they wanted some of the glory of having carried William Quantrill's dying body on their shoulders.

John Slocum was whittling a child's whistle from an alder branch.

Quantrill's face was as white as the sheet wrapped around him. He turned his head to see the men who waited for him, many of whom removed their hats.

"You stung 'em, Bill."

"You stung 'em all right. Damn them to hell."

The ambulance wagon was a high-sided rig with room for twenty dead or half as many wounded. The dead guerrilla was tossed on his horse with his hands and feet tied together under the animal's belly.

Late in the afternoon, they rode into Louisville. Louisville was a bustling port city now that the Ohio was open again.

The procession passed before Louisville's grand

cathedral: an escort of heavily armed men, followed by an ambulance, followed by a lone horse tied to it and a hundred men in wagons, on horseback, trailing behind like a guard of honor.

The Catholic hospital was the finest in Louisville. During the war it had been a military hospital but was civilian now. They hurried Quantrill inside.

Slocum peeled off and rode downtown. He ate a big steak with two eggs, fresh tomato salad and brown bread. He had himself two glasses of beer with his meal and ordered a bottle of good bourbon too.

The black waiter who served him was worried because John Slocum was a rougher customer than they usually saw and no telling what he might do with a full bottle of bourbon and a wicked-looking gun on his hip.

Slocum took a swig straight from the bottle. It was fine. He carried it into the Catholic hospital under his coat.

Some of the early visitors had got into the sickroom armed, but once the nuns understood what was up, they stationed two stern sisters at the door to check the hardware. Slocum gave up his Colt without a murmur. He was smiling. His belly was full. The war was over. What more could a man want?

The hall outside Quantrill's room was lined with benches where his cousins waited. They were all kinds. Some few looked well-to-do, and nervous at a too close association with their notorious kinsman. Most of them were hill people and one, a young blond fellow, Slocum had seen riding with Bloody Bill.

Slocum excused himself through. With men like these, it paid to be polite.

At the door, the jayhawker was doing the honors, as does the man who's captured a bear and wants to be close by when the congratulations flood in.

He waved Slocum forward, self-importantly. He introduced him to a couple strangers as "Someone who rode with us." He added, "He was nearby when I shot Bill Quantrill. I'd suppose you wanted to see him?"

Slocum didn't want the kill credit and gave it away gracefully, "Sure. You brought him down, all right. I saw it."

A big smile. "Go right inside."

It was a big room, facing east, and the afternoon light streamed through the window. It could have been any hospital except for the crucifix above the bed and the second crucifix on the wall where the propped-up patient could see it.

The nun wore a blue habit. She brushed past Slocum, a pitcher of water in her hand.

Quantrill squinted. He licked dry lips. "You one of my dear cousins?" he asked vaguely.

Slocum waited until the nurse closed the door behind her before he said, "No. Your man shot me. I just returned the favor."

The dim light of recognition in the guerrilla's eyes. His mouth was dark—funny colored. His wounds were masked by the perfectly clean white sheet. "Yeah. John Slocum. You rode with me. Lawrence. Was it Lawrence?"

"In a manner of speaking."

"You come to finish me off?" Idle curiosity. Quantrill had no fear in him.

"No. I brought you a bottle of whiskey."

The wounded man almost moved, almost leaned forward. His muscles sure wanted to. "Well then, you are a friend. They won't let me have nothing because of my belly wound. Hell. I ain't gonna live, anyway."

Slocum produced the bottle.

Quantrill's eyes were full of appeal. "You're gonna have to hold it to my lips. One of the bullets has froze up my joints. I can swallow, but I can't move my hands."

Slocum held the bottle to his lips while he had four deep swallows. When he pulled it away, Quantrill gasped and said, "More!" and Slocum let him have a couple more.

"You was the one who shot me. I know you now."

Quantrill's voice was satisfied. The color crept back into his face. "I wanted to kill me a few today, but that damn horse threw me off my aim." He added philosophically, "Sometimes it happens like that."

"Why'd you kill all those men in Lawrence?" Slocum asked.

Quantrill's eyelids drooped. He was puzzled by the question. "Why the hell not kill them?" he asked.

Slocum wanted a drink himself but not from this bottle. Quantrill's voice got soft and sleepy. "This is a Catholic hospital?" he asked.

"Yeah."

"I wonder if I can convert to bein' a Catholic. Do you know about that?"

"Not my line of work."

"Well it ain't exactly mine, either." Quantrill tried a grin. It wasn't big. It hurt him. He choked. "I heard Catholics got to take you up to the very last minute you're alive. If there is a hell, I'd just as soon pass it by."

"I wouldn't think there was much chance of that."

"Probably not. But a man's got to make his try."

EPILOGUE

After converting, Quantrill died of his wounds. His cousins buried the mortal remains in their backyard to foil graverobbers who might stick his head on a picket or sell the body to a carnival. To further disguise their cousin's grave, they threw slops and washwater over it.

Just three weeks later, John Slocum reined in the ugly horse. Slocum's Stand—his homeplace—lay below him in the valley of drowsy August sunlight. He felt great relief. The house was standing and the barn was standing too. Though the springhouse roof had a decided sag to it, it still covered the spring. A deeply satisfied John Slocum climbed down off his horse and walked the last few hundred yards home.